Jumping Ship

Jumping Ship

Julie A Russell

For Aunty Gloria

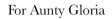

Keep reading and find out how to get hold of bonus material from J A Russell.

THE BRIGHTON AND HOVE ARGUS

DRINK DRIVE DISGRACE

By Trevor Hunt   28th April 2017

Judge Garret, presiding over the inquest of forensic psychologist Clare Fox, reprimanded headteacher Sophie O'Ryan, 49, for her "lack of judgement and blatant disrespect for life". Whilst not legally culpable, he said her encouragement of Miss Fox's actions had resulted in "a tragic, yet potentially avoidable accident".

Fox, 50, from Louisiana, died instantly after losing control of her Vespa scooter on Tivoli Road last October. Judge Garret echoed Sussex Police's criticism of passenger O'Ryan's "skimpy" clothing and Fox's unfastened helmet as "fatal errors". With a previous caution for careless driving, Fox showed nothing but "contempt for the law" that night, bingeing on cocktails just hours earlier.

Miss O'Ryan of Bavant Road, who claims to have no memory of the crash, refused to comment. Her spokesperson, ex-husband Patrick McGovern, told reporters, "We're just grateful this nightmare is over. Our thoughts go out to Miss Fox's family and friends." A verdict of death by misadventure was recorded.

1

6th January 2018. Sydney Harbour.

When I close my eyes, she's falling backwards, her hands slipping mine, screaming *why?* Her voice slides through me like a cold blade, as if I've been asleep for an hour but wake to find it's a lifetime, that everything I know has been rushed by a tide, altered forever. *Why?* There is something in her cry, an impossible question. I don't know, I want to yell. I don't know … I don't know. It's still so raw, like paper-thin flesh covers the pain, the slightest touch, and it will blister and bleed, again.

My aunt places her hand on my knee, kisses my cheek like she's reading my thoughts. 'It'll be okay.'

A wink, a sappy grin, I steal the last triangle of Toblerone from her hand, buck it into my mouth, and swallow the sting.

The ship's theatre swells with new arrivals, cranking it alive. The thunk-swoosh of the doors, musk, over-applied hair lacquer, onion tang sweat heavy on the air-conditioned breeze. Regency chandeliers wink, the mellow glow of a thousand tasselled lamps glint walls papered in gold and black flock. Oriental landscapes raised like Braille, designed to pique passengers' excitement, a nudge to what's coming, and for the first time in months, I feel the slightest twinge of hope.

Aunt Christine jumps up, life jacket swinging around her neck, hands on hips, legs apart. 'I can't do this thing. Sophie-Anne, can you look a bit more hopeless?'

I drop my head, bury my face behind a splayed hand. 'Ainti, please sit down.'

'You flap the straps, and I'll grab the crew's attention before everyone steals all the good ones.'

'Christine. Sit down … Please.'

She spears me to the seat with her eyes. 'Don't do that.'

'Sorry?'

'Call me that.'

I've called her Ainti forever. Christine is the equivalent of a parent scalding their naughty child. From birth, my grandparents, proud of their Irish heritage, tried to teach me the language. Would point to Aunt Christine, repeating, Aintín – Auntie. Ainti, I giggled, knowing it annoyed them. My aunt didn't care, her wide grin suffocating their sour frowns.

'Ainti, sit down. I'll help you.' Tugging the life jacket rougher than intended, my expression ensures she drops her hand. 'Better?'

She sculpts the wisps of grey escaping from the concrete of her chemically shaped hair. 'There she is. Bossy Whatnot. My favourite headmistress.'

'Headteacher. Former. And what do you mean, look more hopeless?'

'Holy kamoley. Lighten up, Sophie-Anne. This is meant to be fun. You remember what that is, don't you? Fun.' She flips my hands away. 'Yoo-hoo, *garçon*.'

'*Garçon*? And you call yourself a feminist.'

She folds her arms, stickers me silent. 'I think feminism is choosing what you do and how you do it, actually.'

Wow. Moments like this transport me back to her sitting on the edge of my bed as a child, assuring me, no, instructing me I could be or do anything I wanted. I believed her in those days.

'Can I help you, ma'am?'

Aunt Christine springs back, hand on chest. 'Strike me pink. Don't do that, young man. You nearly gave me a heart attack.' She jabs a finger into my knee, nudges her head at the concierge. 'We've got ourselves into a bit of a pickle.'

Suit crisp stretched at the buttonhole, the creases on his brow betray his years until I remember we are doubtless the same age. Deep-set brown eyes, the trace of expensive cologne. His raised eyebrows pose a question.

'Not me – I'm fine.' I point to my aunt.

She yelps, bouncing up and down on her seat as he yanks the life jacket tight. 'Thank you, young man. I'll definitely be calling you in an emergency.' He bows, leaves. 'He was nice.' Her gaze follows him as he jogs down the stairs and onto the stage.

I roll my eyes, pull my shawl across my shoulders, digging my nose under the fringe.

'That smells good, Sophie-Anne. New washing powder?'

'Perfume. Peonies.'

'Ah. Yes. Takes me back. Your mother's favourites.'

'Yep.' I rub the itch from my throat at the mention of her. 'What the hell?' A woman lunges across my knees. 'Excuse me. Do you mind?' I snatch the wrap of my skirt dragged open, jam it back under my legs, smoothing the black flannel to my thighs. 'Sorry. I'm … It's … Sorry. It's fine. Please.' I press my legs to the side, wave for her to pass.

'Ladies and gentlemen,' the concierge says. 'Welcome to your muster station. Please, take a seat. Yes. Yes. Come on in. The theatre holds two thousand on show nights. There's plenty of room. Guests, please move along the aisles. Leave the empty spaces at the end of the rows. Let's try to get everyone seated quickly. Thank you.'

A man hovers at Aunt Christine's side, shooing us to move along. I stand, pick up my bag. A thump in my gut, her arm thrusts me back down.

'Stay right where you are, Sophie-Anne. He should've got here earlier if he wanted the best seats.' She cuts to the gentleman, a flip of her hand. 'No. Move along.'

'Sorry,' I mouth. He shuffles down the stairs, a hunch to his shoulders, a chew of peppermint gum. 'I'm going to be covered in bruises.' I rub my stomach.

'Huh?'

'Bruises. If you keep hitting me.'

A silent beat hangs between us; Aunt Christine takes my hand.

'Don't, Ainti.' I tug from her. 'Let's not talk about it. Not now. Please.'

'Good job,' the concierge says. 'I think we're all seated. So, what's next? Right. Yes. Raise your hand only if you don't have a life jacket to try on, please. It's important we all master putting one on before we sail. That's what this part of the drill is for. We might have to leave you in Sydney if you can't do it.' A chorus of laughter echoes across the auditorium.

'What the actual hell? Is that meant to be funny?' I snatch a glance at the clock, 3.30 pm.

'Why? Are you offering to stay behind?'

'Hilarious. Not.' I stick out my tongue at her. 'When do we actually leave?'

'Shush, Sophie-Anne. I'm listening.'

The vibe of this elderly audience is not what I expected. Not a pop sock or pair of elastic-waisted slacks to be seen. These people are bold, an explosion of colour, watermelon pink to forty shades of green, linen pants, cut-off shorts, espadrilles, deck shoes. I bounce my UGG boots over crossed legs.

'Aren't you hot in those?' Aunt Christine fans a hand to her face.

'No. Why? They're made in Australia.'

Should I have worn heels? I don't hate heels. I'm just fed up with wearing what everyone expects me to. Slipping my feet to the floor, I bury them under my seat. It doesn't take much to prod my self-consciousness these days.

'So, that hasn't worked, has it?' the concierge says. 'Ladies and gentlemen. Let's try again. Only those without a jacket raise their hand. Those without a jacket only, please. Only put your hand up if you don't have a life jacket to put on. If you have one on, keep your hand lowered.'

His chuckling behind his hand makes me smile. I follow his eyes, sweeping the auditorium. How many more ways can he say it? They're like a class of children on their first day at school, new clothes, excited smiles, a touch of apprehension, and no clue what to do or where to go. Emotion seizes me, anger, sadness, fear, maybe relief. Back in Brighton, someone else stands at my school gates, listening to my students' stories of Christmas dinner, presents, and soap opera cliffhangers, avoiding the new year, new me buzz in the staffroom of diets and exercise regimes.

My mobile vibrates in my back pocket.

TD: You okay?

Out of Aunt Christine's sight, I reply with a heart emoji. A slip of my finger, I click on Insta. Her face bursts on the screen like a spring flower – image after image of her, me, smiling, laughing. I don't read the messages any more. I should block them, but I don't. Their judgement serves my guilt, I guess. Clare had charged me as her legacy contact years before, said, with her American deep south hee-haw laugh, 'keep my beauty alive and kicking, sweet cheeks. Just in case I make it uber-famous, and someone cares.' I stroke a finger to her face. I care. It's been four hundred and eleven days, twenty-three hours and forty-two minutes since you left, and I miss you. Pain clutches my gut. I swallow the sob bubbling in my chest, snap the phone shut, clasp it to my heart. I close my eyes, and she's falling backwards again, her hand pulling from mine. What do I do now? Without you.

2

Clipboard tucked under his arm, the concierge weaves us across the deck. Waves crowned with white foam mark our course, the growl of sea slapping steel, the ocean breeze, fresh-airy with a hint of garlic from the galley below. He pulls up tall, stabs a finger at the elevator button. No smile. A little taller than me, five seven, five eight. Stout, but who isn't carrying a few extra pounds at our age? Another hit of his luxury cologne reminds me of my father fake-spraying me as a child.

He catches my eye, sucks in his stomach, puffs up his chest. 'Please.' He gestures for us to step inside.

The elevator drops to Magasin deck. As the doors slip open, I step out, spin on my heels, mouth agape at the imperial staircase leading to a stained-glass domed ceiling.

'It's like something from the *Titanic*, isn't it?' I say. 'Oops. Probably not the best reference to make whilst afloat on the Pacific Ocean.'

The concierge smiles, tugs the clipboard from his armpit. He smooths out the sheaf of papers, looks up and down as if checking our direction on a map, shakes it in the air like a tour guide's umbrella. 'This way, please.'

I curl my arm into Aunt Christine's, hook my hand over hers. After forty-eight hours of chaos, knowing we are parading this corridor to find our rooms presents a welcome sense of order.

On either side of the staircase, a gold-flecked claret carpet, the length of one, maybe two, football pitches, lines of small boutiques, all trimmed in the same polished brass. The perfumery and make-up are a popular choice, its customers seduced by vibrant displays of mirrored boxes and honeyed fragrances wafting from its open doors.

Opposite, every shoe colour sits upon illuminated white platforms behind tempered glass. Hours of fun right there, people. I love shoes. I love shopping for shoes, but buying more I'll never wear? Bad idea, Sophie O'Ryan. B-a-d! Your credit card is already a pressure-pinched nerve. Move along.

We pass another. A neon-pink swimsuit, its plunging neckline and high-leg design are a questionable option for the clientele on board. Although, after the safety drill, maybe not. Next, gentleman's fashion offers an eclectic mix of chinos, blazers and woollen sweaters. Women's fashion is at the end of the aisle between branded chocolates, gifts, souvenirs, books and stationery.

The concierge ushers us down a corridor branching off to the left, taps a key card onto a door pad. 'Here we are, 689.' He looks very pleased with himself, his smile not unlike a small child being praised by their teacher for the correct answer.

Aunt Christine pats his arm, waves for him to move aside. 'Excuse me, young man. I'm bursting for a wee.'

I wince, mouth 'sorry,' as the bathroom door slams shut.

The concierge points at the suitcases propped against the wall. 'Your luggage, ma'am. If that's everything, I'll let you get settled in.' He bows his head, turns to leave.

'Excuse me.'

He hesitates mid-stride; a puff of air whistles through his lips, his grin gone. Instead, he forces a corporate smile onto his face. 'Yes, ma'am.'

'I think there's been a mistake.' I flip over the white cardboard tag looped through the handle – 689 written in black marker pen. 'This one needs to go to my cabin, please.' I tap my toe on the silver Samsonite case. Extra-large. Spinner wheels. Fake. 'Sophie O'Ryan. It might be under my aunt's name, Collins.'

The cabin is charming. French windows lead to a balcony wide enough for two chairs and a coffee table, sheltered by a waist-height wall of salt-stained glass. Inside, an ash veneer bedhead and matching sideboard stretch the length of the wall, a wardrobe at the entrance. Swirls of ocean blue and beige wallpaper complement the navy ceiling-to-floor velvet drapes, a weighted throw over white cotton linen. Cheap furniture camouflaged by expensive decoration, uniform, not unlike the fixtures and fittings of a large hotel chain. I don't doubt mine would be a nice, unremarkable, but equally clean replica.

'Apologies, ma'am.' He tucks the clipboard under his arm, tugs a fold of paper from his back pocket, flattens it against his thigh. 'Miss Collins, yes?' He runs his finger down the alphabetical list, taps my aunt's name, highlighted neon yellow. 'Miss C. Collins. Two passengers. Standard double.'

The bathroom door swings open. 'Goodness, I needed that.' Aunt Christine wipes her hands with a towel. 'Oh. Hello. Still here. Ah, the suitcases.' She looks at the concierge, then me. 'Is everything okay?'

'My name's not on the list.'

'Really?' She throws down the towel, signals for him to lift the luggage onto the bed. 'Oh well. Not to worry.' She flips open her bags.

'Sorry?' Smacking my palm on her suitcase, it shuts with a thud. 'What do you mean, not to worry?'

'Right.' He clears his throat, looks at the door, my aunt, me. 'I'll be going then.'

'Oh yes.' She pulls open her handbag, folds a five-pound note in half, and passes it to him like she's doing some undercover drugs deal.

His head tilts to the side, confused. 'Ma'am, I–'

'Buy yourself a pint or something when you clock off later.'

'Ma'am, this is very kind, but I can't accept it. Everything's complimentary. If you want to praise someone for excellent service, there are report cards at reception.' He smiles, hands the money back. 'But thank you.'

'Oh. Of course. I'll do that.' She slips it back into her handbag, zips it shut. 'I didn't catch your name?'

'Oré, ma'am. I'm one of the ship's concierges.'

'Um. Excuse me.' A jittery twitch in my eyelid. 'This is all very well. But I still don't have a room.'

'Cabin.' Aunt Christine avoids my stare.

'Sorry?'

'It's a cabin. Not a room.'

Oré shakes open the paper like a cloth napkin again, scans the page. He observes me, Aunt Christine. 'So, our records show you booked a standard double, Miss Collins. One standard double.'

'Well, that's obviously a mistake. Ainti, have you got our booking details handy?'

Aunt Christine sits back on the bed, tugs a thread from the hem of her shorts, winds it around her finger. The absence of a comeback concerns me. This woman fizzes joy like bubbles in a SodaStream. On the surface, joking and light. Delights at teasing my misfortune. But in recent months, her eyes have lost their sparkle. It's getting harder to see the young woman she'd once been. Wrinkles cut deeper, hair thinning along the parting line. Something in these moments chips at my core. The hunch of her shoulders, her silence.

'Okay. Looks like the error's ours, then. Let's start again.' A crowing inhale. 'Do you have anything available?'

He scrunches his nose, bites his bottom lip, tucks the room list back into his pocket. 'We don't. Sorry. We're fully booked. Five thousand passengers have got on today. Crazy busy. We may have some availability when we dock in Bali, though. But I can't guarantee anything now.'

'When do we get to Bali?'

Oré consults his clipboard. 'The 23rd.'

'What? That's almost three weeks.' I flop down onto the bed, rake a hand through my hair. 'Ainti, what were you thinking?'

She impales me to the bed with her stare, and I'm thirteen again, caught skipping school. 'Where's your accent from?' Aunt Christine turns back to Oré.

Oh, so we're just going to ignore me, pretend I'm not pissed. Cheers, Ainti.

'Chicago, ma'am.'

'Ah. The windy city.' She tails off with a bat of eyelashes.

Oré offers her his hand. 'Right. I'd better get back. They'll wonder where I am.'

She stands, steadies herself on his arm. 'Goodness, don't you have big muscles?'

His grin buried between squeezed lips, Oré pats my aunt's hand. 'I'll take that as a compliment, Miss Collins. Hopefully, we can get the room sorted soon. I hope you won't let it spoil your stay.' He shakes her hand, nods at me. 'Good day.'

My eyes shoot him like lasers as he closes the door. Of course, it'll spoil our stay. I fall back onto the bed, arms and legs wide like a starfish.

Aunt Christine flips open her suitcase, yanks open the drawers on the sideboard. 'I'll take these two. You can have the others, Sophie-Anne.'

'Why am I sensing there's something you're not telling me, Ainti?'

'Is this all the bags?' She turns away, hands on hips, tuts at the door. 'I'm sure I'm missing something.'

'Stop changing the subject. You drag me halfway around the world, and now we're sharing a room. Exactly how is that going to work?'

'I thought I'd told you. Anyhow, it'll be fun, won't it?'

'Or hell, and I know where I'm putting my money.' I thought I told you – seriously? Is that the best she can do? The floating retirement home, the three-month diet of aqua aerobics, bingo and gin rummy, and now we're roomies. For three flipping months. Has she lost her mind?

She folds her clothes into the sideboard drawer. 'I didn't think you should be alone after what's happened.'

I breathe hard through my nose. Back home, I'm sitting on my bed swigging a bottle of vodka, a jagged scuff to the throat, multicoloured pills strewn over the quilt like Smarties. 'I'm not going to do anything. I promise.'

She spins around, places her finger on my lips. 'You scared me, Sophie-Anne. Never, never think that's the answer. I'm here. I'll always be here.' Emotion cracks her voice. 'I know you don't want to talk about what's happened, but I promised your mother and I will do whatever it takes. You might not think it, but this trip is going to be everything you need.' She turns away, tucks her knitted twinsets, identical in various pastel shades, into the drawer. 'Anyway, I'm housetrained and fairly well-behaved.'

'Fairly? Ha. That's a bit of a stretch.'

'Okay. I'll do my best not to annoy you.'

'Or embarrass me?'

'Of course.' She holds up crossed fingers. 'Are we done?'

My head pressed to hers; I slip my arms around her waist, suck in her fruity, baby powder smell. 'I'm sorry, Ainti. I never meant to–'

'Yes. Well,' she flaps me away. 'It's not that bad, is it? We just need to get these beds split.' She stoops down, flips up the valance. 'This is a double.'

'What? I thought they'd just forgotten to separate them?' Dropping to my knees, I run my hand along the divan, hunt for the join.

'Goodness. This definitely won't do – a twin. I ordered a twin. Who do they think we are? Cohabitors?'

I collapse onto the floor, legs wide, back slumped against the bed. 'This just gets better and better.'

'And where are my knickers?'

'What?'

'It's pardon, Sophie.'

'What?'

'Pardon. Not what. I brought you up better than that. Have you got them?'

'Why would I have them?'

'The rucksack. The one I gave you on the coach.'

'On the transfer? No idea. Did you get it out of the overhead locker?'

She throws her arms up, frustrated. 'Why would I do that? I didn't put it up there. You did.'

'Yes. But I didn't know you wanted me to get it down, too.'

'Fantastic. All my underwear's in that bag.'

'It's fine. We've just paraded past an entire floor of shops. We'll get you some new ones.'

She cocks her head to the side. 'No lacy up your bum things, though. I need a strong gusset these days.'

'Oh, my God.' I jump up, laughter hissing from my stomach. 'Too much information.'

3

The shop assistant springs forward, a cheery wave. 'Ladies, welcome. How can I help?'

Aunt Christine leans in, whispers, 'I'm after some underwear, please. Knickers, pants. Oh. Whatever you call them over here. And none of that sexy nonsense.'

'I'm sorry, madam, we don't have any lingerie.' The assistant tugs her red neckerchief, her face flushes pink.

'What? Why not?' Aunt Christine's chin jabs high, a little off-centre.

The assistant clears her throat. 'We don't have any on board. A problem with the suppliers, I believe. We'll be in Newcastle in the morning. They have an excellent selection of shops.'

'My aunt really needs something before then, if possible. She lost them on the transfer.'

'Sophie!'

'What? It's true.'

The assistant's expression softens. 'Perhaps some paper ones from the spa? They're quite comfortable.'

Hot red sweeps from Aunt Christine's cheeks to her forehead, ears. 'No.'

'Some swimwear?' The assistant's eagerness fades at Aunt Christine's scowl.

I raise a sympathetic eyebrow at the assistant. 'Okay. Borrow a pair of mine then?'

Aunt Christine recoils her head, mouth opening to speak before snapping it shut.

'Drop the death stare, Ainti; I hear you.'

'Wait here, Madam. I may have something.'

The assistant returns with a box of novelty briefs. 'We have a few of these left over from Christmas. I'm not meant to sell them, but ...'

Aunt Christine flips open the lid, pinches the knickers stamped with snowflakes and reindeer between her finger and thumb.

'They'll do, Ainti, yes?' I nod at Aunt Christine. 'We'll get some more tomorrow. Perfect.'

She stares at me, her expression not unlike a small child about to cry. 'I suppose so.' She crumples the briefs in her fist, bangs them and the box onto the counter. 'I don't have much choice, do I?' Slaps her charge card on the machine.

'You could always stock up and set up a pop-up on board?' I tug the carrier bag off the counter.

'Pop-up?' She slips the card into her purse.

'Never mind.' I hand her the bag. 'Come on, grab your new undercrackers. Let's get changed. I'm starving.'

The shop's glass door clicks shut behind us, and I'm struck again by the grandeur of Magasin deck – the crack of white light from the spots slicing the shop windows, winking the polished brass trimmings. At the end of the strip, two women climb the staircase, hitch up long, voluminous skirts of emerald green and amethyst satin. The ceiling's vast pendant light fittings glint their sleeveless bodices, embellished with a thousand tiny rhinestones.

'Jesus, Ainti. Do we have to dress like that for dinner?'

Aunt Christine flicks her eyes. 'No. Look at them prancing around like they're in an episode of *Downton Abbey*. It just says something smart for formal nights. Did you bring anything bright and cheerful?'

'By that, you mean colourful? You know I don't do colour.'

She waves her hand for me to follow, like an obedient lamb. 'Ah, yes. The wardrobe of doom and gloom. How about that navy one? A present from Clare, wasn't it? Have you ever worn it?'

'Once,' I say.

***

Slumped down on the bed, I kicked out at the contents of my wardrobe scattered across the bedroom floor. 'I can't go.'

'What the hell?' Clare flung open the door. 'Don't be so silly.'

'I can't. I've nothing to wear. Nothing fits. I'm not going.'

'Right. We're not doing this again. Not tonight. It's a drink. Just a drink.'

'But he's gorgeous, could turn up in his flipping muddy football kit and still look fab. Why did he even ask me? There're a trillion other girls better than me out there.' I flop back on the bed. 'Argh. What was I thinking?'

'Get up.' Clare dragged me rag-doll-like from the bed, handed me a silver bag tied with a wide pink ribbon. 'It was meant for your birthday, but needs must.'

'What is it?' I looked at her, the bag, untied the ribbon.

'Enough with the questions. *Allons.*'

I look up at Clare, lifting out the layers of pink tissue paper. 'Oh my goodness. This is way too much.'

'Nah.' She flipped me off with her hand. 'I saw you looking at it last week, knew you'd never buy it.'

I drew the fabric through my fingers, stroked the navy-blue organza tumbling over silk against my face. 'Clare, it's flipping perfect. But it's so expensive.'

'So? I think you're worth it, even if you don't.'

I jumped up, held it against me, watched it fall like water over my skin. 'Is it a bit too booby, do you think?'

'Hell no. You've got a magnificent set of bamboobers. Now get it on, or you're gonna miss happy hour.'

'You're the best, do you know that?' I hesitated at the bathroom door. 'It's not a bit showy for a first date? What if he's wearing jeans and a T-shirt?'

'Then he can kiss my ass.' She stepped forward, pushed my hair behind my ears. 'It's beautiful, just like you. Sophie O'Ryan, you've got this.'

***

The door clicks closed behind me, and we're back in the cabin. A buzz from the dresser breaks the silence.

'Sophie. Your phone's jumping about over here. Who's TD?'

'No one.' I snatch the mobile open, cancel the call. 'I didn't think these things worked at sea?' I tap – *I can't talk right now.* Sensing her glare scald the back of my head, I look over my shoulder.

'Okay?' Her stare makes my chest tight.

'Absolutely.' I throw the phone into my rucksack. 'So, are we getting ready or not? I'm starving.'

'Let's do it. I can't wait for you to see the restaurant.' Aunt Christine disappears into the bathroom, humming 'Let It Snow! Let It Snow! Let It Snow!'

A series of pings echo from inside the bag. I smile at the bathroom door, my aunt's singing, press the rucksack to the back of the wardrobe. Tonight, I need to show her I can do this trip, will enjoy myself. I've misjudged how important this is for her. I slip the navy dress from the hanger, lean against the wardrobe door, snap it shut. 'Okay, Sophie O'Ryan, you've got this,' I whisper.

4

'I told you it would be lovely, Sophie-Anne.'

The restaurant is stunning – a blaze of grandeur. Every detail is carefully blended with exquisite elegance. The purr of a grand piano, high ceilings peppered with enormous torched-crystal chandeliers scattering soft shadows to the restaurant's edges, gold embossed wallpaper complementing swirls of blue and green fabrics. And the air … the air is mouth-wateringly delicious. A blend of aromas to drink in, brawny carved meats, buttered carrots. The hiss of garlic rolling from pan-fried salmon, the sugariness of caramel parading on dessert trollies along walkways of polished oak. The tuneful clink of glass, cutlery, plates.

'Ah. Here we are. Communal tables are all part of the fun.' Aunt Christine circles a hand in the air for me to follow, and my day takes another unexpected swipe to the left.

A repetition of polite hellos and good evenings, a gentleman in a white tuxedo, a crushed red velvet bowtie knotted under a stubbled chin, rises from his seat and pulls out our chairs. Next to him, a woman in a red satin halter-neck gown, heavy make-up, a darker tint than the pale skin of her earlobe. To her left, a woman, a little younger than my aunt, wearing a crushed black-leather biker jacket with polished chrome buckles, the smell of stale cigarettes seeping from the pelt. Her contempt for the dress code hints at rock festivals and Harley-Davidsons. I catch her eye, smile, yank my dress down over my thighs.

Chin held high, the lady in red turns her head with opulent slowness to look at me. 'I'll get the introductions started, shall I?' She composes herself, pitches forward on her seat. 'I'm Candice. This is my husband, Roy.'

'Howdy,' Roy salutes.

'We teach dancing on board, ballroom and Latin. Obviously, not tonight. We couldn't do that in here.' She snorts, a noise somewhere between a donkey's whinny and a husky's yelp, stopping when she catches Roy's disapproving glare. 'You?' She gestures her hand to my aunt.

Aunt Christine's horrified stare flicks from Candice's face to her outstretched palm and back again. 'Christine.' She turns to face me, mouths 'what the hell', before turning back with a half-smile. 'And this is Sophie.'

'I'm Beatrix. But everyone calls me Bea.' The older woman wiggles her fingers hello.

Candice drops her tone, nudges my shoulder. 'I saw you and your mother in the theatre earlier.'

'Oh. She's not my mother. I'm her niece.' I neglect to tell her she's as good as. The solar system around my galaxy, the stone in my peach.

'Oh. Really?' She stiffens, slaps a hand on her chest like this revelation has electrified her. 'Well. Well. How lovely. On holiday with your auntie.' Candice's laughter shrills across the table.

'It's aunt.' Aunt Christine dagger-eyes her silent, clears her throat. 'I've always hated the *ie* on the end. Sounds like a litter of hungry piglets squealing at you.'

'It's her birthday soon,' I interrupt, sensing the tension.

Candice looks down, flips a napkin one-handed onto her lap. 'A birthday, Christine. Is it a special one?'

Without looking up, Aunt Christine opens the drinks menu. 'Eighty. Is that special? It's old.'

'Of course it's special, and nobody's old on here, Christine. No. No. No. We're all as young as the man we feel. Isn't that right, Royston?' She turns to Roy, pinching his cheeks with a loud 'ouchy'.

'Good grief,' Aunt Christine mutters under her breath.

'Are you having a party? You must, must, must. Come have some lessons. We'll help you wow them on the dancefloor.' Candice hip kicks off her seat, shimmies her shoulders.

Aunt Christine shakes her head at the menu, flips over the page. 'Sophie has a birthday coming up too.'

I knock my foot against hers under the table, throw her a thanks-for-that glare.

'Two! Do my ears deceive me? Did you hear that, Roy, Bea?' She gestures her hand like she's striking a match in the air, 'Two birthdays. One cruise. Well, I never. It's a total dream. What a team you are. May I ask how old you'll be, Sophie? You don't look a day over …' She hesitates, studies my face, neck, shoulders, tilts her head. 'Fifty, fifty-five, maybe?'

Aunt Christine slaps a palm on the table, scooting her napkin onto the floor. 'How dare you?'

Candice slithers down her seat like an inflatable losing its air. 'Sorry? I don't understand. Why shouldn't women celebrate their age?'

I flash be-kind eyes at Aunt Christine. 'Fifty, Candice. I'm going to be fifty.'

'Goodness. Well. You must both come and find us in the ballroom. We'll have hours of fun.'

I lift my napkin over my mouth. 'Not flipping likely,' I mutter.

Bea winks at me, smiles at the waiter stepping to her side. 'Wine, anyone?'

I raise my hand like a nervous child. I have no idea what the protocol is for splitting the bill on somewhere like this. 'Or I can get my own if you prefer?'

'Nae. The drinks are on me. Let's call it a welcome on-board gift. Um. We'll start with a bottle of the Pinot Noir, please, Charles. The Bass Philip,' Bea, says.

'Softies only for us, remember?' Candice straightens, drums her index finger on the table.

'Of course. Stupid rule,' Bea replies.

'Scotch on the rocks, please.' Aunt Christine slaps the menu shut, hands it to the waiter. 'I don't really drink, but it might help with the jet lag, I guess.'

'Ahem.' Candice smirks, flicks her eyebrows at Bea, Roy.

Woah! Don't be judging my aunt, people. There's no outing anyone in their near eighties. If she wants to believe it's jet lag, so be it. 'Aren't you allowed to drink?'

'No! Absolutely forbidden. One, one and a half maximum.'

Candice places her hand over mine, nods at my stomach. 'You really should think about coming to our classes, Sophie. It's tremendous exercise. Will tighten up all those wobbly bits.'

My brain stutters, a clunky gear change. Is she saying I'm fat? My mantra, Mrs Candice Floss, is to ignore said wobbly bits. Don't trust a mirror, don't wear clothes that show them off, and avoid talking about bodies, food and diets with anyone. Not in a million, trillion years will I be stepping into one of your classes. I've humiliated myself quite enough just by being here without shovelling on any more. But of course, I don't say that. Not to her. 'I don't think so. Dancing's not really my thing.'

The waiter emerges at my side. 'Are we ready to order, ladies and gentlemen?'

Conscious of Candice's observation, I ignore the battered calamari, leg of lamb and point to the grilled salmon with a side of green salad. Adding, 'Can you hold the dressing and new potatoes, please?'

He nods. 'And for a starter?'

'The soup. Please.'

'Pea and watercress soup.' He accents the ingredients as if questioning why anyone would come on here and choose these options. He snatches his eyes to Bea. 'Madam?'

Aunt Christine runs a finger around the rim of her tumbler. 'I didn't realise the staff could eat with the passengers.'

Candice adjusts the strap of her dress around her neck. 'Oh, yes. We have a cafeteria too. But it's nice to come upstairs occasionally.'

'So, how long have you known each other?' Aunt Christine points her glass at Bea, Candice, Roy.

'Too long, Bea would say,' Candice shrieks, her head nodding like a horse laughing with its teeth.

Is this place for real? It's like I've stepped into a dinner party from an Agatha Christie novel, and we're waiting for one of us to be murdered. I'm happy to volunteer! 'So, whereabouts in Scotland are you from, Bea?'

'Ha. My cover's blown.' She pushes back her glasses, hands the waiter her menu. 'A small village just outside Glasgow. It's a bonnie place. Although I haven't been back in a while. Canada's my home.

It's lost its edge, but it's a hard accent to lose.' Bea tidies her napkin onto her lap. 'So, Sophie, tell us about you. How have you ended up on here with us oldies?'

Their eyes turn on me, biting like a dull blade. The dread of the truth being discovered stabs in and out in time with my heartbeat, pounding in my head. Stab. Stab. Stab. If that happens, it's over, proof enough that I'll never escape. That my timeless sentence will follow me – everywhere. What was Aunt Christine thinking? The youngest passenger on board by at least two decades, I stick out like a splash of lipstick red in a pot of black paint. It was only a matter of time before someone asked the question, curious, snooping. I've always been a terrible liar; the hesitation in my voice, lack of eye contact, my finger coiling through my hair, not saying enough, saying too much. 'Well.' I place my glass down, tidy my cutlery. It's hard to keep the story Aunt Christine and I had agreed on the flight over straight in my head. 'My aunt duped me,' I laugh. 'A short break, she said. Majorca, the Canary Islands. But here we are. Halfway across the world. I almost fell off my chair when I discovered it was a cruise.' I shuffle straight, tidy the tablecloth smooth. The shame of the lies slipping so easily from my lips rips through me like a plaster torn from a child's knee.

Candice turns to Roy, her cheeks sucked in like she's slurping on a Sherbet Dip Dab. 'Goodness. What an unexpected adventure. What is it you do again?' She savours her drink, searches my expression. 'For a job.'

'I'm a headteacher.'

'How interesting.' Candice circles the rim of her glass with the tip of a glossy red acrylic nail. 'Of course, I know little about schools, but I'm surprised you're allowed to take time off in term time.'

Aunt Christine puts down her tumbler. Her glare steps between us like a mamma bear shielding its cub. The cub she would die for to save it from harm. 'And that's your business because?'

Candice tosses her hair, drops her eyes, admitting defeat. 'Hmm. Quite right, Christine.' A whinny of laughter. 'My imagination can run away with me sometimes.'

'Compassionate leave,' I say, deviating from our agreed script. My aunt turns her body to face me, a what-did-you-say-that-for roll of her eyes. 'Sorry,' I mouth.

'Oh.' Candice looks at me, Aunt Christine, taps her napkin on her lips. 'Of course.'

'Ignore them, Sophie,' Bea whispers in my ear. 'Right.' She addresses the table. 'Now the introductions are over; top-up, anyone?'

'Have fun.' Candice blows us a kiss, slips her arm around Roy's waist before disappearing down the stairwell.

Bea pulls a gold key card from her back pocket, taps it on the pad of a glass bullet-shaped lift. 'Nightcap?'

Aunt Christine, elbows high, muscles her way past me. 'Absolutely.'

I grip her shoulders, tug her back to my side. 'Ainti,' I whisper. 'What are you doing? We can't just rock up to a stranger's cabin. It's almost midnight.'

'Oh, for goodness' sake, Sophie-Anne. How else are you going to get to know people on here? She's offering us a drink, not her body. Anyway,' she cups a hand to my ear, 'that is a private lift, which only works with one of those golden key cards. So, you might want to err on the side of caution, but I'm going up in that baby and seeing what's at the top of that beanstalk. Come on. Time to live a little dangerously.' The glass doors slip open, and she bundles me inside.

Bea waves the key card against the gilded control pad, and the elevator fires skywards. Below, the ship's mock cityscape is alive like a festival stage. Chandeliers, snowflake-cut pendant lampshades, walkways stained by outfits the colours of an artist's palette. Ding! The elevator slides open onto a mezzanine of aqua-frosted glass walls housing three sets of double oak doors. The cabin numbers replaced by names scribed onto polished brass plaques.

Bea swipes her card, pushes open the doors to the Regency Penthouse. 'Come on in.'

Inside, breezy, fresh air wafts through a wall of pushed back bi-fold doors, a melody of slapping waves. Lampshades the size of race day hats, complement dozens of ivory pillar candles, burning golden on side tables and cabinets lining the walls. Bea tosses her jacket on a sideboard next to a vase bouquet of spicy-perfumed yellow chrysanthemums, a display of silver-framed photographs.

Aunt Christine runs a finger along the dark oak surface as if checking for dust. 'Beatrix. This is very fancy.'

'Our cabin's a postage stamp compared to this.' I step into the lounge area, a plush purple rug merging into a charcoal L-shaped sofa, snaking the back wall to a spiral staircase.

'Is this a suite?'

'A presidential apartment. Indulgent for one, I know. But I'm worth it.'

'Are those bedrooms?' I point up the stairs.

'Aye. Two. Please. Sit.' She swings open a mini fridge integrated into a marble-topped wet bar set into the far wall, waves a punnet of strawberries, a bottle of white rum. 'Daiquiri?'

Aunt Christine kicks off her shoes, shuffles back onto the sofa, hugged by a wall of plush cushions. 'Make mine a large, Beatrix.'

'Comfortable, are we?' I tut at my aunt's toothy grin, sit down opposite her on a wingback armchair of royal-purple velvet. Its vibrance nods to the full-length drapes and scatter cushions in the same colour. 'Are you sure you don't mind us being here, Bea?' I sticker stare my aunt silent before she dares to speak. 'We don't want to get in your way.'

'Nae. It's lovely to have some company.'

'Your cabin's gorgeous.' I nod at the sideboard. 'Are they your pictures?'

'Aye. I like a few creature comforts.'

Weird, it's not the first thing you think of packing, is it? I must remember to slot in three of my favourite framed photographs. 'Are they your family?'

Bea's stare lingers on the frames for a beat before returning to the counter. 'Here we are.' She hands us both a tall-stemmed cocktail glass, points a remote at the wall, flicks on some music.

My eyes follow her from the bar to the couch. Her deflection from answering my question does not go unnoticed. I suck the strawberry garnish, take a sip. 'Fuck me. This is really good.' I slap my hand over my mouth. 'Shit. Sorry. Sorry.'

'Sophie O'Ryan!' Aunt Christine puts down her glass, folds her arms across her chest, hands tucked tight under her armpits. 'What in heaven's name?'

'I know. I'm sorry. I forgot where I was for a minute.'

Bea giggles, spluttering her drink. 'Fuck me, indeed. I couldn't have put it better myself, Sophie. Cheers, ladies.' She holds up her glass to mine, side stares Aunt Christine's pinched eyes. 'Are you telling me you've never sworn, Christine?'

Aunt Christine sucks in her cheeks. 'Hmm.' She hauls herself up, walks over to the wall of open glass doors. 'Is that a terrace outside?'

Bea stands, sweeps the cocktail shaker from the bar, tops up my aunt's glass. 'Come see.' She flips on the spots hidden into the slate grey flagstone floor, beckons for her to follow her outside.

Aunt Christine glances back at me, points to the doors. 'You, okay if …?'

I bat her away, take a long, slow sip of daiquiri. Ha. Something tells me my aunt may have met her match with Bea.

The guitar intro to 'Wake Me Up When September Ends' rolls from the sound system. One of my go-to songs this past year, I stand, run my hand slick along the back of the velvet couch, the satiny sheen of the oak furniture, singing like I've been transported into a music video. The silver photo frames flicker in the candlelight, photographs of Bea smiling, a child swinging from her hand, a woman clasped in a warm embrace.

'Green Day fan?' Bea says softly, stepping up next to me.

I spin to face her. 'Sorry?'

She waves her finger at the sound system, me. 'The song. It's one of my favourites. Do you sing much at home?'

'No.' I laugh, shake my head.

'Well, you should. That's a gift of a voice, Sophie.'

Aunt Christine flops back on the couch next to Bea, swings her glass like a flag. 'Isn't she fantastic? My very own Shirley Bassey. I haven't heard you sing like that in years, Sophie-Anne.' A quiver to her lips, she places a hand over her mouth, takes a moment. 'Lovely. Just lovely.'

'Oh, stop it, Ainti. I thought you were both outside.'

I smile at them, kicked back on the sofa, chatting like they've known each other forever. Holidays can do that, can't they? Strangers turn into friends overnight, or, in this case, dinner, wine, scotch and cocktails.

30

Bea plumps a cushion behind her back. 'So, tell me, how are you settling in?'

'Don't ask.' Aunt Christine flicks her eyes skyward. 'They messed up our booking. Can't sort it out for weeks, apparently. Did you know they've run out of knickers too?'

'That's not strictly true, is it, Ainti? Anyway, we're going to hunt down M&S in Bali, remember?' I tidy my hair into its clip. 'Do you always travel like this, Bea?'

She straightens, brushes lines into the nap of the fabric. 'I get off for a couple of months to catch up with family, but otherwise, aye, I go wherever it takes me.'

I study the cabin. What seemed like a thousand questions bubble into my mind. 'You mean you live on here? On your own? Don't you get lonely?'

'Nae. It's much lonelier living a life that doesn't suit, I think.'

'But it must be so expensive?'

'Sophie!' Aunt Christine taps a finger to her lips. 'Shush. It's none of your business.'

'I was only asking. Sorry, Bea.'

She flaps a hand at my aunt. 'It's fine, Christine. It's nae a secret. I sold my businesses a few years ago, treated myself to a world cruise, and here I am.'

'Seriously?' I sit down on the armchair. 'That was brave.'

'Ha. Most call it stupid.'

'Don't they just. I have exactly that problem at—'

'Yes, well, the less said about that, the better, hey, Sophie-Anne,' Aunt Christine interrupts. She clinks her glass with Bea's. 'Good on you, Beatrix. I'd love to do something like it.'

'So, why don't you?' I say, sipping the last of my cocktail.

'Don't be silly. It's not that easy, is it?'

'Why?'

'Because.'

'No. Not because. You could downsize and free up some money. Maybe not enough for this, but—'

'We can't all just up and leave, Sophie.' She looks over at the sideboard of chrysanthemums and photographs, crosses, uncrosses her legs. 'Can we talk about something else, please?'

'Is it because of what's …' Irritation grinds my words. 'Is it me? I've told you I'm not going to–'

'Enough!' She tugs her glass from the coffee table, daiquiri splashing over its edge. 'Now look what I've done.' She sucks her hand, hoovers up the spilt drink.

'More music?' Bea punches the controller, the soothing intro of Aerosmith's 'I Don't Want to Miss a Thing'. 'There we go. How apt. Another one of my favourites.'

I slip off my shoes, fold my legs under me, fingers fitted together in my lap. Some of my earliest memories are of my aunt returning from holiday discarding storybooks in favour of her own adventures, real and imagined. She didn't go for years after Mum died. I knew I'd got in the way. She started again when I went to university, before stopping after the accident. I gathered it was her age, her wanting to slow down, but … She clears her throat, twists away from me. How can I be so stupid? So selfish? So wrapped up in my own grief that I haven't stopped to think about how all this has blighted those around me, her. Strangers' and our once friends' judgement – I blame the parents, they had said; behind every bad egg is a village of trouble, written on her garden wall. As if anyone could blame her for this. 'Ainti–'

'No, Sophie-Anne.' She doesn't turn around. 'Not another word. Please.' She watches her drink swirl around her glass. 'Anyway, there's plenty of life left in this old dog, so maybe one day.'

'Cheers to that, Christine.' Bea heaves herself from the sofa. 'Another daiquiri, anyone?'

5

Cruising the Coral Sea

The ocean breathes dark blue in the amber light of sunrise. The surface, a rhythmic rise and fall not unlike Aunt Christine's chest as she lays splayed across the duvet, a slip of mascara under each eye. Her hogging the bed had forced me to scoop up the spare covers and pillows around 3 am, settling down on the armchair. It's been almost seven years since I've shared a bed. Longer for my aunt, I suspect. The final shapes of moonlight swim across the ceiling, and the emptiness howls in me. Full of need, I pull out my phone, type, 'Are you awake?' He doesn't respond, and like a wave, the need is gone.

Our unpacked suitcases sit on the floor, bathed in hushed arcs of daybreak. The leather of Aunt Christine's is smooth, shabby, walnut brown. I wiggle a finger under the frayed seam of cream cotton. Each crease and scuff echoes her boldness, heartache, despair. Our conversation last night taps, the irritation in her words. What have I done to her? I should be helping her to love life, make the most of every moment.

I rest against the French doors, recalling the first time I encountered these bags, strewn across the hallway – the day my mother died, one week before my thirteenth birthday. I can still taste the air stained with sickness and disinfectant, see my aunt hunched over the kitchen table, an arm thrown over her eyes. Her sobbing sliced forever in my memory. 'She couldn't fight any more,' Aunt Christine said, her tears trickling hot on my skin. Her baby sister, my mother, gone, the cancer creeping through her body until her soul stopped breathing. My dad was away sorting stuff, she said. It took her eyes breaking from mine to realise it's impossible to hear someone you love lie.

I kiss her time-weary skin, arrange the quilt under her chin. 'What would I do without you?' Panic thunders through me, hot dread charging my veins.

I slide back the door, step onto the balcony. Touched by the golden fingers of sunrise, the sea and sky unite. Silhouettes surf, scuffing waves, splinters of silver fracturing the surface, tossing salty dampness skywards. Bodies arc, tails flip, a cascade of water droplets from the dolphins' white underbellies. I've never seen them like this, wild. They're more of everything – majestic, alive, free.

'Sophie.'

'I'm out here,' I call over my shoulder, catching the emotion in my voice. 'Look. You're missing the dolphins. They're swimming alongside the boat.'

'Ship.'

'Sorry?' Like a tripwire, darkness flattens my mind as I step back inside.

'It's a ship. Not a boat.'

'Right. You're alive then.' I prod her arm. 'How are you feeling?'

She observes me through the slit of one eye. 'Not good.' She whimpers, rubs her thigh. 'Please tell me I'm not in yesterday's clothes?' A slap of her hand on her forehead, a dramatic pose of woe. 'Oh, the shame, Christine. Was I awful?'

'No. Hours of fun were had by all.'

'Aw.' She twists her head to me. 'Everything hurts.'

'I'm not surprised. A shortage of knickers is the least of their worries after last night. You must have drunk Bea's cabin dry.'

'Please. Don't say any more.'

'Can I get you anything?'

'In my wash bag. Paracetamol. Please.'

'It's empty. What do you say about putting the empty packets in the bin?'

'Enough with the lectures. My handbag?'

'Nope. Nothing.'

'I'm dying.' Aunt Christine buries her face in the pillow.

'I hope not. We've got a long way to go.' I set a glass of water down on the bedside cabinet. 'Drink this. Sips, or you'll be sick.'

She wriggles onto her side, nuzzles into the pillow. 'Thank you.'

She clutches my hand before I pull it away. 'Did you enjoy yourself?'

'Last night? I did. It was just what I needed,' I lie.

How can I tell her that nothing scours the ache? Of my sitting for hours, chewing my nails sore, dragging blunt blades across my thighs and stomach, of gorging bad foods, all to slay the pain surging through me. Being here hasn't stopped it. I feel everything, and without the distraction of life, home, work, I dread feeling it even more.

'I can't believe you told them you don't drink, Ainti. What will they think?'

'Don't care.'

'I know.' I pat her hand, pull on my boots. 'Stay there. I'll pop down to reception to see if they have anything.'

She turns over. 'Fabulous. Just do it quietly, please.'

It's 6.30 am, and the foyer is a whir with pre-breakfast activity. Staff in white overalls edged with gold rope, steer vacuum cleaners and buff polished surfaces to a high sheen, the scent of lemon and pine thick.

'Hello. Can you help me, please?' I peer at the assistant sitting on a swivel chair, his back to me, on the other side of the reception desk. 'Hello,' I say louder, attempting to drown out the vacuum's whine. Nothing. 'Hello,' I yell, flinching as the room falls silent.

A folder thumps onto the floor. 'Give me five.' He kneels. His beery paunch strains against the white cotton of his shirt, black skin jutting through stressed buttonholes, navel to torso. He slaps at the papers spilling from his hands across the floor. 'No. No. No.'

'Oops. Are you okay?' I lean over the counter. 'Oh. It's you.' I straighten, flick the hair from my shoulders.

'Sorry. Can you give me a minute?'

He's doing that thing when people talk but don't look at you. The frustration of being here with him is starting to cramp my insides.

He lumps the loose sheets of paper onto the counter, scrunches his nose at me. 'Sorry. I should've done my homework. How can I help?'

'Paracetamol.' I clear my throat. 'Please. Any painkiller will do, I think.'

He punches the papers back into the lever arch file. 'Bear with me.'

I turn from him, take a long, sharp breath through gritted teeth, spin back, place a splayed hand on the counter. 'It's Oré, isn't it?'

His eyes narrow, trawling his memory for me. 'Ah, yes. 689. Miss Collins' friend.'

My stomach hardens. It's nice to see I made an impression. 'It's Miss O'Ryan. Sophie O'Ryan. And I'm her niece, not her friend.'

'Ah, right? Of course. I remember.' He slaps down his palms next to mine. 'Ha. That was passive aggressive, wasn't it?' He slides his hands to his sides. 'Sorry. How can I help?'

'Paracetamol, please. Can I buy some on board? A shop, or a medical centre maybe.'

He points to the stack of loose papers. 'It will probably tell us in there. Let's have a look.' He flips through the pages, looks up, a question on the bridge of his lips. 'How's the cabin?' When I don't answer, he stops. 'That good, ha?'

My eyes fix on his. I fold my arms. 'Yep. That good.'

'Have you tried setting up the bed like two singles? I know you can't split them, but I can organise for more pillows, and you could build a wall between you.' He turns back to the papers and says, 'Build a wall,' in his best Donald Trump impersonation.

'Okay.' I slap a hand on the desk. I have no problem with being passive aggressive because I'm not in the mood for your idle humour this morning, Mr Oré, I haven't read the manual, concierge. 'So, here's the deal. My aunt's back in the cabin, dying. Well, not actually dying, but she has the hangover from hell and is waiting for me to save her.' I suck in an irritated wheeze. 'Can you help me or not? Please.'

Eyebrows lifting like he's having a lightbulb moment, he spins on his heels. 'Stay right there,' and he disappears through a doorway behind him.

Rage cracks and fizzes under my skin. I laugh rather than cry. I just want some paracetamol, people. Come on. Help me. Please.

A young lady sweeps out of the doorway. 'Madam, hello. How can I help?'

Again? I have to repeat it all? Really? I close my eyes for a beat. Rein it in O'Ryan. This is not their fault. You're not pissed with them. Well, not her, anyway. 'Yes. Sorry. I mean, yes, please. Paracetamol. Can I buy some on board? Your colleague wasn't much help.'

'Sorry about that. Oré's new to the team. He's still learning where everything is.' She looks behind her, checking he's not listening, leans across the counter, and whispers, 'Very slowly.' Reaching under the desk, she pulls out a box of paracetamol. 'We keep a small selection under here for emergencies. That'll be six dollars, please?'

'Six dollars?' What the actual hell? It's one of those times when you're stuffed, right? They'll be two dollars on shore, even less in bulk. Oh no, we'll add on at least another four dollars to cover the cost of walking them up the gangplank and down a few corridors. Exploitation of the elderly, alive and kicking right here, people. 'Thank you.' I swipe my charge card, slip it and the paracetamol into my pocket, pace across the lobby. 'Well, that was an utter car crash.'

'Have a great day,' Oré calls.

Ah, so he reappears just as I'm leaving, the coward. I stab a finger at the elevator call button.

'So-o-phie. Perfect timing.'

As if my morning couldn't get any worse. 'Candice.'

She lifts my hand, slaps a flyer into my palm. 'Two thirty in the playhouse theatre. A ballroom come Latin beginner's master class. A-maz-ing fun. I'll see you there. Don't be late.' She tosses her hair, marches towards reception. 'Oré.' She snaps her fingers like he's a puppy in training. 'Yes. You. I need you to do something.'

The ping of the elevator doors opening masks the growl rising in my stomach. I crumple the flyer into a clenched fist. 'Two months and twenty-four days and counting, people.'

6

Knife slices of sunlight stab through skylights edged with salt-stained chalky halos. Legs crossed, I shuffle back on the toilet. A blaze of white light flows through my fingers like water. I left my aunt lounging by the pool in oversized sunglasses and a headscarf, flipping pastries around her plate and have been hiding in here for almost an hour, avoiding her suffocating supervision.

Outside of the cubicle, I twist on the tap, a rush of warm water like summer rain. Each step I take on this journey should be a reason to forget, to soothe the panic that keeps me awake, Clare's voice in my head. Yet it feels impossible to believe I will ever get over this. That I can forgive myself, her. I toss the hand towel into the laundry bin, step outside. An explosion of music, 'Roxanne', The Police, screams into the corridor from the doorway opposite. I inch through the double oak doors, slip my sunglasses back onto my head. Another couple of minutes won't hurt, will it?

Below, Candice, graceful in a mid-calf emerald satin gown, swerves her students, correcting flaws in posture, sliding hands into position. I slip onto the back row of the playhouse theatre. A haze of sweet floral, minty perfume catches my throat, the stagehands placing bunches of freesia and eucalyptus around the stage for tonight's shows. The music stops just as my sunglasses clatter onto the wooden floor, amplified by the silence. I fall to my knees, out of sight, peep through the gap between the seats.

Candice cups a hand to her eyes, masks the spotlight's glare. 'Hello,' she calls. 'Come on down. We're all beginners here.'

My head spins from side to side, willing another eager spectator to be looking on, but no, she's talking to me. I stoop lower, bowing like a worshipper on a hassock at Sunday service. A thud of footsteps climbs the stairs.

'Hi. Come. Come. We're just warming up.' Candice motions her hands at me like an airport marshall.

I clear my throat, jut my head above the folded seats. 'Sorry.' I wave the glasses. 'They fell on the floor.'

'Sophie?' Candice shields her eyes, squints me into view.

She recognises me. Just brilliant. I clamber to my feet, wiggle my fingers hello. 'Hi.'

'You came. Let's go, go, go. We're just warming up.'

I'm stuffed. She's blocking my only escape route, locking me into this dance class purgatory. 'Oh Candice, I'm awful at this type of thing.' I cringe at the quiver of desperation in my voice. 'I'll just get in the way.'

She tugs my forearm. 'They all say that in the beginning. Come. Come. You'll love it.'

I grab it back, rub away her pinch. 'I can't. My aunt will wonder where I am.' I snatch a glance at the watch I don't own on my wrist. 'She'll worry if I'm too long.' Jesus. Listen to me. I sound like I'm five years old.

Candice drops her arms to her hips, shrugs. Her smile fades as her legs extend like a ballerina, making her way back down the stairs, the bounce gone in her step.

A heaviness sweeps through me. Teeth clenched, I raise a slow hand into the air, puff a what-am-I-doing exhale through pursed lips. 'Candice, wait. I'll stay for a few minutes.'

'Yay! Super-duper-trooper.' She reaches out, grabs my wrist, jerks me out of the row. 'Once you start, you'll lov- lov- love it. I promise.'

I duper-trooper doubt that. I force a smile as she pushes me down the stairs. And just like that, I'm making someone else's day while ruining mine, again.

'Right, ladies and gentlemen, eyes on me. We're learning one of my personal favourites today.' Candice drums the edge of the stage, throws up her hands, 'It's the T-an-go.'

What? Shoulders hunched, I cross my arms, clamp my hands under my armpits like an irritated toddler. Of all the dances you can choose, Candyfloss. You thought the dramatic, seductive one was the way to go, did you? Have you seen your audience? What the actual hell?

'Right.' Candice shoos her students into two lines, tuts at my reluctance to shuffle forward and conform. 'Front for the ladies. Back for the gentlemen.' She grips my hand, swings me into the front row. 'Go, go, go.'

Hot, fiery blood injects my veins. As she turns away, my scowl brands her like a blacksmith's hot iron. Why do the men get to watch us make clowns of ourselves whilst they hide behind our backs? Sexism alive and kicking right here. Do equality laws not apply on this boat? Women lost their lives to save us from this crud.

'Okay.' Candice claps her hands.

The lady beside me waves her arms up and down, on and off her hips, like a child being told to make space in a PE lesson.

'That will have to do. Let's make a start.' Candice's face pinches as she scans her rows of pupils. 'Stand tall and pull your stomach in like so. Shoulders squared. Lift your ribcage high. A slight bend in the knee. And exhale.'

My attempts to mimic Candice's fluid movements from rounded back to elevated ribcage, of thrusting back and forth, are not pretty, elegant or even a dance move.

'Excellent. We can also go from side to side like this. These are called ribcage isolations. We move through the core of the body like so.' Candice places a hand on her middle, transfers her weight like a swathe of floating silk.

'Oh. Oh. I know this one.' I turn to the woman, thrusting at my side. She tilts her head, eyeballs me from head to toe, sceptical of my claim. I gyrate my hips and realise she's right. I haven't had core muscles for over twenty years. This is an utter disaster. I scrunch my eyes shut, wishing myself anywhere but here.

'And stop. Right. I have a super-duper surprise today.' Candice sweeps a hand to the stairs. 'Bring in the dancers.' She claps like a sea lion performing for fish. 'Whoop! Whoop! Let's give them some encouragement, shall we, ladies and gentlemen?'

Down the stairs comes a random selection of staff. Some mimic Candice's howls, springing two steps at a time, high-fiving each other as they bound onto the dancefloor. Others, shadows of dragging feet, hands pressed in pockets, chins on chests – my crew, right there.

Everyone shuffles to a partner. I stay rooted to a small square of the dance floor, desperate not to catch anyone's attention and exit whilst Candice's not looking.

A hand taps my shoulder. Oh, for goodness' sake. This can't be happening. I turn around.

'Miss O'Ryan. Fancy seeing you here.'

'Oh.' I straighten, sweep the hair from my shoulders. 'It's you.' Of all the people on this flipping ship, it had to be you.

'Wow.' He bites his bottom lip, scans the room before his eyes find mine. 'That's the second time you've greeted me like that today. Don't look so disappointed.'

'Oré.' I shake his hand. 'I didn't know the concierge danced as well.'

He grins, strokes his clean-shaven chin. 'I'm a little offended you haven't noticed my gliding around reception?' He leans into my ear. 'Candice thought it would be a good way for passengers to meet the crew. If it helps, I had a few lessons in my youth. Can do a mean foxtrot to 'Fly Me to the Moon'. You?'

Great. That's all I need. An Anton Du Beke wannabe at my side. 'Nope. This is my first and last. It's not as easy as it looks on the television.'

'So, I won't be singing 'I Bet You Look Good on the Dancefloor', then?'

Is he mocking me? I dagger-eye the smirk from his lips. 'No.'

He slaps his arms to his sides. 'Well, I've never tangoed before, so we can be terrible together.' He skims the room. 'Where's your aunt?'

A jolt of irritation courses through me. 'We don't come as a pair. I get time off for good behaviour.'

He smiles, looks away. 'Glad to hear it.'

Candice claps like a flamenco señorita, and my spine stiffens.

'Here we go. Poker face on,' Oré whispers.

'Right.' Candice runs her hands over her waist and hips. 'The tango is a serious, passionate dance. There is no room for smiling or laughter.'

'Or enjoyment,' I mumble. Chuckle as Oré snorts a soft laugh.

'So,' Candice waves her hands like she's conducting an orchestra, 'face your partners and drop a little in the knees like so. Shoulders back, lift the ribcage, and don't forget to breathe.' She steps forward, places a hand on the small of my back. 'Don't be shy, Sophie. Step in a little closer. I want to see the passion smoulder between you.'

She presses Oré into me. There's no reservoir of cologne today, just a delicious coconut lotion twitching my nose.

'Lift your elbows. Ladies, your hand should look like this. Place your thumb under his arm, and your elbows will interlock, like so. *Voilà.*'

Still stuck on what to do with my hand, I play for time. I can't think of anything worse than sticking my thumb into his armpit, regardless of how fragrant he might smell.

Candice snaps her fingers in the air. 'If you're still unsure, look at Elsie and Tom, who are doing an excellent job over here.'

Oré drops his hands, steps to my side. 'Elsie and Tom are definitely not beginners.'

'You're not kidding. Our very own Gio and Debbie McGee in the house.'

'Who?'

'Strictly finalists. 2017.'

He frowns, shakes his head. 'Nope.'

'Strictly Come Dancing? The BBC? Lovely jubbly. Paul Daniels. You'll like this. Not a lot. But you'll like it.'

His brow creases, as if trying to find any link in his memory to what I've just said. 'Ah. I get it. Like Kym and Mr T.'

'Who?'

'Mr T. DWTS 2017. His cha-cha-cha to the A-Team theme was real bad, but total genius.'

'What? What's DWTS?'

'*Dancing with the Stars.* Keep up.' Oré presses a finger to his lips, motions for me to zip it, concentrate on Candice and her prodigies.

My stomach tightens. I shoot him a sidelong glance, whisper, 'Rude.'

'Very good. Ex-cell-ent.' Candice extends her neck like a giraffe trying to reach the top branches of a tree. 'Now, ladies, hold that chin high, turn your head dramatically to the left, like this.'

She grips my hips, lunges them into Oré's groin. I cough, suppress a yelp. He stabs his chin into the air, a grimace of gritted teeth. How is this even happening?

'Good, Sophie. Surprising, considering your,' she waves a hand up and down, lost for words.

'Body?'

'Yes. That,' she says, not a hint of remorse in her tone.

Are all the staff this rude? If I wanted to be insulted, I could have stayed at home.

Candice slaps my back, propels me into Oré. 'Now, let me see you ache. You must throb with the burning desire to be with him. Only him.'

Oré spits out a stifled laugh.

'Not funny,' I giggle.

The body comment I can take. I get it. But ache for him? What the actual hell, Candyfloss? I was ready to thump him a few minutes ago. The only aching is in my neck as he tosses me from side to side. Please. Get me out of here. His lips draw into a thin line. Is he still teasing me or taking this far too seriously? Ainti, where are you when I need you? Make this stop.

'And,' Candice hesitates, hands on hips, 'step away from your partners.'

'Thank goodness for that.' I pull from his hold.

Candice takes a moment, a hand on her stomach, bends over as if she's just run a marathon, panting. 'Okay. Nothing like a workout to get the juices pumping, is there?' She snaps her fingers above her head. 'Now for the feet.'

'The what? Are you flipping kidding me? Feet? Do we have to use our feet?' My head, shoulders and arms droop forward like an uncoordinated zombie. 'I want to go home,' I whimper.

Oré takes my arm. 'You're funny. Come on, Ginger. Fred'll save ya.'

Twenty minutes later, my torso is plunging, my head lolling, not snapping, and my feet are slow, slow, quick, quicking over Oré's toes. He doesn't appear to notice, marching me from corner to corner, propelling me over his arm. It's hard to tell if he's ultra-focused or in pain behind those clenched teeth.

I cup my mouth, laughter prickling from my stomach.

'Are you taunting me, Miss O'Ryan?' He turns away, tries to

quash his chuckle.

The more I laugh, the more he swings me around. 'Stop. Please stop. You're killing me.'

'I can't. Candice is looking.'

'Are you scared of her?'

'Absolutely.' Oré looks away, pretend shakes with fear. 'Although I think she's concluded, we're no Rashad and Emma.'

'Who?'

'Rashad Jennings.'

'Nope. Not a clue.'

'What! New York Giants, NFL legend. DWTS winner 2017.'

'Why would I know that?'

'Seriously? Can't you get it over in the UK?'

'On some obscure cable channel, maybe. What are you? A dance show groupie?'

He pulls me into him, lifts his chin high to the side. 'What can I say? I'm home alone a lot.'

'In your own bed, no doubt.' I push from his arms. 'For goodness' sake, my shoes are crippling me. That's it. I'm totally done with heels.'

'So, take them off.'

'What?'

He steps in front of me, waves a finger at my shoes. 'Take them off.'

'I can't.'

'Of course you can.'

'But what will people say?'

He looks from side to side, shrugs. 'Who cares?'

Over his shoulder, Candice weaves between couples, observing exposed necklines and thrusting upper bodies.

'All right.' I pull off my fake suede wedges, fling them onto a chair. My once-rebellious self squeals inside, rocking a rolled-up school skirt, a flash of contraband electric pink cycling shorts. 'Hey!' I cry as he jerks me back into his arms, spins me around.

'Oré, let's leave the Viennese waltz for another day, shall we? You'll make Sophie dizzy, twirling her like that.'

He tips an imaginary hat. 'Spoilsport.'

'And stop.' Candice waves her hand. 'Everyone, into position.

This is our last piece.' She disappears behind the stage. 'It's time to show me what you've got.'

Heads bob, and the floor pulses to the beat of Robert Plant's 'Addicted to Love'.

'Crikey. This is a blast from the past.' Oré taps his foot. 'Haven't heard this in years. The 90s?'

'80s. 85.'

Oré takes my hand. 'Someone knows their music.'

'Not really.' A wave of sadness tenses my shoulders. 'It was in the charts when I started uni. Was always playing.'

I lean backwards, snatch my head into position. Clare and I first met in the student union bar during freshers' week, surrounded by wet, sweaty bodies, cheap cider and music pounding from floor-to-ceiling speakers. She had sidled up to me, a cigarette pinched between her lips, puffing smoke rings to the side. She was so cool. It was as if she had ice flowing in her veins. In high-waisted jeans, a white T-shirt and trainers, she was straight off the cover of *Vogue*. Me, in my black netted puff skirt, slouchy off-the-shoulder rainbow hoodie, the geeky back pages nobody read in *Smash Hits*. She became obsessed with the smell of my hair, would follow me into the bathroom, slip out with another bottle of my apple shampoo in her pocket, and her nickname for me, *Soap*, was born.

Oré releases me from his grasp, and I stumble back into the room.

'Miss O'Ryan, it's been an unexpected pleasure. Alas, our scores are rubbish, and we have crashed and burned in the dance-off. So, no glitter ball trophy for us. Plus, I've got to get back to the day job. But thank you.' He bows. 'Enjoy the rest of your day.'

I pull on my sandals, smile as he strides up the stairs, one hand on his stomach, one bent as if still in hold.

Candice steps to my side. 'Well, that was a pretty good start, Sophie.'

I can't help but think she says this to everyone, but I'll take it. 'You're very kind, but I don't think they'll be signing me up for Strictly, will they?'

'No. Probably not. Oré looked like he was having fun, though.' She frowns, watches him hold open the auditorium doors, questions in her eyes. 'You never quite know how the new ones will blend in.'

'He's quite the mover, isn't he?' I say, interrupting her thoughts. 'I'm not sure what moves he was doing, but he was definitely in the room.' I push my slingbacks over my heels. 'No Roy today?'

She gathers up discarded clothing from the seats. 'We take it in turns doing these. They're exhausting but easy.'

Wow. A double slap to the face for all the novices. 'Right.' I smack my knees, stand. 'Thanks, Candice.'

Her eyes dart to mine, fingers tapping the clothing hung over her arm. 'Did you like it?'

'I didn't think I'd say this, but I did.'

'Fab-u-lous. Then you must come again.' Her head slopes to the side, checking my expression. 'I'll turn you into a dancer before the cruise ends.'

'Ha. That's a stretch. Anyhow, I better go. My aunt will wonder where I am.'

'Oh. She looks fine to me.' Candice nods to a couple sitting mid-row halfway up the auditorium.

'Ainti?' I throw up my arms. 'How long have you been sitting there?'

'Long enough,' she says, pressing her tongue into her cheek. 'Long enough.'

7

'Coffee, ladies?' Bea guides us into the coffee lounge, a scatter of burgundy couches, low-slung tables of rich, deep browns. The customers' chatter and swirling dark, aromatic perfume, a warm, familiar hug.

A wall of gold scatter cushions, I sit down beside my aunt. 'Water for me, please. I daren't have any more caffeine. I'll bore the pants off you.' My penchant for blustering like I'm on the podium at Speaker's Corner after just a mouthful of coffee is a longstanding joke at home.

'I doubt that, Sophie.' Bea sits opposite, hands us the menu. 'Ever had an affogato? They're great on board.'

'What is it?'

'Do you like ice cream?'

I swallow hard. Bea, you have no idea how much I flipping worship ice cream. 'Ha. Just a bit. But I have to watch the calories these days, so—'

'No, Sophie-Anne. Absolutely not.' Aunt Christine tosses the menu across the coffee table, off the edge and onto my feet. 'You did this at dinner last night, too. And I'm not having it.' She waves a spikey finger at me. 'This self-dissecting nonsense. You're on holiday, for goodness' sake. Give yourself a break.'

Bea slaps the menu to her chest, laughs so hard she rolls forward, holding her stomach.

I shake my head, clasp my aunt's hand, disarming her pistol finger. 'Ainti, I love you.' I retrieve the menu from the floor. 'It's deprecating. Self-deprecating.'

Bea breathes in and out of her nose a few times, composes herself. 'Oh, Christine. You're such a tonic. You both are.' She signals for service. 'She's right, though, Sophie. Don't let the bastards win. You're a bonnie lassie. Let no one tell you otherwise.' She holds up her palm, signals for the barista to wait. 'Now. Are you sure I can't tempt you?'

The barista wipes down our table, a dust cloud exploding into a shaft of sunlight. It reflects my mood, erratic, frequently changing direction, before floating back to earth with a moment of resumed calm.

'Oh, go on, then. I'll have one of those affo thingies, please.'

'That's what we like to hear. Three affogatos, please,' Bea leans in to read the barista's name badge, 'Robyn. Make them large with double shots all around. Let's start how we mean to go on. You'll love it, Sophie.'

I push back between two plumped-up cushions. You bet your affogato double vanilla flipping mind I'll love it, Beatrix. It's the shame hammering me in a couple of hours that I'll loathe.

Aunt Christine tidies today's baby-pink knitted twinset over her oversized beige cargo shorts. 'Tell us about the dancing, Sophie-Anne?'

'There's nothing to tell. I came out of the bathroom and got hijacked. End of.'

'By a rather dishy-looking concierge. I saw.'

'No. You didn't.' I dagger her silent. 'I didn't know the crew was going to be there.'

'I see.'

'Stop it. I didn't go on purpose, if that's what you're insinuating.'

Aunt Christine holds her chest as if I've shot her. 'Moi. I didn't say a word.'

'You didn't have to.'

'Oh, Sophie-Anne, stop being a bore. It'll do you a world of good to muck in. Anyhow, you love Strictly.' She turns to Bea. 'She was quite the expert at the macarena in her youth.'

'Bore! Really? And what's the macarena got to do with anything? It's hardly the same, is it?'

The waiter puts down our drinks, pours a small jug of hickory espresso over scoops of pillowy vanilla ice cream. A syrupy nutty aroma spins into the air. A heaped teaspoon of the thick caramel liquid strokes my throat like a shot of tequila – the bitterness of the coffee combined with the sweetness of the gelato. 'That is so good.' I nod at the book on the table. 'What're you reading, Bea?'

She flips it over. 'It's a journal.'

'Ha.' The gold embossed LOVE YOU printed on the cover makes me cringe. 'I have the same one in the cabin. I'm meant to be writing something in it every day.'

'How's it going?'

I gulp a mouthful of coffee. 'Badly,' I splutter, hold up my mug like I'm about to clink it in celebration to another. 'I'm not great at all this touchy-feely emotional stuff.' I place down the mug, pick up the journal, slapping it on my lap. 'What does *love you* mean, anyway? Is it a term of endearment, as in, the person who gifted it loves you? Or is it imploring you to love yourself?'

Aunt Christine wrestles the book from my hand. 'Sophie, you're—'

'And what if you're the one who bought it? How does that work?' I tap the mug on my lips, down the last dregs of coffee. 'I'm convinced that fifty years from now, they'll reflect on my generation of women and be like, what the actual hell? As if we've been some transitional experiment, sold the dream of having it all – education, careers, families, youthful skin. Never mention Botox in my company. We're doing more than ever before, and does anybody care? Do they hell! Who decided hot yoga, restorative yoga, chair yoga, squeeze-the-next-forty-years-of-potential-disasters-which-will-never-happen-anyway-from-your-mind yoga was a good idea? That we'd need a library of self-help manuals, a zillion podcasts, and inspirational thoughts pinging up on our screens every minute, which incidentally aren't as nice as they used to be. Have you had your five-a-day because kale and avocadoes are flipping superfoods? When did someone conclude it was wise to talk about how we feel? That we need to love ourselves. And then there's the menopause – the final insult. Who really understands that?' I bang my mug down on the table. 'No. People will look back and say, thank goodness we tested this out on them. Devastated those women.'

'Woo-hoo! You go, girl.' Bea bucks a complimentary pretzel into her mouth.

'And there she is. Now and then, Sophie-Anne, there's the slightest glimmer. Just the smallest twinkle,' says Aunt Christine, a proud parent smile.

'Sorry.' I throw my arm over my eyes. 'Rant over. Ha. I warned you. Caffeine rage.' My mobile pings in my pocket. 'I've got a text,' I say, giggle.

Aunt Christine shrugs, side-eyes Bea to see if she understands the joke. 'Well, answer it then. The suspense is killing us.'

I pull it out. 'Do you mind?'

Aunt Christine flicks a hand at me, turns to Bea. 'So, Beatrix ...'

I scroll the WhatsApp threads, friends surmising what I'm doing and with whom. I tap back – *All good. Call soon.* I keep it short, knowing they will chew on this slither of news for hours before moving on. What would I say anyway? Hi, I'm hanging with my buddies, Aunt Christine and Bea, with an average age of seventy-eight and more zest for life than I've ever had. No siree. I can berate myself well enough without their diagnostic opinions. Another chime, like a magician's ta-dah.

TD: Sorry I missed you. What's up?

Me: Just having a moment. Speak later?

TD: Sure.

I mute the conversations, slip the phone back into my pocket.

Bea jolts forward, swipes at the hand grasping her shoulder from behind. 'What the ...'

A man, dark caramel skin, bright eyes and sharp cheekbones holds out his arms. 'Beatrix.'

Bea jumps from her seat, grips him around his neck. 'Anton, you little tinker.' She plants a kiss on each cheek, smooths his untucked white linen shirt against his chest. 'When did you arrive?' She glances from side to side. 'No Jed?'

Boyishly handsome, his eyes weighed down by wrinkle folds, his posture erect like a man who goes to the gym for fun rather than necessity.

'*Ce matin.* I'm only staying a few stops, then flying onto Dubai to see Jed and co.' His voice is strong, plummy like an army colonel in a TV war drama. Anton scans the nest of couches, drops his grasp. 'How rude. I'm interrupting you.'

'Not at all. Come and sit down. Coffee?'

He lifts his shirt cuff, checks his gold-rimmed wristwatch. 'I'd love to, but I've got water polo in fifteen.' He grips the back of the empty chair, two hands. 'But what are you up to tomorrow? The Andersons have chartered a yacht. You know, Ted and Anna from Bridgetown last year. Come with us.' He nods at Aunt Christine, me. 'Bring your friends.'

'Braw. Fancy it, ladies? The snorkelling's to die for.'

'My aunt can't swim,' I say, abruptly.

'There'll be turtles.' Anton wiggles his eyebrows at Aunt Christine. 'You can always watch from the boat.'

I adjust in my seat. 'I don't—'

'I'll think about it,' Aunt Christine interrupts.

His gaze lingers on my aunt, hers on his. 'Excellent. Well, we're leaving at eight. It would be lovely to see you. All of you.' He thrusts his hand at me. 'Anton. I'm one of Bea's long-suffering travelling companions.' He gestures for Aunt Christine's hand, pulls it to his lips. 'And you are?'

Her face softens. 'Christine. I'm, we're, friends of Beatrix's.'

We are? Goodness, you're a quick worker, Ainti. I look at him, her, recall a scene from my childhood, of her sitting on the knee of a man, him stroking her hair behind her ear, kissing her neck, the same doughy half smile.

'Well, Christine and—' Anton turns to me.

'Oh, sorry. Yes. Sophie. I'm Sophie. Christine's niece.'

'Well, Christine and Sophie, we would be delighted if you could join us. Don't forget to pack your bathers.' He squeezes Bea's shoulder, nods goodbye, and with a spin of his hips, he's gone.

'Well, that sounds lovely, doesn't it, Sophie-Anne?' Aunt Christine signals for the waiter. 'Another?'

I slide my mug across the table, slap a cushion over my stomach, thighs. 'Lovely,' I repeat, silently chanting one, two, three, one, two, three at the riotous dread pounding my head.

8

Whitsunday Islands. Queensland. Australia.

'Remind me why I came again, Ainti?'

'Hmph, hmph, hmph.' Aunt Christine reclines on a sunlounger, cobalt one-piece swimsuit, black sarong, full-face diver's mask and snorkel.

'The mask.'

Her shoulders bounce, hiccupping laughter as she pulls it over her head. 'Just getting in the spirit, Sophie-Anne.'

I peer over the side of the catamaran, the fish weaving over ridges of sand carved like waves on the ocean floor. 'Are you going in? I don't think it's very deep.'

'Goodness no. I don't do seawater. My legs are meaty enough to attract a shark from a mile away. You go, though.'

'So, it's okay for me to get eaten?'

'Absolutely.' She drops her head back, a wry smile, eyes closed.

The lounger creaks in agony as I slide onto the one next to her. 'I don't think so.'

'Whyever not?' She flips open her sunglasses and slips them onto the lacquered rock face of her hair. 'Oh, go on. You'll enjoy it. I'll be fine. Get changed inside. People are coming in and out of there like a revolving door.'

'No, thanks. I'm not feeling it today.' I stare at the yachts scattering the shoreline like decorated swimwear speckling the beach.

'Don't be so silly. Go.'

My spine stiffens like a steel rod is being inched through me. 'I don't want to.'

'But why?'

My breath catches at her question. 'Is that anyone's business? Can we just focus on the people who want to?'

'Sophie?'

I wipe at the mist of sweat prickling the back of my neck and chest. 'What?'

'Sophie?'

'What?' The air fogs thick with difficult, the question stills on the bridge of her lips. I look down; my knuckles clenched tight. 'I don't have a swimming costume, okay?' Frustration sharpens my words. 'And before you start, I don't need a lecture.'

'You forgot to bring it?' Her head falls to one side, inspecting my reaction. 'Or you didn't bring one?' When I don't reply she turns to face me. 'Sophie?'

I sit up straight, push my hands under my thighs. 'Enough, Ainti. I don't like the sea.'

'Which isn't true, is it? You used to be a right little mermaid.'

'Four decades ago, maybe.'

Aunt Christine stares deadpan at the shore. 'Is it because you think you're fat?'

The dirge pounding my veins screeches to a stop. 'And how's that helping?'

'Well, is it?' A twitch in her eyelid. 'Sophie, you've lost all that weight. Too much, if you ask me. Isn't it enough?'

I stare up at the sky, my breathing a silent whistle through gritted teeth.

'You look fantastic. You did before, and you do now. Is that what you need to hear? Because I can do that. I'll tell you every minute of every day if that's what it takes.' She yanks off her sunglasses, entangled with a knot of silver hair. 'For goodness' sake, Christine. You can't be losing a single strand at your age. You fool.'

I pick up the mask, twirl the strap between my fingers. 'It's beautiful here, isn't it?'

'Don't change the subject. Why don't you use one of those rubber suit thingies?' Aunt Christine points her glasses at a rail of dripping wetsuits swinging like a line of hung men. 'Come on. I'll help you find one.'

'Please stop. It's not about that.' Which isn't entirely true. This body has been crushing me for a lifetime, the unfortunate container that carries my head around. God knows, I would have designed her better. It's part of it, yes, but it's not *that*. I calm my tone. 'Sorry. I don't want to be like this.'

Aunt Christine pats my hand, lays her head against mine. 'I know.'

'Ladies, how are we doing?' Bea strides towards us, Anton on her arm.

Aunt Christine places down her glasses, purrs like a teenager swooning over a poster of their first celebrity crush. 'Leave this to me.' She shuffles her legs off the lounger until seated, feet flat on the deck. Chin low, she bats her eyelashes. 'Anyone would think you're following me around, Anton.'

He kisses the back of her hand. 'I assure you, my intentions are completely dishonourable, Christine.'

'I hope so,' she coughs, winks at me.

'Hey. Behave.' I dig her playfully in the ribs.

'So, ladies,' Anton rubs his hands together, 'coming in?'

My aunt's arm circles my back. 'Not today. We're going to watch from up here.'

Anton's face washes with confusion like the cogs in his brain can't turn fast enough to process what she said. 'It's pretty shallow and the water's fantastic. Are you sure?'

'Perfectly.' Her grip tightens, squeezing my waist.

'Sophie?' Bea says.

Before I open my mouth, Aunt Christine stands, blocks their path. 'Sophie's staying with me. Can't be trusted on my own and all that.' She stares them down, flicks her hand. 'Go. Have fun.'

In moments like this, I slip back into being that scared twelve-year-old under the kitchen table. The sureness of her voice, slender fingers curling around my hand. My welcoming her need to mother me, even if she doesn't understand why. None of this is her fault. She has, despite our differences, my indiscretions, done a beautiful job raising me.

Anton rubs his forehead, looks at the well-loved bodies, all shapes and sizes, hurling themselves overboard. 'If you're sure?'

Aunt Christine nods. 'Please. You go.'

'Okay.' Anton takes Bea's hand, gives us a two-finger salute goodbye. 'Ready?' They leap over the side. '*Pousse-toi!*'

My aunt grips the guardrail, giggles at them smacking their hands in the water, the sunlight winking the ripples like tiny mirrors.

I throw my head back, stare unseeing at the sky. 'I'm so sorry, Ainti. I'm spoiling this for you.'

She taps my shoulder. 'Did you see the six-pack on him, Sophie-Anne? Wowsers.'

'Ainti!'

On the horizon, a twenty-something couple from a neighbouring boat frolic in the sea. He smooths back her hair, hoists her legs around his waist. A kiss, a reuniting of knowing lips. It's the kind of moment when the world stands still, falls silent. There's no one else, just you and them. The memory swells up in my throat, and I'm outside myself, watching me, watching them, watching us.

***

'I missed you on the weekend.' A fork of spaghetti carbonara hovered at Patrick's lips. 'What did you get up to?'

When Patrick sauntered into school for the first time, clean-shaven, thick sandy hair framing sky-blue eyes, heads turned. Thirty-nine and three years older than me, an English major, I watched him coach the school football team from the staffroom window for months. I never expected anything from him, but then one day he looked up, his T-shirt stretched taut over his sporty frame, and drank me.

'Not much. Clare, a friend from uni, came down.'

Patrick spooned parmesan over his food. 'Want some?'

'No.' I heaved. 'It smells like vomit.'

'Charming!' He waved his fork at my plate. 'Says she, being as adventurous as ever.'

'I like pizza.'

'I know.' He grinned, wiggled his eyebrows. 'You have it every time.'

'Hardly. We've only been here twice. So. What did you do?'

'Played football. Drowned my sorrows in a kebab of saturated fat.' He picks up the wine, hesitates like he's looking inside me. 'It wasn't the same without you.'

Heat rose on my cheeks; I tore off a slice of pizza. 'Ahh. Sweet.'

'I am sweet.' He pours me another glass. 'I've been meaning to ask you, what are your plans for the summer?'

'Not sure. I might head up and see Clare for a bit. Why?'

'I'm going to see my folks the week after we break up. Come with me?' His expression turned serious, his words falling like an axe between us.

'Oh.' I ripped off a mouthful of pizza, let it fall.

'Yeah. They're itching to meet you.'

An awkward silence. I stumbled over his words. 'Right.'

'Problem?' His eyes didn't leave mine as he heaped a fork of spaghetti into his mouth.

I drank some wine, bought myself some time. 'We break up in two weeks.'

'We do.'

Lowered eyes, I put down my glass. 'It feels quick, Pat, doesn't it?'

'Oh.' He set the fork down on his plate, adjusted in his seat. 'Okay. I get it. You don't want to. It's fine.'

I breathed hard through my nose. 'Please don't do that. I'm just not sure we're at the parents' stage.'

He downed his wine, topped it up again, scanned the room. 'No. You're right. I'm getting over-excited.'

What did he expect? We'd been seeing each other for three weeks – three flipping weeks. We're not teenagers having a first crush. But the pain slicing his eyes punched my gut. 'No. It's me. I'm sorry. You've just taken me by surprise.'

Patrick spooned more parmesan over his pasta. 'Aha. Brilliant weather, hey?'

I took a long, slow sip of wine, mulled over his invitation. Did I want to go? No. Was I ready to meet his family? No. And what did that mean, anyway? A flipping lot for me. I searched his face. His wounded expression made me feel a multitude of things all at once. 'Okay.'

He stopped prodding his food, his blue eyes framed by feathery eyelashes meeting mine.

I crushed my napkin under my palm on the table. 'Why not? Sounds fun.'

He slumped back in his chair. 'Really? You're sure?'

'Aha.'

He reached into his pocket, pulled out his phone. 'I'm going to let them know before you change your mind.'

A couple at the next table kiss, a prick in my stomach, jealously.

'So.' Patrick put down his phone, took my hand, his thumb rubbing my skin like a suggestion. 'Tonight …'

Electricity burned under my skin. 'I've a ton of marking, Pat.'

'Me too.' He pulled me from the table, placed his jacket over my shoulders. 'It can wait.'

***

A roar of laughter drags me back to the revellers below, to Aunt Christine bent over the side, squealing at Anton and Bea, soaking her with a pumped-up water pistol. A youthful glow to her skin, a glimpse of her once untroubled cheerfulness.

'Sophie-Anne.' She wags her finger between Anton and Bea. 'Can you see what they're doing to me?'

Their screams are not unlike the excitement I see every day on the playground at school. The thought of home cracks like glass being struck by a rock. I had seen on the playground. I had seen. It still feels uncomfortable to think about my life in the past tense.

'Why don't you get in, Ainti? Put a life jacket on. They'll look after you.'

'Come on, you two,' Bea shouts.

'She won't come,' Aunt Christine calls back. 'We need to sort her out, Beatrix.'

Bea winks, taps her nose. 'Don't you worry, Christine. Leave it to me. I think I know just the thing.'

9

Bali. Indonesia.

'So, Sophie. We've got a surprise for you,' says Bea.

I turn from the car window. 'Oh?' The day had started with the three of us bundling into a taxi at sunrise on a mission to replace Aunt Christine's yuletide-themed knickers at Marks & Spencer in Badung. 'I thought we were heading back.'

'We are. But we thought we'd treat you to a witch doctor on the way.' Aunt Christine pats my knee, a wide, toothy grin.

'A what?'

'A medicine man, Christine, not a witch doctor.' Bea chuckles.

'Is there a difference?' What the actual hell are they talking about? And what does Aunt Christine mean by a treat? A bar of chocolate or a new scarf is a treat, not a trip to a flipping medicine man. Whatever that is?

'Aye. He's a wise man. A kind of fortune teller. The Balinese love them.'

Aunt Christine's expression turns serious. 'There's no voodoo-hoodoo, Sophie-Anne. He won't stick pins in you or anything like that. Just sort you out.'

'Sort me out?' I cut to the window, the soothing hillsides of refreshing greens capped by a sea of white clouds. 'Nothing to worry about then.'

'Sarcasm is never attractive, Sophie-Anne.'

I turn to face them. 'And we have to go now?'

'We are, and we do.' Aunt Christine hones her authoritative parenting pout, flicks hair from her eyes.

'We've already travelled up and down half the country already.

Aren't you tired?'

'Sophie. You need to get a grip. Beatrix and I are used to this pace of life. You have to max it when you get a couple of days in port, no time for lounging around.'

I dare you, Ainti. I dare you to call me lazy. I've played my part on this voyage *désastreux*. When did I become the one not wanting to get off this ship? Remember Darwin? Who snoozed all day under a golden eye mask? Not me, that's for sure. Oh, the irony.

'Well, ladies.' Bea points out of the window. 'We need to decide. We're here.'

We step out of the car. Heat floats like a gassy fume from the dusty road. Shopkeepers perch in open doorways, savouring the shade under wooden signs hanging loose on rusted chains.

'Put a helmet on,' Aunt Christine hollers at a young man speeding past on a moped, her eyes meeting mine.

I close the car door, a long whistling sigh. As much as I want to hate this trip, each new place draws me in, screwing at the want I've long ignored. Is it the power of this beauty which will help me dream again? Only the most inquisitive among us dare to step beyond the tourist hot spots and discover places like this. It takes energy, courage too. I felt the same longing as a child lying in bed, rolling the uncharted journeys I would one day take over and over in my mind. Why do we let our hopes fade with others' expectations? Until they disappear. Until time runs out. Aunt Christine and Bea did not perhaps personify the crusading adventurers we see on screen, but they were like them in many ways. It's also why I suspect they're growing closer by the day.

Bea points to an open doorway, scarcely the width of a person, motions for us to follow her through. On either side, a child-sized statue, one a welcoming hand, the other a pinched brow. Lofty walls of rendered concrete rise to the sides, still sturdy despite the chiselled pits of decay. Beyond, a tunnel of verdant foliage and the medicine man.

A courtyard of manicured green lawns and plumeria trees, every shade, shape and size of petal lay thick like fallen leaves on our path. I scoop them to my nose, silky, cooler than expected, their perfume a floral orchestra tumbling through my fingers. A woman ties back her thick black hair, bows her head. She ushers us up onto a porch to a man sitting cross-legged on a mat of white carpet. Early twenties, he pulls on a turban of white cotton, adjusts a necklace of red and brown beads. He is not what I am expecting.

My throat cakes with thirst. Climbing the steps, I wipe away the trickle of sweat dripping from temple to chin. 'You're kidding, right? He's just a kid,' I whisper to Bea.

He pats the floor. '*Om swastiastu*. Please. Sit.'

Aunt Christine circles like a dog, trying to find the most comfortable resting place. She mouths 'thank you' to the woman with black hair, thrusting a plastic chair into the back of her knees. Cross-legged, Bea and I settle on the floor.

'Very good.' He holds his hands in prayer, ruby-jewelled silver rings pinching his fingers. I rub my left hand, my ring finger, steal it to my side.

'I am Kadek. Thank you for coming.' He strokes a palm down his washed-out red T-shirt, a faded mustard yellow batik sarong. 'Where are you from?' He opens his hand, beckons for our reply.

'Canada.' Bea lifts a hand hello.

'England.' I point at me, my aunt, follow the blink of his eyelids, the concentration of his stare.

'So, how do you know of me?' He looks down before flicking his eyes back to mine. My stomach cramps, a tightness in my heart, and I can't move. I look down at the floor, stretch back my shoulders, brush away the dust coating my feet.

Bea hands Kadek a photograph, folded into quarters. 'I've been here before.'

'This is you?' He smooths it against his hand.

'Yes. About six years ago. I came with my girlfriend, Alice.'

How old is this man? Wise men are ancient. Well, they are in movies. Six years ago, unless Kadek has the elixir of eternal youth, he would have been only a teenager, sixteen, seventeen. I couldn't even decide what to wear at that age, let alone offer counsel. Years of hustling the tourist trade is sitting right in front of us. Fair play, Kadek. If they're gullible enough to pay, hey? He stabs me with a sharp stare as if reading my thoughts; my limbs stiffen.

A waft of perfumed incense pitches deep into my nose and throat.

Over my shoulder, the cry of an infant. A group of women swathed in pale pastel sarongs sit sheltered on a porch across the courtyard, toddlers pulling at their hands. Spinning back, I catch my reflection in a mirror propped against the wall, the loose skin wrinkled under my chin drums at my own mortality.

'I can see you've not been before.' Kadek's gaze falls on me. He places his hands of manicured nails onto his knees. 'Your eyes, they are sad.'

Ice trickles down my spine. 'Sorry?'

He takes my hand in his, points to my palm. 'Can I?'

A thump of caution in my head tells me to leave, not to listen. He unwraps my fingers, his grip gentle, smile soft. I nod, 'Ahem.'

His thumb strokes my palm, and my whole body feels it, a throb, a yearning for something, something I cannot trap to speak.

Kadek blows across his fingers. 'You have experienced pain. Much, much pain.' He looks up. 'It's time to let go.' A quiver trims his voice. He cups my hand in his. 'You are a good woman. But until you believe this, nothing will change.' He peels his hand from mine, points to my ring finger. 'Married, yes?'

'Not any more.' My shoulders lift, tense.

'Yes. I see that. You will marry again.'

'Ha.' I shake my head. 'I don't think so.' Is he for real? I don't need his or anyone's pity. Look at her, almost fifty and single, poor you, poor Sophie O'Ryan, who just needs a man to complete her, save her troubled soul. This isn't a flipping scene from *Jerry Maguire*, Kadek. Can a woman not be unattached in peace?

'Heartbreak makes us fearful, no? Your heart will mend. Find forgiveness, and you'll live again. It's not easy. Will take great patience. Many give up.' Kadek's voice relaxes. 'But not you.'

I snatch my hand from his, stumble to my feet. I'm not the first to have their heart broken, Kadek, am I? Such is life. And who are you to comment, anyway? You don't have the life experience to dissect my choices. And what does he mean by forgiveness? I can forgive. I have forgiven. Many times. That's the simple part. It's the forgetting I need to master.

I bow my head, wipe sweaty palms on my thighs. 'Thank you.' I've no energy left within me to argue. Pissed, like a kettle about to blow on a hob, I turn to my aunt, Bea. 'I'm done. I'll wait over there.'

At the end of the porch, birdcages of reedy bars hang from a roof made from the same layered bamboo. A man sits cross-legged in front of a shrine of china deities and strikes a wooden pestle on a tarnished metal-coloured bowl. I close my eyes at the hypnotic pull of his chant. My pulse thumps in my ears. A mind-flash of Clare, calling to me through thrashing rain.

A roar of laughter. 'Sophie-Anne. Come over here.'

Bea throws a hand across Aunt Christine, rocking in her chair.

I smooth down my dress. 'Are you okay?' I steady her chair, glance at Bea, Kadek.

'He says I'm going to get married too.' Aunt Christine slaps a hand on my thigh.

'Ouch.'

'Sorry.' She steals her hand away. 'I wasn't thinking.'

Aunt Christine prods Bea's arm. 'Ha. I've no energy for me these days, Kadek, let alone a new man.'

Seriously! Nobody's buying into this junk, are they? Look at her. She's almost eighty, for Christ's sake.

Aunt Christine gives Kadek a lighthearted punch on his chest. 'You're a hoot. Me married. Well, I never.' She hoists herself up from the seat. 'Let's go. Before he marries you off too, Bea.'

Kadek nods towards the narrow entrance, grips my wrist hard as I pass, places his palm on his heart. 'Listen to what this tells you. Remember lessons learnt.' His eyes, entrancing ovals of hazel, fine lines of rust-red bleeding into brown, green and gold, pupils stated, scraping like fingernails on a chalkboard, vexing my core raw. 'May forgiveness and gratitude light your path.' He drops my arm, turns away.

'No.' I clasp his hand.

He stops, looks at my hand holding his.

'Sorry.' I drop my grip. 'Sorry.' My head is cotton. I smooth my hands over my hips, cross my arms. My voice breaks with emotion. 'What do you mean by lessons learnt?'

'Listen.' He taps a finger on his temple. 'You are a good woman. Believe, and everything changes.'

Kadek bows, walks away, my eyes not leaving him.

'Stick two fingers up to that, hey, Sophie-Anne? What a load of old twaddle.' Aunt Christine slaps my back. 'What would he know, anyway? He's barely out of nappies.'

Kadek enters the bungalow, drops the curtain door, is gone.

I shake my head. 'He's just doing his job,' I mutter to her, to me.

'Well, at least Bea's happy. She's coming into money, apparently. Not that she needs it. Good God, I'd rather that than see my last days washing some ungrateful geriatric's dirty pants.'

The sky jolts dark, knotted clouds, a crack of lightning like a searchlight, and my mind skips. A knife of colder air, the rain sheets off the leaves and buildings, like thunder.

Aunt Christine marches over to the driver, waves both hands in the air. 'Jazz hands all the way, Sophie-Anne. Come on, let's go. You're getting soaked.'

I hug my arms around me, sodden fabric sticking to my skin. 'Lessons learnt,' I whisper, throw my face skywards into the rain.

***

Our wedding reception had been a day of blue skies and silver clouds, the grass a carpet of wintry white crystals. Patrick stood propped against the bar, observed us from the depth of his blue eyes.

'Well, I'll be damned. You've really gone and done it, Soap.' Clare embraced me, eyebrows lifted, gritted teeth.

'Yes, I have. Crazy to think we hadn't even kissed a few months ago.'

'Bonkers.' She patted my back. 'You look superb, by the way.'

The Master of Ceremonies clinks a knife to glass. 'Mr and Mrs McGovern, please make your way to the dancefloor for the first dance.'

Clare swept her hand in front of me. 'Let the good times roll.'

Patrick twirled onto the dancefloor, bowing to the crowd, arms outstretched, champagne bottle in hand.

'The bottle, darling? You might want to put it down.'

'Oh, yes. Good point.' He kissed my cheek, tossed the bottle at his best man.

'Crikey, how much have you had, Pat?'

'All right. All right. It's a party.' He tapped my chest, gripped me around the waist. 'You're my wife today, babes, not my boss.'

A wave of laughter and applause erupted as the band struck up Kool and the Gang's 'Ladies Night'.

'Soph. What the?' Patrick's words were hot in my ear. 'I thought we'd agreed to change this?'

'We agreed we didn't have a song.'

'You could have told me?' A curled lip, his hands shifted to my shoulders. 'Everyone's laughing at us.'

'I did tell you.' Our high-spirited guests spilled onto the dancefloor, whooping, glasses lunged in the air. 'It's funny. They're just having a good time.' My kiss was soft on his lips.

'At my expense.'

'Come on, Pat. It was my mum's favourite.'

'Like this, Sophie-Anne. Jazz hands.' Aunt Christine wiggled her hips, weaved past us, Clare in tow.

'Looking fabulous as always, Ainti.'

'You're right. Of course you are.' He spun me from his grasp. 'And now the cavalry has arrived.' He wiped the back of his hand to his mouth. 'I need a drink.' His stare fixed on Clare.

***

'Come on, Sophie-Anne. You're getting drenched.' Aunt Christine tugs my arm, pulls me from my thoughts.

The mist twists into fog. I climb into the car, wipe the wetness from my face. The rainstorm outside spins me dizzy. Kadek's words stirring memories of Patrick, rain-slicked hair, the stroke of a blood-stained hand. I close my eyes, press my forehead to the window, and my tears, for the first time in months, fall unchecked.

10

Tucked into a booth in the top deck bar, I swallow spoon after spoon of ice cream. The honeyed taste, syrupy with a bitter crunch of dark chocolate chip, hasn't hit my stomach before I lunge the next scoop into my mouth. The spoon falls, clank onto the table. Three deep breaths, I pinch sharp, jagged, bitten-down nails into the purple, fleshy underside of my wrist. The dragging sting is enough to shock the urge for another bite or ten. For now. I stack the six empty cartons inside each other, kick them under the chair. The revulsion throttles me. Tears prickle my eyes tender. Nobody knows. Nobody cares. Not even me. Not enough to stop. Eating like this has nothing to do with hunger, nothing to do with gratification, and everything to do with gouging at the grief, and guilt, and pain, deafening inside me. My need to not feel … anything. I pull the fringed shawl around my shoulders, drink in my mother's ghost scent.

It's standing room only at the bar, evening gowns traded for summer dresses, tuxedos for cotton shirts hung slack over casual trousers, the flutter of hand-held fans in decorated fabric. Bea pushes through the crowd, her eyes scanning the throng for me. Since getting back, I've dodged them both. Aunt Christine's repeated attempts to check in with me, tearing my patience. I have no desire to talk about something neither of us understands. I lick the last creamy drips of ice cream from my fingers, turn away, rub the ache in my forehead.

Beads of water from the earlier rain hang like tears from the handrails. Each drop fashions a hundred mirrored rainbows in the setting sun. I swipe up the crystal tumbler, suck the ice cubes laced with the last traces of vodka. In a few hours, the shame will sting, but not now. Now, I ignore the agitation waiting to rip and thunder out of me.

'Sophie. Thank goodness.' Bea hunches over me, a hand on my shoulder wheezing like a gush of wind through an open door. 'Geez. I've been looking for you everywhere. It's Christine. She's had a fall.'

'What? Is she okay?' I hurdle off the chair, weave after her past customers, down the stairs into reception. Mum's shawl flapping like a flag, clamped under my arm.

Bea points to a nest of settees. A familiar cackle cuts through the buzz of passengers returning from today's excursions. Oré, Aunt Christine's handbag looped over his arm, lowers her onto an armchair, ice pack on knee. A nurse dressed in white scrubs kneels at her feet.

'Ainti! Are you okay?'

'I'm fine, Sophie-Anne. Just a bump.'

'Is it bad?'

The nurse shakes her head. 'No. She knocked her knee on the table as she went down. She'll be fine. Luckily, Oré caught her. The ice pack's just a precaution.'

I turn to Oré. 'What happened?'

'Hmm. Yes. Well …' He pulls at his shirt collar. 'There was some sunscreen on the floor. I'm so sorry, Christine. It was totally my fault. I got distracted.' He looks at me, an uneasy laugh. 'I hit her with my mop.'

'Ha. I told him I already had a shower.' Aunt Christine takes hold of his hand. 'I should've been looking at where I was going.'

All the anger bubbling in my gut from the past few hours blasts from my mouth. 'You did what?' Feet astride, I kick the mop and bucket, throw my hands in the air. 'You idiot. You absolute idiot. You could have really hurt her. Do you know how serious a fall can be at her age? A broken hip could literally kill her.'

'Sophie. What on earth?' Aunt Christine drops the ice pack, stands. 'It was an accident.'

'I hear that, Ainti. But I think you should see a doctor anyway.' I usher her to sit back down, place the ice pack back on her knee.

'Have you been drinking?' She sniffs my breath. 'We haven't been back an hour, young lady. How much have you had?'

'What? Nothing … One. Maybe two.'

Aunt Christine leans into me, lifts my left eyelid. 'Or have you been on the wacky-baccy again?'

I sweep her hand away. 'Don't be so ridiculous. This isn't about me. It's about him and that delinquent mop.' I twist to Oré. 'Have you sorted out our beds? Or have you conveniently forgotten about that, too?'

He jerks his hand out of his trouser pocket, looks at Aunt Christine, me. 'Well–'

'No,' I interrupt, my voice clipped, knuckles itching. 'Didn't think so.'

'Stop fussing.' Aunt Christine heaves herself back up. 'I told him he can do it anytime if it means I get those lovely arms wrapped around me.'

'That's not the point. It could have been much worse.'

Bea steps forwards, grabs my arm. 'Sophie, why don't you take Christine back to the cabin?'

'But–'

'Enough.' Aunt Christine's glare insists I don't say another word. 'Thank you, nurse, Oré.' She loops her arm into mine. 'Come. You can finish your tantrum in private. Apologies everyone. Beatrix, I'll see you in the morning.'

My silver trainers thump the cabin wall. 'You could've told me about this before I ripped into him.' I examine our new cabin through a splayed hand. One floor below Bea's, we now have two king-sized divans, a two-seater sofa, and a circular dining table, four chairs.

'Sit down.' Aunt Christine pats the bed.

'I don't want to sit down.' I snatch up the trainers, lob them into the wardrobe. 'Did you know about this?'

'I thought it would be a nice surprise.'

'Is that why you dragged me out this afternoon? So someone could rifle through my underwear. Christ. Was it him? Did he do this? Ainti!'

'Don't be silly. Sit down. Look, two beds.' She slaps the white cotton duvet. 'Enormous beds. And a settee. Happy?'

I unscrew a bottle of water, take a long sip. 'I look like a total idiot.'

'No.' She tilts her head, scrunches her nose, pinches finger to thumb. 'Well, maybe a little.'

'Thanks for that.'

'Come. Make an old lady happy and sit down.'

I slump down next to her, curl a loose thread from my capri pants around my thumb until it pinches the skin white.

She strokes strands of hair from my cheek. 'I'm curious, Sophie-Anne. Who are you angry with? Oré, me, yourself?'

'What's that supposed to mean?'

'Goodness, you stink.' She fans her face. 'Drinking yourself silly won't help, will it?'

'Are you really going to lecture me about drinking?'

'Ha. Good point. Maybe not.'

'Anyway.' I rub a stain on my trousers. 'I'm not drunk, if that's what you're insinuating.'

'I was merely–'

I stick my palm between us. 'No.'

'Well, that told me.' She stands, swings open the wardrobe. 'Zip it, Christine,' she mumbles, slides our laundered clothes onto hangers. 'Where did you go, anyway?' She stops when I don't answer, crosses her arms. 'Is this really about what Kadek said?'

I pull Mum's shawl onto my lap, pick at the knotted tassels. 'It doesn't matter.'

'Oh, Sophie-Anne. It's a load of claptrap. Ignore him.'

'I'm fine.' I hold the shawl to my nose, draw in its scent.

Aunt Christine shuffles down next to me. 'You're not fine. Talk to me.'

I shrug, fold the shawl into quarters.

'Argh, Sophie-Anne.' She slaps her palm on the bed, shakes her head. 'You can't go around shouting at people like that. Not every man is out to get you.'

'Excuse me?' I slam the shawl down. 'You make it sound like I'm some kind of deranged man-hater.'

'Well. You've been on your–'

I cut across her. 'I am not a man-hater.'

She shakes her head, mouths, 'No,' giggles as I turn back and catch her nodding.

'Stop it. You're terrible,' I say, trying not to laugh.

'A sorry wouldn't go amiss, though, missy, would it?'

'For whom?' Her pinched lips answer my question. 'Absolutely not. I'm not apologising to him.'

'You're a stubborn old goat, Sophie-Anne. I can't imagine where you get it from.'

'Hmm, I wonder?' I fold the shawl on the bed one way, then the other. 'I'm not apologising.'

'Please.' She holds her hands in prayer. 'For me.'

'No, Ainti. He could have really hurt you.'

'It was a mop, not a machete, Sophie-Anne. He made a mistake. You're pretty good at them yourself, remember?'

'Ouch! Really?' I drag my eyes from her, pull the shawl onto my lap. 'That's not fair.'

'Maybe not. But come on, give him a break. He's gone to a lot of effort to get us this upgrade.'

'Okay. Okay. Can we just stop.' I grip my head in my hands. 'I don't know what came over me.'

Aunt Christine dramatically draws back, fans her nose as if she's smelt a stink bomb. 'Too many V and Ts if your breath's anything to go by.'

We fall into silence except for the ticking clock. 'Great. We've missed your pre-dinner big band show thingy.'

Aunt Christine pats the back of her hand on her forehead like a damsel in distress from a silent movie. 'The highlight of my whole cruise, been and gone.'

'Don't say that. I feel awful.'

'So you should, you eejit.' She takes Mum's shawl, tucks it into the bedside cabinet. 'I'm joking. They'll be another show. Let's get changed and see what else is happening. Or, we could, of course, track down–'

'Now, hold on. I never said I'd …' I stand, shake my head. 'No. Absolutely not.'

She hiccups laughter, aims the remote control at the television, pulling up this week's itinerary. 'Goodness. We're in Singapore tomorrow. Where has the time gone? I tried to book a table at the Raffles Hotel, but it's full.'

'Have you been before?'

'Singapore? Oh, yes. They have the most beautiful gardens. The trees are so high you can barely see them from the ground. They illuminate them at night. One of my favourites.'

'And Raffles?'

'I've never been inside. It's quite a spectacle, I hear. Not to worry. Next time.'

'I'll take you one day, Ainti.' I stand, push open the bathroom door. 'It's getting late. I'm going to take a shower before dinner. Shall I run you a bubble bath?'

The swish of an envelope sliding under the door interrupts our conversation.

'Is that someone knocking?' She pulls out her adjustable loafers from under the dressing table.

'It's a letter.' *For the Attention of Miss Christine Collins* written in blue ink. 'It's for you.'

'Put it on the side. It's probably a bill.'

'I don't think so. It's hard, like there's a card inside.'

'Let me see.' She sits, rolls the envelope in her hands, slips a fingernail under the gummed seal. 'Can you read it for me? I haven't got my lenses in.'

'It's an invitation.' I drop next to her on the bed. 'From Oré.' I turn to her, stumble over my words. 'For afternoon tea at Raffles. An apology for today apparently. We need to be on the dock at nine. Someone called Asher is picking us up.'

'Nine's a bit early for afternoon tea, isn't it?' Aunt Christine releases an excited squeal, pulls the card from my hand. 'Are you sure it's not for breakfast?'

'Positive. Look.' I point to the words *afternoon tea*. 'But you said it's fully booked?'

'It is. Has a three-month waiting list, they told me.'

'So how's he …'

'The cruise company has a contact, perhaps?' Aunt Christine slips the invitation back into the envelope.

'But there still needs to be a table. They can't just squeeze another cover in, can they?'

'Oh, I don't know. A last-minute cancellation, maybe?'

'True. Anyhow, we can't accept it.'

'What? Why not?'

'Hold on. A few minutes ago, you said he had nothing to apologise for. Absolutely not. This'll make us indebted to him for the entire trip.'

'Or perhaps he's just being kind.' She presses the card to her heart. 'Look. I don't care if I have to clean the toilets for a month.' She pulls me to my feet, spins me as if in a game of Here We Go Round the Mulberry Bush. 'Sophie-Anne. We're going to the Raffles Hotel.'

11

The winged lady figurehead glints like a brilliant-cut diamond in the sunshine. The Rolls-Royce pulls up at our feet, cream paintwork, polished alloy spiked wheels. I expect Bea to appear behind us, but this seems a little ostentatious even for her. The female chauffeur, black hair tucked under a peaked cap, gets out of the car, adjusts her off-white uniform with burgundy trim. 'Miss Christine?' She retrieves a fold of paper from her back pocket. 'Miss Christine, Miss Sophie?'

What the actual hell? I look on either side of us, chancing that someone else has the same name. 'There must be some mistake.' We can't afford this. 'Wait here, Ainti. I'll sort it.'

The chauffeur opens the car door, gestures for us to get in. 'Yah. Compliments of the Raffles Hotel.' She bows, clicks her heels.

They give you a car? I glance at Aunt Christine, her grin buffing her ears. She slips onto the backseat, signals for me to do the same.

'Please. Miss Christine. Come.' The chauffeur holds out her hand.

'Actually, I'm Miss Sophie. I mean, Sophie. Christine and Sophie. Are you sure this is for us?'

'Ah, yes. Yes. Yes. Good morning.' She places a hand on her chest. 'I'm Asher.' She shuts the door behind me, jumps into the driver's seat, continues the conversation. 'I will take you anywhere you want to go. But first, I'm told to take you to the gardens.'

Aunt Christine squeals, claps her hands. 'Aw, Sophie. One of my most favourite places in the world. How did he know? That's why the pickup was so early.'

The car pulls from the dock, the *Tutum Of The Sea*, a line of passengers scurrying down its gangway onto coaches fading into the distance. I push back into the cradle of soft cream leather cushions, draw in its earthy, fresh off-the-production line smell.

'If you look to the left, Miss Christine, Miss Sophie, we are passing the most popular restaurant in the whole of Singapore.'

We squint through the privacy glass, the glossy wooden veneer satiny cold against my fingertips. 'We're not sure where to look, Asher?'

'There.' She explodes in a fit of giggles. 'Maccas. It's the most favourite restaurant in the whole of Singapore.'

'Oh, Asher. You're teasing us.' Aunt Christine turns to me, a cheeky grin.

'Yah. It's true.' Asher slaps a hand on the steering wheel, wheezes laughter. 'Maccy Ds. Most popular restaurant in the world, methinks.'

Aunt Christine looks out of the window. 'Isn't it wonderful? I'm having such a lovely time, Sophie-Anne.'

'Don't get your hopes up too high, Ainti. We haven't actually done anything yet.'

'It doesn't matter.' She taps my hand. 'I just love being with you.'

Until this trip, I hadn't considered that Aunt Christine and loneliness could exist in the same breath. She's always been so active, surrounded by love, the life of any gathering. In moments like this, when someone does something selfless for her without expectation, she radiates gratitude, a brightness in her smile. The smallest gestures mean the most, a heartfelt poem on a birthday card or driving her across town to the one place serving her favourite rum and raisin ice cream. These things matter to her more than I perhaps realise.

The door swings open. 'Come, Miss Christine. Miss Sophie. I'll get you a shuttle to the armadillos.'

I climb out of the car, slip on my sunglasses. 'Armadillos? I thought we were going to a garden.'

'Ha. Yah. It is Miss Sophie. But from above, the buildings look like sleepy armadillos in the sun. I think so. Please, come. This buggy is for you.'

I fasten my seatbelt. 'That was incredible, Asher.'

Asher nods, turns onto the highway. 'They are special, for sure. Did you see the surfboard from the walkway?'

'The surfboard?'

'Yah. The surfboard in the sky.'

After Asher's earlier reference to armadillos, I realise this might not be an actual surfboard. 'Do you mean the hotel?'

'Yah. That's it, Miss Sophie. The giant surfboard held by three powerful arms. Most famous hotel in Singapore, I think. Lots of people stay there.'

'I thought Raffles was the most famous?'

Asher pouts, rolls her head from side to side, considers my comment. 'Yah. True. Raffles is very important. But the surfboard's on all the posters nowadays. Very famous.'

'What's it called?'

'The Marina Bay Sands,' Aunt Christine says, stares out the car window.

'Have you been, Ainti?'

'I have. It has the most terrifying infinity pool.'

'Miss Christine, you are so right. It is chilling.' Without looking around, Asher grimaces, shakes her head in the rear-view mirror. 'You feel like you are falling off the edge of the world.' She rolls her shoulders, shudders. 'Most alarming.'

A succession of clicks and we turn off the main road again. The drop in speed also suggests we're stopping. A building of brilliant white rises over three lofty floors in front of us. Not the soaring spectacle from earlier, but it's clear why it features in every tourist guide, why visitors stop and turn their heads.

The passenger door swings open. Asher sits tall at the steering wheel, entranced by the spectacle she must have seen a hundred times, its charm still rendering her speechless. The doorman offers his hand to my aunt. A white jacket, pristine against black trousers, with gold-roped shoulder lapels, a brass buckled burnt-orange belt. My eyes fix on him like the first time I saw the guards outside Buckingham Palace as a child. When we got home, I trawled every book I could find about London, studied every iconic landmark until I knew its history in the minutest detail.

At the entrance, Aunt Christine pauses, pats my arm. 'Oh my goodness, Sophie-Anne, look at it. Isn't it wonderful?'

We step inside onto a floor of glassy white marble. Foliage in vast decorated blue and white urns rise in swirls across the foyer's arched recesses on either side.

'Miss Collins?' A gentleman dressed in a cream suit, burgundy tie, leather-bound folder under his arm, approaches. 'Welcome to the Raffles Hotel. Please. Follow me.'

I stop, look up at the ceiling like a child seeing dew sprinkling a spider's web for the first time. A woman looks over the gallery and runs her hand along a banister of polished ebony crowning a carved woodland scene worthy of the most magical fairy tale.

'Madam.'

Sunlight slices through the glass roof, the floor ignites icy, the chandelier glittering tiny mirrors across the walls.

'Huh?'

'Madam. Your table. Can I?'

'Oh, yes. Sorry.' My eyes drift skywards again. 'I'm … It's quite something, isn't it?'

He bows, gestures for me to follow.

We parade through the central lobby to an alcove of cream, copper-trimmed couches, a coffee table edged with intricately carved ivory-white feathers.

A waiter places down two highball glasses, menus. 'I'll be back in a few minutes. If you have any questions, just ring.' He points to a small silver bell at the far end of the table.

I pull out the pineapple and glace cherry garnish from the crystal glass, sip the frothy pink cocktail through a straw. 'What is this?'

'A Singapore Sling. The hotel's famous for them.' Aunt Christine lifts the glass and sips it with an 'Ah. I've waited a long time for you.' She pulls out the straw, sucks it clean, places it on the table. 'It's gin, cherry brandy, lime and soda, and …'

I lift the glass to my nose, draw it in. 'Cointreau?' I take another sip. 'It tastes herby.'

'Yes. Yes.' Aunt Christine points her finger at me. 'Benedictine. I knew there was something else.'

'You seem to know a lot about it, Ainti,' I say, study the menu.

'Yes, well. As you know, I do like a cocktail or two.'

'And every other spirit on the bartender's shelf, hey?'

She stares out of the cubicle. 'Isn't this spectacular, Sophie? Even better than I imagined.'

'It's stunning. I'm glad we came.'

'Madam. Have you decided which tea blend you would like?' says the waiter, collecting the menus.

'I'll have the Orange Pekoe Ceylan, please.' I've no idea what it'll be like, but what's not to like about orange tea? Orange tea!

'The Casablanca blend, please. I'm feeling all "play it again, Sam",' Aunt Christine giggles.

The waiter smiles, bows his head as if it's the first time he's ever heard that joke. He places down a silver cake stand, describes every tier. Sandwiches in various coloured breads, curried crab, cucumber and smoked salmon, tuna and mayonnaise, egg salad with chives. Scones, regular and raisin, served with clotted cream and the hotel's signature rose petal jam. Mixed fruit tartlets, hazelnut rolls and spiced orange marmalade cake. Aunt Christine slips her napkin to her knee, nods at his every word.

I mouth 'thank you' as he finishes pouring our tea, a waft of peppermint churning with the scent of caramel, citrus, sweet and sour.

'Are you having a good time, Ainti?'

Aunt Christine slouches back on the cushions, her white china teacup clinks the saucer, joy fizzing her face. 'Oh yes. The best day ever. You?'

'Yep. It's been great.'

'Worthy of an apology?'

I sip my tea, turn away, try not to smile.

'Sophie?'

'I'll say thank you, okay? Happy?'

Aunt Christine cuts a fruit scone in half, taps on a teaspoon of jam, clotted cream. 'I hope no Devonians are watching.'

'Not like you to turn down a heated debate.' I pick up a triangled curried crab sandwich. 'You used to travel a lot, didn't you? I remember you'd be gone for weeks. Mum would say you were always off gallivanting.' I place down the uneaten crab sandwich. 'Do you have a favourite?'

'Cake?' She glances up, motions for me to pass the jam. 'I'm teasing. Switzerland.'

'I wouldn't have guessed that. Why?'

'The sun and snow. The views are fantastic, and it's spotless.'

Our eyes lock. 'Spotless?' I repeat; such an Aunt Christine thing to say.

'Spotless.'

'Anywhere you still want to go?'

Aunt Christine's stare sits frozen over my shoulder for a few seconds before the corners of her mouth soften. 'Canada. The Rocky Mountaineer train.' She sighs, takes a bite of her scone, piled high with cream and rose petal jam.

'Well, maybe your new bezzy mate could take you, hey?'

She places down the scone, scans the alcove, every part of her face ablaze with a brilliant smile. 'Look at all this, Sophie-Anne. Oré has certainly pulled a few strings.'

'Indeed.' Yesterday, Kadek, was an earthquake, a storm of muddy waters weaving the past into the present. Today, like a skimming stone, Oré has charged me into the sunshine. Why would he do that? The afternoon tea, the car, Asher, the city tour, everything. I mean, I realise he wants to make amends, but this is not an act of regret. This is a full-on celebration, a special anniversary, a marriage proposal. How am I going to recover from this? Am I like, excuse me, Oré, but what the fuck? Are you kidding me? I fall back in my seat, study the extraordinary scene playing out around me. Things like this don't happen to people like us, do they? I mean, this is a Loro Piana cashmere sweater, a luxury Jo Malone gift set, dinner at the Fat Duck in Bray, not a takeaway pizza and a bottle of cheap wine on Brighton beach like I'm used to.

I smile at Aunt Christine, press a napkin into her hand to catch the cake crumbs falling from her mouth. Candice, watching Oré leave the dance class, flashes my mind, the question hovering on her lips, now on mine – who are you, Concierge Oré Zadzisai?

12

Laem Chabang. Thailand.

Thud, thud, thud. The bus shudders to a halt.

'Apologies, ladies and gentlemen. We've a slight mechanical hitch. Please stay seated. Another coach is on its way. In the meantime, we'll be coming around with a complimentary drinks service.'

Aunt Christine heaves herself up, one hand on the seat in front, the other on her hip. 'Excuse me, young man.'

I know that look, cheeks drawn in like she's sucking on a lemon wedge. 'Ainti, please sit down.' She ignores me, and here we go.

The tour guide edges down the aisle, steadying himself on the seat headrests. 'Yes, madam?'

'How do you know the next coach isn't another clapped-out old wreck?'

He takes a moment to mull over her candour. You have no idea whom you're taking on, sir. Not when she's in this mood. Spin around and go back to where you came from.

He clears his throat. 'Apologies, madam. Another bus will be here shortly. We're still on schedule to be in Bangkok for lunch. There's no need to worry.'

Not looking at him, she pats her hair. A cone sculpture today, set with an entire can of Elemis. 'But I am,' she side-eye stabs him, 'worried.'

'There's really no need. Once the replacement coach arrives, we'll transfer everyone over. Everything's in hand. Can I get you some refreshments?'

'Ainti. Please.' I tug her arm. 'See. They're sorting it. Come on, sit down. Everyone's staring.'

We left the port of Laem Chabang at 9 am on the first leg of our Bangkok overnight excursion. Forty-five minutes later, we're sitting on the side of the highway, and her glare is the sharpest blade. I tried, sir, but brace yourself. She is about to roar.

'As I thought.' She flips my hand away, shuffles sideways into the aisle. 'No. I refuse to get on another one of these death traps. Out of my way.'

And here we go. 'Ainti, please don't.'

Aunt Christine drags her handbag from the floor, its contents spilling over my feet.

'Here. Let me help you.' I slide onto my knees, clamped in a bottom-width vice of stale velveteen chairs, bundle everything back into her bag. 'Jesus, Ainti. Can you try to fit a bit more in here next time?' I wave a toilet roll, a jar of Nutella, a glue stick and a stapler at her. 'Do you really need these?'

'Bless you.' She pats my head, loops the bag into the crook of her arm. 'I'll meet you outside.' A palm pressed on the tour guide's chest she manoeuvres him backwards down the aisle, ignoring his protests. 'Don't be long, Sophie-Anne,' she calls over her shoulder.

'Sorry. I'm so sorry,' I say, clambering to my feet, thumping my knees and hips into our fellow passengers' backs. I throw my rucksack over my shoulder, a packet of travel tissues and a fold of paper fall to the ground. 'Ainti, wait. You've left–' Hand held high over her head, she doesn't turn around, beckons for me to follow. 'Perfect. I'll bring these, shall I?' I push them into my pocket, weave down the aisle.

A gust of hot wind, the whoosh of lorries and cars, slaps me backwards as I scramble down the steps. 'Ainti, what are you doing out here? It's dangerous.'

'Madam, please get back on board. It's not safe.' The coach driver motions to the vehicles charging past a couple of metres from our feet. He places his arm around Aunt Christine's waist, attempts to guide her up the steps.

'Excuse me! Hands off.' She strikes him with her handbag. 'How dare you manhandle me. I'll be speaking to the Captain about you.' She stabs a pointy finger into his shoulder. 'I am not. I repeat. I am not getting on that or anything like it. Get me a taxi this instance.' She drops her hand, straightens her handbag on her arm. 'Please.' When he fails to move, her stare slaps him across both cheeks. 'Now!' She points at the bus. 'You can poke your lousy coaches where—' The roar of a truck's engine cuts her silent. 'Sophie, come.' She taps the driver's chest, tapers her tone. 'Oh, yes, and I'll have a gin and tonic when you're ready, please. Large.'

I steer her onto the strip of scorched grass verge, under the dappled shade of a fig tree. 'One day you'll go too far. Do you know that?'

Aunt Christine tugs open her handbag, fumbles inside. 'Where are my tissues?'

I pull out the packet, the fold of paper from my pocket, hand her the hankies.

She wipes a rectangle of tissue across her brow. 'Goodness. I'm sweating like a baboon.'

'And this.' I unfold the paper, *Chrystal* scrawled in blue fountain pen across the envelope. 'Why do I know that name?'

She snatches it from me, folds it along the crease, rams it to the bottom of her handbag. 'I've no idea.'

'Ainti. Have you been pinching someone's letters?' I cross my arms, nudge her shoulder, try to lighten the mood.

'Not funny.'

'It was a joke,' I protest.

She turns away, presses the bag back into the crease of her elbow. 'Some things are private, Sophie-Anne. Ah. Perfect timing.' She takes the gin and tonic from the tour guide, tosses the lemon back at him, groans about it being served in a plastic cup. 'Now, where's our taxi, young man?' She looks at me, her elbow clinching the bag tight to her side.

I pull a bottle of water from my rucksack. What was that all about? Someone's in a good mood, not. I thought I was the complicated one, but this cruise is one unfolding mystery after the other. Forget about Oré Zadzisai; who the heck is Chrystal?

The ceiling fans in the Crow's Nest bar spin with the soft hum of after-dinner conversation. It's quieter than usual, with most passengers staying onshore soaking up Bangkok's nightlife.

'May I?' He tosses a book, a pager, onto the bar.

His spicy cologne hits thick in my nose and throat. I groan, look down at my glass, self-conscious of my lack of make-up, uncombed hair, sweat-stained beach dress.

Oré slips onto the chair next to me. 'How's the room?'

'Cabin.'

'Sorry?'

'It's a cabin. That's what my aunt keeps reminding me.' I look up, smile. 'It's good, thanks. Who knew two beds could mean so much?'

He signals to the bartender. 'Another?' Points at my half-empty glass.

No. No. No. I'm quite happy sitting here on my own, drowning today's catastrophe in the vodka and tonic I've paid for. 'I'm fine. Thank you.'

'Sure, I can't tempt you?'

I place the tumbler down, a wheezy huff like the closing of an accordion. 'Am I really your best option?' I wipe my palms on my thighs. 'Sorry. It's been a long day. I'm not in the best of moods.'

He flips a beer mat onto its edge. 'Another of those and a small beer, please, bartender.'

'I said no.'

'I know.' He turns his entire body towards me. 'Are you ever gonna give this up?'

'Sorry?'

The bartender tosses the crown off a bottle of beer. Puts ice in a tall glass, a large measure of vodka, a splash of tonic. He raises an eyebrow like he's saying good luck to Oré, pushes the glass in front of me.

I look at the drink, Oré. 'Why are you doing this?'

He takes a sip, hesitates as it slips his throat. 'What?'

'Being nice. Cabin upgrades, day trips, and now you want to have a drink with me. Why?'

Oré turns back to the bar, his fingers slipping lines through the bottle's condensation. 'Bad day, hey?'

'You think?'

'I was on duty earlier. It looked tense.'

So now he's spying on me. What am I meant to say to that? No, everything's fine. My aunt is always having meltdowns on the road to

Bangkok. Just another typical outing for us.

'Look.' His head tilts to the side, his eyes, dark pools, drill into mine. 'Can we start again?' There's a bit of ache in his voice. 'I'm new here, and, well, let's just say I've not had the best start.' He lifts his bottle to my glass. 'I apologise if I upset you.'

He looks different tonight, relaxed, dressed down in a blue and white NY Giants shirt, dark denim gripping the shape of his legs. My body reacts, even though I don't want it to. I study his expression as he looks away. He seems genuine. But what would I know? I'm hardly the best judge. I lift my glass, clink his beer. 'Sure.' I take a sip, sigh as the alcohol numbs my throat. 'Ignore me. I'm tired.'

He offers me his hand. 'Oré.'

'I know.'

He slides his hand to me again. 'Humour me.'

I lift my shoulder in a half-shrug. 'Sophie.' A small smile, two firm pumps. 'Night off?'

He dips his chin at the pager. 'On call. So, what happened? She looked upset.'

'Her upset? Do you reckon? Yep, we were all upset. Including your poor colleagues. She's sulking back in the room, sorry, cabin. Demanding a full refund and to speak to the Captain.' I hold up my drink. 'Cheers.'

'Has she seen the Captain?'

'No. He'll be hiding if he knows what's good for him.' I giggle, shake my head, catch his reflection in the bar's mirrored wall. The creases around his eyes, soft, dark, betraying a man who perhaps laughs often. I rest my elbow on the bar, chin in hand. 'Anyway, you've saved me a journey. I was going to find you to say thank you for Raffles.'

He looks down before lifting back to me. 'Was it okay?'

'Um. Yes.' He laughs at my squeal. 'Flipping amazing. All of it. Our driver had us in stitches. It was fantastic. Thank you. How did you do it?'

'Ah, I called in a few favours.' He leans forward, peels the label from his beer, side-eyes me. 'So, what's the deal with you? You're quite the paradox on here, aren't you?'

And there it is. The real reason you're plying me with alcohol.

The room instantly feels like it's been lit by strobes, his question hot on my tongue. I should have known. All this, can I buy you a drink? Oh, and while I'm at it, tell me why you've ended up on holiday with a shipload of pensioners. It's all over the internet, Oré. If you want to find it, you can. Google my name, and the first five searches will give you the tabloids take on the whole sordid affair. I don't need you or anyone else to feed the remorse corkscrewing my sanity raw. My guilt is palpable, a claw tearing at already blistered skin. I get it. I'm a convenient way to pass the time, but the fact he's asked is disappointing.

I stumble off my seat, slip my key card into my back pocket. 'And that's my cue to leave. Thanks for—'

'What? No. Please don't go.' Oré holds up his palm. 'I'm prying. Ignore me.'

I feel the panic tighten around my heart. What will I do? Run away every time someone asks why I'm here.

'Stay. Please,' he says. I study his hand, offering to help me climb back up. 'Please.' He motions for me to sit back down.

His hand is cool in mine as I climb back up, the silence stretching between us.

I tap the tumbler on my chin. 'Of course, I could say the same about you.'

He watches me in the mirrored wall, sips his beer. 'I'm not sure what you mean?'

'Oh, I think you do. You're not very experienced, considering your ...'

'My?' He smiles. 'Age?'

I lift my glass, congratulate his deduction. 'Yep, that.'

'Busted.' He laughs, flips over the beer mat. 'So, what're you up to tomorrow? Another try at Bangkok?'

'I don't think so. My aunt's not feeling it.'

'I'm off to Wang Nam Khiao in the morning. It's not Bangkok, but it's very pretty. You're welcome to tag along.'

Heat rises on my face. 'Oh, I don't think she'll do that.'

'And you?' He stabs me a sharp stare.

'Sorry?'

'Come on your own.'

'Me?' My breath itches. 'I … I'm … I'm not sure. She gets funny about me going off alone.'

The pager bounces, a flash of blue light. 'Sorry.' He glances at the message, flips it off. 'I've gotta go. If you change your mind, I'll be at reception at eight. It's a long drive. I'd welcome the company.' He downs his beer, slips off the stool, pulls the pager from the bar, clips it on his pocket. 'It's been a pleasure, Miss O'Ryan. See it as a thank you for Raffles if you like.' He thumps his book to his chest, nods goodbye, leaves.

Head back, I tip the last dribbles of my drink into my mouth, crunch the ice. Why is he doing this? And why is he spinning it like some kind of repayment deal? I thought Raffles was him saying sorry for maiming my aunt. So why should I pay it back?

I jump down, catch my reflection in the bars mirrored wall, drag a hand through my hair. Warmth seeps like hot melted butter through every inch of me. 'I hear you. I'll think about it, okay?'

'Sorry, madam? Can I help you?' says the bartender.

'What? Oh. No.' I tap my temple. 'My friend. She's …' I drop my hand, slide the key card off the bar. 'Nagging me.' My words trail off, registering how ridiculous I sound.

He nods, polishes a pint glass. 'Of course. Good night, madam.'

13

Wang Nam Khiao, Thailand.

'Come here often?' Oré steps on the accelerator, tears out of the dock.

It's 8.15 am, and I'm an edgy mess, not unlike a teenager going on a first date. Not that this is a date. Because it isn't, a date. I shift on the leather seat, worn past the point of distress with its frayed rips. My conscience conquered me in the end. Although, the thought of spending all day with my aunt sulking in the cabin had been a contributing factor. Bea distracted her at breakfast, aiding my escape. Courtesy of her butler Gino, we also established Oré is not a psychopathic murderer currently. However, she suggested carrying my phone with me just in case. Although, how useful that will be if he disposes of my body in Thailand's remote countryside is questionable.

I smooth my dress over my knees. 'So, why are we doing this? It's a long way for a day trip.'

'Have you been checking up on me, Miss O'Ryan?'

'Of course. I don't get into a stranger's car easily.'

'Good to know.' He glances sideways, smiles. 'So, how do you fancy lunch with my son?'

'What?' I look away, shift my hands under my thighs. 'Won't he mind me rocking up with you?'

'Who Brad? Nah. He's chill. Anyway, he loves London.'

I snap back to him, frown. 'I'm not from London.'

'Oh, right? Then he'll probably hate you. Anyway, England, London, it's all the same, right?'

I make a sound like a whale spouting water. 'Like Chicago, San Francisco and New York are all the same?'

He rakes a hand through his dark chocolate hair, disturbs the grey surrendering to age. 'Yeah. Fair point. You've got me.'

I lower my eyes, smile, listen to him chuckle. 'How old is he?'

'Twenty-four.'

'What's he doing out here?'

'Working. Some charity gig. Something to do with helping kids who've experienced trauma. Lost a parent, trafficked, witnessed war, that kinda stuff.'

'Interesting. Do you see him much?'

'Nope. Not now.' He taps the steering wheel. 'So, Sophie, are you ever gonna tell me why you're holidaying with the cast of *The Best Exotic Marigold Hotel?*' His face beams a cheeky grin.

'That's a bit disingenuous of you, considering you're staff.'

'True. But I'm getting paid to be here. Anyway, I like hanging with the old folks.'

What does he mean by that? 'I don't hate old people.'

He nods his head, rubs his chin. 'Right. My mistake. So, why are you here?'

Look at him testing me. Make some shit up, Sophie. Make it quick and make it good. 'It's my aunt's birthday soon. Her friend dropped out, and she didn't have anyone else to go with. I had the time, so here I am.'

'Okay. Tell me more?'

I lean out of the window, the warm breeze floods my face. 'There's not much else to tell.' The car jolts, vaults us into the air. 'Shit!' My skirt lifts, exposes my thighs. 'What the hell are you doing?' I yank down my dress, grip the seat.

'Hole in the road. Should've got something with better suspension, perhaps.' His mouth contorts into a goofy grin. 'And air-conditioning. You, okay?'

'Can you please slow down?' Letting go of the seat, I tug on the seatbelt to make sure it's tight. 'And keep your eyes on the road.'

Oré takes his foot off the gas. 'Better?'

'Much.' He's biting his lip, glancing at me like there's something he wants to ask. 'What?'

'No. It's nothing. I'm just curious. Are you some kind of carer?'

'No. And don't let my aunt hear you say that. She'll push you right off your pedestal.'

'A nurse? Personal trainer?'

'Hilarious,' I mutter sarcastically.

He stabs me a sharp stare. 'Sorry?'

'Road!' I turn from him, pinch my eyes shut.

'Oh, yeah.' He stares straight ahead for a long moment, his knuckles bleeding white gripping the steering wheel. 'I like your aunt. She's funny.'

'Sometimes.' I turn around and drink him in. His arm rests on the open window. Slip-on loafers, no socks, knee-length denim shorts, a white linen shirt unbuttoned at the neck. There's a waft of his spicy cologne in the air, a silky gloss to his skin and hair. Stop it, Sophie. I cough the thought of him away, adjust in my seat.

He darts a look at me. 'So, what do you do for a job?'

'I'm a head.'

'A head?'

'Headteacher. Principal. I run, ran, a school.'

'Wow.' He pushes his lips together, suppresses a smile.

'Wow? What does that mean?'

'Nothing. You just don't look like one.'

'And what's that?' Oh, go on, surprise me. I've heard it a hundred times.

'Tan-coloured tights, hair in a bun, thick glasses. A moustache.'

'Not that you're being stereotypical or anything. When were you last in a school?'

'True. So, you've given it up?'

I shrug, press my hands under my knees, look out the window. 'It's a long story.'

'And that told me.' He turns up the radio. 'Yeesh! Only two hours, twenty minutes to go, Zadzi, and you're crushing it, dude. Music?'

As we turn down the lane, a line of palm trees stands guard on either side, leaves stabbing high into the sky like a guard of honour. At the end of the driveway is a house built of dark wooden slabs. No glass in the windows, open doorways, 'Tonlon' is written in big white letters. I check myself in the side mirror, adjust my hair, my make-up smudged like I've braved the most ferocious rainstorm. I did, I fear, not look my best.

'Now for the main event.' Oré pulls up the handbrake, gets out of the car. 'Hungry?'

'Oh. It's a restaurant. Starving.' I rub my lower back, driven up into my ribcage from his hammering around the dirt tracks.

At the top of the staircase, cooler air chases around us. A ceiling of weeping vegetation casts natural shade, intertwined into swinging bamboo chairs hung from a slatted roof. Plants scatter the walkways in enormous terracotta pots, no doubt lifted into place by a small crane.

Oré pulls out my chair. 'For you, ma'am.'

'Thank you.' I thumb the menu, attempt to decipher the words, any words. 'Is it all in Thai?'

Oré leans over, points at the page. 'The dumplings are good, and the chilli prawns. They'll calm the spice if you don't want them hot.'

He continues to translate each of the dishes as if a native. I follow his gaze, flitting between me and the menu, nodding.

'Oré.' The lady's voice is light, bubbly. A slender arm raised from a baby-blue vest into the air, ankle-length skinny white trousers, skim athletic legs. She strides towards us, sweeps long braids of golden hair from her shoulders. I study the menu with increased interest. This is not his son.

Oré jumps up, throws out his arms. 'Tap.' Their clasp is filled with energy and known affection. 'Where's Brad?'

'Ah. Yes. That.' She grits her teeth. 'There's a teensy-weensy problem. He's not coming.' She pats Oré's arm, sits down. 'He got called to Phnom Penh last night. Said he'd call you. I guess he forgot.'

Oré shakes his head, the joy slips his face. 'Jeez, Tap. Couldn't he have waited for one day? We've driven hours to get here.'

'I know.' Tap pops an olive into her mouth. 'It sounded important. He'll tell you when he calls. Besides, I'm here, aren't I.' Her eyes fall on me. 'Are you going to introduce us?'

'Oh. Yes. Sorry. Tara, Sophie. Sophie, Tara. Better known as Tap because she constantly leaves them running. Which makes no sense, as we call them faucets in the States. Anyway, Tap is my very-hard-to-track-down son's extremely patient girlfriend.'

'Hi.' Her attention flicks between us. 'So, this is interesting.'

'Stop.' Oré swipes the menu from the table. 'Sophie is a passenger on the ship. She offered to come with me on my extraordinarily long drive to have lunch with my absent son and,' he flips the menu playfully on her arm, 'his overly nosey girlfriend.'

Tara sticks out her tongue, bucks another olive into her mouth. I should drop my gaze, but their devoted regard charms me. His lips melt into a soft smile. The harsher layers of this normally suited man float away on the flow of their conversation.

Tara crunches another olive. 'So, Sophie. Where are you from?'

'England.'

'England's awesome. Who are you here with?'

'My aunt.' As I say it, I realise how pathetic it sounds.

She looks at Oré, me. 'I see.' Lifting her eyebrows, she tilts her head. 'Okay.'

'Ha. Yes.' My tittering tapers off into a drawn-out sigh. She thinks I'm weird. Some crazy cat lady who has no friends and sits at home knitting.

'Hey. Enough questions. Sophie came along for the ride, not a Spanish inquisition.' Oré squeezes the tip of Tap's nose. 'Let's eat. I'm starving.'

'Defo. Let's do it, Pops.' She bats his hand away, wiggles her nose at him.

'Watch it, oh so smart one. Otherwise, you'll be taking an early bath in that water feature.' He rubs his hands together. 'Do you trust me to order, Sophie?'

The two of them converse with the waiter, their eyes bobbing between each other, the menu.

'#Pops is hungry.' Tap hands the waiter her menu.

'#Pops is starving.' He chuckles, looks at me. 'Iced lemon tea, juice, soda?'

'Great? Yes. Tea. Sounds good.' I look like a sarcastic fringehead fish staring at them both. I've never learnt another language, I haven't needed to. Unless you count O-level French, which, seeing as I got a D, isn't relevant. A punch of garlic and chilli itches my nose, and for the first time in forever, I'm not stressing about calories, sugar content, complex carbohydrates or fat.

'Right, I'm off to the restroom. You two behave whilst I'm gone.' Tara laughs at Oré, rolling his eyes.

'Oré, where did you learn to do that? You both sound like locals.'

'Self-taught. I'm a hell of a rusty, though. But I like to try when I'm back.

'Tap seems a lot of fun.'

'And trouble. Nah. She's a good kid. Met Brad in tenth grade. She's like a daughter to me. Let's hope they don't split up – awks. Anyhow, they finished uni, went travelling, didn't come home. Two years later, here we are.' He stumbles over his words, clears the grittiness from his throat. 'There's that fine balance between letting them find themselves and wanting to keep them close, isn't there?' He scrubs his hand across his face.

A heaviness in his eyes makes my chest tight. 'Do they talk about coming home?' I adjust the cutlery, suppress the urge to touch his arm, to tell him it'll be okay.

'No. And I don't blame them. If I were their age again, I'd be doing the exact same thing.'

'Where's Phnom Penh?'

'Cambodia.' He pops an olive in his mouth.

'We're heading there next, right? Can't you see him there?'

He pulls out the olive stone, drops it onto his side plate. 'Maybe. If I can swap a shift.'

I tuck a napkin over my knees. 'You seem to know a lot about this place.'

'A bit. I lived here when I was younger.' He leans back, his smile gone. 'I met Brad's mum here.' He jumps up, pulls out Tap's chair. 'Hey, just in time, Tapster. Here comes the food.'

Oré strolls down the steps, swings Tara's hand in his.

'Great to meet you, Sophie.' She glares at the car looking like something from an 80's cop show, cloaked in more dust than the track it's sitting on. 'What the heck is that, Pops? Couldn't you have got something a bit more impressive?'

'What? It's authentic.'

'It's a dump.' Her elbow nudges my arm. 'Make sure he takes you out in style next time, Sophie.' She winks at him. 'He can afford it.'

'Okay. Enough. Can I give you a lift home in my dump of a car?'

'No thanks. I've got my bicycle. I've been feeling a bit off lately. The fresh air does me good.' She throws her hands around Oré's neck, kisses both his cheeks. 'Damn, we miss you, Pops.' She grins, looks over her shoulder at me. 'Can't wait to hear more about your little adventure, you two.'

Oré groans, lifts a hand goodbye, climbs into the car. 'Be good and tell my wayward son to call me.'

Tap wiggles her fingers. 'Bye, Sophie.' She bounces past the car, blows kisses from her hand. 'Love you, Pops.'

I slip into the passenger seat, fasten my seatbelt, check it's taut against my chest, waist. 'Thank you for lunch.'

A hand on the steering wheel, Oré turns to face me. 'You're welcome.' He wipes a hand to his mouth before looking away. 'Good. Well, we're not finished yet. You've got another four hours in the car with me, so you might wanna hold off on the compliments.'

He reverses out of the parking space. The wing mirror grinding the trunk of a palm tree, splintering into three knife-like shards.

'You airhead, Zadzi.' He cracks it off, tosses it onto the backseat. 'I hope that's not another bucket load of bad luck.'

'Bad luck?'

He winks, cranks up the radio, sings a medley of rock classics. I say singing. It's more of an untuneful shriek. I giggle at the concentration creased into his brow as he bobs his head. His tapping the steering wheel along to the beat, makes me smile deep inside. So, I'm not the only one with a story, Oré Zadzisai. You call me the paradox, but the more I get to know you, the more I think you may have just as much to hide as me.

14

A slight skip to my step, I poke my head out of our balcony door, Aunt Christine and Bea stretching out on two reclining chairs.

'Sophieeeee,' Aunt Christine wheezes. 'How wonderful to see you. Come here.' She pats the small square plastic coffee table at her side.

I frown at the table's short stubby legs, admire her confidence that it will hold my weight. 'For me? How kind.'

She pulls a goofy grin, falls back against the chair. 'Your bum's not that big, is it?'

'Thanks. I think. Is everything all right? You wanted to string the Captain up by his braces when I left. And now …' An earthy smell of tobacco strokes my throat. 'Have you been smoking?'

Aunt Christine sniggers at Bea, who pretends to zip her lips together. 'Nooo. Anyway, I think you've got something to say to me, young lady?'

I look up at the sky, breathe hard, the heat of nightfall strokes my face. I'm a toddler twisting free of her hand, her fingers stretched wide, trying to haul me back. 'Sorry. I should have told you I was going.'

'Yes, well, that was naughty.' She throws her hand out to the side, slaps my bottom, almost topples the chair. 'You're back safe and sound, so no harm done. I've had words with your co-conspirator, though.' She side-eyes Bea.

That was easier than I expected. 'Are you okay?'

'Aha. Tell me, how was your date?'

And, just as I dare to let my guard down, here we go. 'It wasn't a date. If you've spoken to Bea, you'd know that. I went to keep him company. Payback for Raffles.'

Aunt Christine looks at Bea. They erupt with laughter. 'What do you say, Beatrix? My bad. Of course, it wasn't a date.'

'Stop teasing.' I push her hand from the armrest, perch on the edge of the lounger. 'It's nice to see you smiling again. Bea's cheered you up, I see. Did you catch up with the Captain?'

They clasp hands, hold them aloft like a boxer and referee, signalling triumph. Another thunder of giggles.

'Right.' I jump up. 'Am I missing something?'

Aunt Christine, shuffles straight, attempts a more serious expression. 'No. Why?'

A fragrant waft fondles my nostrils again. 'What's that smell? It's all over the cabin.' I spin from side to side, look over the balcony. 'Is there something happening on shore?'

Aunt Christine stoops lopsided over the side of her chair, pulls out a hand-rolled cigarette from the ashtray underneath.

'What the actual hell? Is that what I think it is?' I grab the roll-up, hold it to my nose. 'Bloody hell it is. God help me. I can't leave you for one flipping day.' I toss it back into the ashtray, lower my voice. 'It's weed. You know that, right?' Another bellow of laughter. 'Shush. For Christ's sake, this isn't funny, you two. We're in bloody Thailand. They'll put you in jail for that here. Have you any idea what prison looks like in Bangkok?' I lean back on the guardrail, check if anyone is listening on the neighbouring balconies. 'How did you get it on board?'

Aunt Christine taps a finger to her nose. 'Beatrix knows a man who knows a lady who knows–' She glances sideways at Bea.

'A lady. Or perhaps it was a man.' Bea weeps with laughter.

'Bea, I'm surprised at you. You're meant to be the sensible one. I thought you'd at least try to keep her out of trouble, not roll her in it.'

Aunt Christine looks confused, opens her mouth to speak, but decides against it.

Bea drops her head, places a hand on Aunt Christine's knee. 'I think we've upset her, Chrissie.'

'Chrissie? When did that happen?'

'Sophie-Anne, sit down. We're not doing any harm. It's purely medicinal.'

I scowl at her, laughing behind her hand. 'Everything's flipping medicinal with you. Do you think they'll care when they're dragging you off this ship? Anyway, what the hell for?'

'Stop cursing.' She rubs a hand on her shin. 'My leg's sore.' Her frown cracks into a wide grin. She falls backwards, another spasm of giggles.

'And an ice pack and a couple of paracetamol were out of the question?'

'Don't roll your eyes at me, young lady.' Aunt Christine straightens. 'Just because you're missing your boyfriend.'

'I am not missing anyone, and, for the last time, he's not my boyfriend.'

'But he could be.' She nods at Bea, taps her nose.

'Enough!' Hands on hips, I attempt to take control of the situation. 'Give it to me.'

Aunt Christine takes a drag of the joint. 'Methinks she protestests too much, Beatrix. Take a chill pill, Soph. Here, have some.'

'This isn't funny.' I snatch the roll-up, hold it in the air. 'Any more of these?' Bea shakes her head. 'The last thing I need is to be visiting you two in the flipping Bangkok Hilton.'

'Oh, I like them. I stayed in one in London once. Mind you, thinking about it. It could have been a Premier Inn.'

'What are you talking about? How strong is this stuff?' I roll the joint between my fingers. 'It's got nothing to do with the Hilton Hotel in London or anywhere else. Remember that book you read?'

Aunt Christine frowns. 'I've read lots of books.'

'*Forget You Had a Daughter*. You remember that one?'

Her tight face softens slightly. 'Ah, yes. Wasn't it on TV too?' Aunt Christine looks at Bea. 'A true story. Terribly sad.' She pauses. 'Oh. Is that …'

I nod, take a drag of the roll-up, toss it over the railings.

'Sophie-Anne! You spoilsport.'

'This isn't funny. Bea, tell her.'

'Oh, Sophie, let it be. She sacrificed so much to bring you up. More than you'll ever know. Surely, she deserves a bit of fun?' She smacks her hand over her mouth, stickered by Aunt Christine's death stare. 'Oops. Sorry, Chrissie. A slip of the tongue. Moving on. Sophie's right. We must do better.'

'Quite. We will try harder.' Aunt Christine salutes, slaps her lips together. 'Did we miss lunch?'

'Fabulous idea. Aye. Let's eat.'

'Hold on. Bea, what do you mean by more than I'll ever know?'

'She means nothing, Sophie-Anne. Beatrix,' Aunt Christine places a finger on her lips, 'shush. Let's eat, yes?'

I grip the handle of the French doors. 'Absolutely not. Stay right where you are. You stink of dope.'

'I can't smell anything.' Aunt Christine sniffs her top, offers it to Bea to inhale.

'Of course you can't, you're pie-eyed. So, we're just going to ignore Bea's comment, are we?'

'Oh, Sophie-Anne, it's nothing. Ignore her.'

'Aye. A bit of foggy brain-itis.' Bea drops her head, mutters, 'Note to self, keep mouth shut about things that don't concern me.'

'Hmm. Well, neither of you are stepping out of this room tonight. You'll get us all arrested.'

'The top drawer of the dressing table, Sophie-Anne. My emergency snack bag.'

'Please.' I pull out an unmarked carrier bag jammed with chocolate bars, crisps, biscuits, cup-a-soups. 'Ainti, what the actual hell is this?'

'Just a few snacks from home. You never know if they'll have your favourites, do you?'

I toss her the bag. 'Unbelievable.'

She unwraps a Galaxy bar, offers me a bite. 'Here. Have some.'

'No, thank you. That's never going to fill you up. I'll get the room service menu.' A bang on the door. 'Really? Right, you two, don't move.' I slide the balcony doors shut behind me, blast the smell of marijuana with half a can of deodorant, inch open the front door. A woman, white-haired, with a sun-toasted face, clasps an envelope to her chest.

'Hi. Is Christine around?'

'She's a bit caught up at the moment. Can I help?'

She glances at the brown envelope before handing it to me. 'Can you give her this and say thank you?'

'And you are?'

'Tamsin. Tell her I'll catch up with her later.' She winks, turns away.

Watching her walk down the corridor, I flip open the unsealed envelope, edge out a £20 note. I thump my hip against the door, click it shut. 'Ainti. What the hell have you been up to? This better not be what I think it is.' My mobile buzzes, dancing frantically on the sideboard. 'Perfect timing! Saved by the bell, hey?'

15

Aunt Christine asleep, I collect my mobile from the sideboard, step out onto the balcony, the sea undulating on the horizon, black, torched by a path of golden moonlight. The balcony door ajar, I lay back on the lounger. 'Hey, you. Sorry about earlier.'

'Are you ignoring me?' he says.

'What? No.' I turn down the volume, click the mobile to speaker phone. 'Don't be silly. We've been at sea and the internet's rubbish on here.'

'How's it going?'

'Yeah. Okay. Hot.'

A drawn-out inhale. 'Nice.'

'Are you smoking?'

'All right, Miss Marple. Give me a break.' A hissed exhale. 'I dreamt about you last night.'

I cringe, imagine the smoke belching into his mobile at the other end. 'All good I hope?'

'Not really. You drowned.'

'Well, let's hope it's not a premonition.'

He hesitates, the whistle from another drag of the cigarette. 'I guess it's still playing on my mind. Have you told anyone yet?' His long-ragged inhale is a painless cut.

'About?' I sink my face into my hand.

A thin laugh. 'What happened, babes.'

I coil my legs under me, click the speakerphone off, pull it to my ear. 'No. Why would I do that?'

There's a drumbeat as if he's bouncing the phone on his chin. 'So, where are you now?'

'Thailand. Although it sounds like they're getting ready to leave.'

'Thailand. Cool. What've you been up to?'

'Oh, you know, swimming, sitting around the pool. Normal holiday stuff. Aunt Christine's having a great time. I caught her smoking flipping dope earlier.'

'AC? That's mad.'

'I know, right?' My laugh fades, an awkward silence. 'How're things at home?'

'Oh, you know.' His voice pitches as he shifts position. 'I haven't been around much, to be honest. But someone's always got something to say.' A beat hangs between us. 'I miss you.'

My heart flutters down my chest like it did the first time we met. 'What are they saying?'

'The usual. Look at the bitch carrying on with her life. That kinda stuff. Ignore it. I do.'

His words worry the wound I'm here trying to heal. 'I'm sorry, Pat. I thought people would have moved on by now. How about the press?'

'All quiet. I did a good job there, right?' He takes another long draw of nicotine. 'It's okay. I've got you.'

I curl into myself; the sadness rushes me like a wave of cold seawater. 'I thought I'd feel different out here, but it's like she's inside me. Not in a bad way but …'

'Hmm. You need to let it go. Time to move on, babes. So, when are you back?'

I close my eyes. A flutter of bird wings, their calls, and Clare's falling, the darkness churning as she slips from my hands. 'I don't …'

'Sorry?'

I open my eyes, let my silence hang, draw in the scent of sea, the taste of gasoline. The clang of metal on metal, dockers cussing on shore.

'You don't what?' Irritation sharpens Patrick's words.

I grip my knees to my chest, my heart races. 'I don't–'

'Sophie,' Aunt Christine calls.

'Shit. She's awake. I've got to go.'

'She still doesn't know, does she?'

'Sophie!' Panic quivers her voice.

'Coming,' I call over my shoulder. Snap the phone shut.

16

Sihanoukville. Cambodia.

'You okay, now, Ainti?'

The panic ripping across Aunt Christine's face last night when she realised I wasn't in bed had stretched my heart so tight I thought it might crack. After pouring her a medicinal miniature of whisky from the minibar, I'd crawled into bed, tugged a pillow over my head. The memory of the accident thumped for hours, the screech of rubber on wet tarmac, the metallic taste of blood, petrol, of people screaming, crying. Like the therapist showed me, I breathed in slowly, exhaled long and hard, but it made no difference.

Aunt Christine presses her head to mine, staring at the shoreline. 'I'm trying to let go.'

'I know. Me too.' I squeeze her hand. 'It's okay. Everything's okay.'

Last night, she and Bea had laughed off my concerns about the envelope of money, assuring me it had nothing to do with the drugs floating on the Gulf of Thailand. She stumbled into the bathroom after escorting Bea out of the cabin, ignoring my questions about Tamsin and the £20. I gave up when she slipped into bed, pulled on her eye mask, and turned over. Today we agreed no more drama, just a stroll along the shoreline. Sit, take time to watch the waves breaking on golden sand, the sunlight rippling the surf.

'It's quite the perfect picture, isn't it, Ainti?'

She pouts, hunches her shoulders. 'Until you turn around.'

Behind, the road rolls thick with traffic. Vehicles of all shapes and sizes speed past a long, suffocating line of cafés and bars. Clouds of smoke spit from exhausts, clashing with the swirl of scented roasted meats, candied sweets. The blue sky is cut with scurrying wisps of cloud over sun-scorched roofs punctured by cranes the size of skyscrapers.

Aunt Christine turns back to the sea. 'It used to be so pretty. It's such a shame.'

'The price of tourism, I guess. The more people come, the more of everything you need.'

'I was here, maybe ten, fifteen years ago. It was sandy beach after sandy beach. And look at it now. A building site.'

I slip off my shoes, slip-slide my feet in the sand, study the horizon. 'Ainti, what did Bea mean about you sacrificing more than I know?'

Aunt Christine zips up her handbag, places it between us on the bench, catches my sideways glance. 'It's nothing. I promise. What could she possibly know about it, anyway? Was she there? No. Anyway, back to you. You were very aloof about your date last night.'

'Why are you doing that?'

'What?'

'Changing the subject?'

'I don't think it's me who's avoiding the question, Sophie-Anne. Come on, spill. I'm tired of asking.' Aunt Christine clasps her hands in her lap, shuffles back on the seat until her feet swing off the floor. 'I'm not moving until you give me all the details.'

'Please, let it be? It wasn't a date.' I avoid her stare, push the sand through my toes like a friendly hug.

'Oh, come on, Sophie-Anne, I'm just interested. I don't care either way. I've lived perfectly well without a man all my life. But it's nice to have some company sometimes, isn't it?' She runs a finger along the edge of the bench between us. 'Oré seems very charming.'

'I had a good time, okay? We had lunch, and I met his son's girlfriend.' I plump my rucksack into the small of my back like a pillow. 'He really surprised me, actually. He can speak Thai, you know. Like really, really well.'

'Oh. I guess speaking languages is a bonus in his job.'

'True. The only downside is I now have bruises the size of rugby balls on my bum. And before you say anything, the car he hired had rubbish suspension, nothing else.'

'I didn't say a word.' She zips her lips.

I nudge her with my shoulder. 'You didn't have to. I can read your filthy mind.'

Aunt Christine presses her palms onto the bench. 'Well, this is lovely, isn't it? When do we just sit and talk like this? Crazy when you think we live by the sea. Do you remember when we used to go to Weymouth when you were little?' She nods at a mother and child sitting on the beach, scooping handfuls of wet sand to make a river at the water's edge. 'Now, Weymouth, that's a beautiful beach.'

I draw in the sea air. 'Hmm. I remember the first time I saw it was from a shop window. I thought it was a painting until I noticed the people moving around like ants.'

'There was nothing better. You playing in the sand. Me and your mum in deckchairs, a flask of tea in hand, talking about everything and nothing.'

We fall into silence, Aunt Christine lost in thought.

'I can't remember Dad ever being there, can you?'

Aunt Christine's lips pull into a thin line. She sweeps hair from her face, not a styling product in sight today. 'Rarely.' Aunt Christine pulls her handbag over her arm. 'I think we should start heading back. It's getting busy.'

I slip on my red ballet pumps. A screech of tyres, a crunch, and we spin around to the road. Two motorbike tuck-tucks stand nose to nose, crumpled on the tarmac. I clasp my throat, my pulse punching fast. The sound of raised voices, hands thrown high, the drivers' faces creased with disbelief. I run a hand down over my stomach to my thigh, wince at the squeal of sirens, the people filling the space around us, desperate to watch the conflict unfold.

I tilt my head from side to side, attempt to ease the stiffness rising in my neck. 'I can't be doing with this. Let's go.' I turn to grab my bag from the seat, a vacant space where it had sat.

I look under the bench. 'Ainti, have you seen my bag?' Tightness grips my chest. My palms pressed to my temples, I twirl back and forth, wrenching my hands through my hair. 'No. No. No. This can't be happening. Ainti, where are you?'

In all the unrest, like my bag, unseeing hands had dragged her into the swell. Bodies bumping, the smell of hot, perspiration-soaked skin. I press my palms over my ears, blur the incessant babble of the swarm, the roar of police sirens.

'Ainti!'

'Sophie?' Aunt Christine spirals out of the mass.

'For the love of God. Ainti.' I grab her to me. 'Where did you go?' A tremor quivers on her lips. 'I couldn't find you.'

'Come here. Sit down.' I guide her over to the bench, people climbing either side of us, chancing a better view. A chorus of mumbling voices, revving engines.

'Can we just go, please?' she stutters.

I kiss her hair, pull her hand into mine, look back at the space where my bag had been. 'Come on. I've got you. Keep hold of your handbag.'

Back on the ship, the atrium is a buzz of quiet conversation, soothing against the mayhem unfolding at the beach. Aunt Christine waves to a couple lounging on easy chairs, sun hats tossed onto the coffee table, beach bags at their sides.

'How do you know all these people, Ainti?'

Everywhere we go, the bar, the restaurant, the pool, someone's saying hello. A woman clad head to toe in black Lycra stuck her head out of the gym yesterday. Aunt Christine couldn't remember her name, shouting, 'Hello, you fitness freak!' Fitness freak thankfully saw the funny side.

I guide Aunt Christine to a couch. 'I'll get you some tea, yes?'

'Or perhaps a small brandy, Sophie-Anne.' She pinches her thumb to forefinger, peels them apart, chances a double.

'Hmm. Someone's feeling better. Back in a minute.'

I place my palms flat on the reception counter, the rush of coolness welcome against my hot skin. 'Excuse me?'

'Yes, madam, how can I help?' The receptionist glances at my fingers, tapping erratically fast on the desk.

I snatch my hand away. 'Sorry. My aunt's had a bit of a scare. Could someone get her a brandy, please? A small one. Even if she asks you for a large, it's small.'

'I'm sorry to hear that. Of course. Does she need the doctor?'

'I don't think so, thank you.'

'Sophie.' Oré strides out of the backroom. 'I thought I heard your voice. Good day?'

'Not really.' The young lady smiles at Oré, hurries over to the phone. 'There was an accident at the beach. My aunt got lost in the crowd.' I hesitate for a beat. 'And someone stole my bag.' A thick grey fog darkens my thoughts. Rubbing a hand on my forehead, I try to focus. 'I need to cancel things, don't I? My cards?' I turn to the elevator. 'Can you look after my aunt whilst … Sorry. I–'

'Hey, it's okay. I can help you with that.' He lifts the counter flap. 'Come on in. We'll get it sorted.'

I turn to Aunt Christine, who has moved over to the couple lounging on the easy chairs, deep in conversation. 'What about my aunt?' Laughter erupts from the corner.

'She'll be fine. I'll ask the others to keep an eye on her. Come on, let's get you sorted.'

The backroom isn't anything like I imagined. No plush seating area or bubbling coffee machine. No rows of executive desks, rotating leather chairs, flat-screen monitors. Instead, a boxroom, a faint trace of lemon polish in the air. Three tall filing cabinets stand against the wall, two pedestal desks pushed together, each with a phone and desktop computer. No kettle, tea caddy or biscuits, just a tabletop fan recirculating the air-conditioned breeze onto hot skin.

'This isn't how I imagined it. You and your colleagues are forever running in and out of here. I thought it was a grand fleet of offices or a state-of-the-art staffroom.'

'Nope. Just a not very exciting cupboard. The main offices are below deck, but us lowly front-of-house workers don't get invited in there. Right. Have a seat.' He taps a pen on a notepad. 'What was in the bag?'

I consider his question for a few seconds. 'My wallet. A sun hat, sunglasses, suncream.' I pause, visualise my earlier steps. 'We were going to the beach, so I'd left my phone in the cabin and I gave my passport to my aunt to look after. She's got one of those zippy compartments in her bag.'

'Useful.' He taps the pen, lifts his eyes to me. 'Okay. So, that doesn't sound too bad. What was in the wallet? Cards, cash?'

'Um. Yes. A debit and credit card, both HSBC. Oh, and about

fifty Australian dollars. I …' A knot grows in my throat. 'I … I …'

He drops the pen, places an arm around my shoulders. 'Hey. It'll be fine. The cash is gone, but the cards are easy to sort out. I'll get them on the phone. Cancel everything and ask to pick up replacements in Hong Kong. They'll sort that for you.'

I stare at the phone in his hand. 'I …'

'Sophie? Are you okay?'

As he says it, I see the scene of her and me play out as if it happened yesterday, my sitting in her bedroom, holding her hand. 'No. I don't think I am.'

No child should watch their mother die. No matter how often I sat at her bedside, flattened out her covers, tidied the fringe of her shawl, I never got used to it. Her heart pumping stubbornly in her chest, skin lucid, bruised by anything but the slightest of touches. Bunches of pale-pink peonies, her favourite, stood tall in vases of elegant simplicity on the windowsill. I knew when she handed me the swirl of yellow and white gold, time was short. Until then, she had worn it always.

The pain explodes within me like a silent grenade. 'My Ailm. It was in the pocket of my wallet.' I push up off the chair. 'The clasp broke. I meant to get it fixed, but–' Sliding back down onto the seat, I falter. 'I put it in the back pocket, so I wouldn't lose it.' My voice is scratchy. 'It's gone, isn't it?'

He places the phone receiver down, a deafening click. 'Is it insured?'

I wipe the back of my hand at the fat tear rolling down my cheek. 'How could I be so stupid?'

'Shall I call the police?'

My breath rattles as it enters and leaves my chest in sharp jags. I shake my head. 'No. Can we just call the bank, please?'

Oré places a hand on my shoulder, picks up the phone.

17

Ho Chi Minh City (Saigon). Vietnam.

The midday heat strikes hard as I step out of the car. A lack of sleep is tearing at my already fragile state of mind, the shame of not telling Aunt Christine about my losing Mum's Ailm necklace, Patrick. I fear her face crumpling with disappointment will crush me beyond repair. So, I'm doing what I do best, ignore it, keep myself busy, eat a ton of ice cream, a few extra vodkas. Numb the guilt scratching me raw inside.

I slap a hand on my back pocket as my mobile starts to vibrate and ring. It's the fifth time Patrick's called since we spoke in Thailand. He knows me well enough to sense something's off and I'm ignoring his calls.

'Keep up, Sophie-Anne. Stop skulking behind like some hormonal teenager, and either answer that phone or switch it off. It's bleeping getting on my nerves.'

I cancel the call, tap back – *Can't talk now.*

'Stop!' Bea throws out her arm. 'The traffic's crazy. They drive straight at you, even on the crossings. Hold your hand up like the locals, be confident, and you'll be fine, my friends.'

The tincture of gasoline belches from zipping motorbikes, tired cars, the smog of traffic-choked roads searing the throat. Mopeds crammed with families of three, four generations dance in a pattern of quick, slow, quick, in fitful lines.

Aunt Christine's shoulders hunch. Hands wide from her sides, she struts high knees into the road like an overgrown chicken. I cover my mouth, laughter heaves from my stomach. Vehicles weave around her shouting, 'I'm crossing. I'm crossing. I'm crossing.' Stepping onto the kerb, she spins around, arms held aloft, and cheers. My aunt, the Rocky

Balboa of Ho Chi Minh City.

I whoop, clap my hands above my head. 'Go, Ainti.' Who needs therapy when you can laugh until your stomach hurts?

'That's the first time I've seen you smile in days, Sophie-Anne. Come on. Over you come. You're holding us up.'

On the other side is Ben Thanh Market. A warren of cluttered gaudy booths separated by walkways paved with grey and blush pink tiles. Sunlight flashes bright through skylights onto thoroughfares saturated with chatter. Rows upon rows of garish scarves, handbags, towels, jewellery, souvenirs in ordered displays. The shopkeepers perch on red and blue plastic footstools, fanning cardboard ripped from today's deliveries against the heat and perspiration-infused humidity.

'Young man. That's not the way to get a lady's attention.' Aunt Christine tuts at a shopkeeper, tugging on her cardigan sleeve. 'Right.' Legs wide, she wags a finger at him. 'Enough,' releases a wheezy snort as he drops his head, steps away. 'Oh, very well. Come on. God knows I'm a sucker for a bargain. What have you got?'

He tugs at a pile of neatly folded T-shirts, holding up a black one with the words 'Screw January' embossed in large gold metallic lettering.

'What do you think, Sophie-Anne?'

'Perfect. They'll love me walking around at home in that, won't they?'

'Two.' She holds up two fingers, follows his beckoning hand down an alley at the side. 'Do you, by any chance, sell women's underwear?'

'Ainti.'

'What?' She shrugs. 'Sophie-Anne, I've learnt my lesson. Never again. I …' Her words drift until she and Bea are out of sight.

At the end of the row, raised voices grow from nowhere. A woman scurries past, tugs an orange silk scarf tied slack around her neck. Her raised eyebrow advises me to turn around, go back. A man in a pink shirt and faded blue jeans paces in and out of an alleyway. A woman in a knee-length yellow cotton dress stands pressed against the wall, her handbag held across her stomach. She squeals as two rats the size of small cats scamper across her path. They stop, sniff at the smell of fried food snaking around us. The sound of shattering china behind me makes my mind skip bright, like the sun in my eyes.

I unpacked the fish and chips, settled in front of the television. The front door slammed.

'Hi. In here,' I called. 'I've got food.'

'What the fuck?'

9.30 pm, he was late. I jumped to my feet, chip paper still in hand, edged into the kitchen. 'Hey. What's wrong?'

Patrick swiped the tap, threw a cloth into the sink. 'Do you do anything around here? Couldn't you at least do the washing-up?'

'I've only just come in. Sit down. I'll do it later.'

'That's the story of your life, isn't it?' He slammed a cup onto the draining board.

'Pat, be fair. I've only been back a few minutes and I'm starving. What do you expect me to do, work all day, come home and start playing housewife?' I flinched, a plate shattering on the flagstone floor.

'Oops.' He turned to face me, reclined on the sink, wiped his hands on a tea towel.

'Was that really necessary?' Knelt at his feet, I collected up the broken pieces of china.

He shrugged. 'What? I dropped a plate. Making a drama out of nothing again, are we? No. If I'd wanted to break something.' He hurled a mug at the wall.

Hands covering my head, I cowered. 'Patrick. Please.'

He tossed the tea towel into the sink, turned to the stairs. 'We can't all be as perfect as you, can we?'

'Why are you doing this? You've been home less than ten minutes. Why are you shouting at me?'

'Oh, and here she goes.' Spit flew from his mouth, his face flushed red. 'I want to sit down too, you know, but I'm the one having to clear up your fucking crap.'

I froze, knowing leaving would have made it worse, jabbed his rage. Head down, his voice thundered, spicy wet on my face. The back of my head pressed into the wall, his words sunk into my skin. Their invisible wounds layered upon those already sliced.

***

107

'Stick um up.'

Something stabs my back, I freeze. 'What the fuck!'

'Sophie-Anne. Language.'

'Ainti.' I spin around, a hand on my heart. 'You scared the flipping life out of me.'

'Always so dramatic. Look. You'd better take us back to the car.' Red-faced, Aunt Christine and Bea hold up six oversized carrier bags. 'Don't ask. Let's just say the traders of Ben Thanh Market will eat well tonight. Anyway, what happened to you? We turned around, and you'd gone.'

I scratch my head, take a bag from each of them. 'Look at you two. I can't turn my back for two minutes. What is all this stuff?'

'Ah.' Aunt Christine taps her nose. 'Nothing for you to worry about. Let's take these to the car and go get a drink. Apparently, Bea knows a spectacular place.'

'Is this it?' Aunt Christine groans.

Large grey letters on a well-weathered red sign read 'Note Café Bar'. Thousands of sticky notelets hang like wallpaper below the windows. Two storeys, it sits nestled between open-fronted jewellery shops and lines of abandoned mopeds. To the right, the footpath widens, spotted with maple trees shading locals and tourists from the late afternoon sun.

Bea tugs open the door. 'Come on, you two. You're gonna love it.'

Aunt Christine grits her teeth, dips her head for me to go first.

The uneven concrete step leads to a sun-blistered wooden floor, a shock of nutty caramel swirls the air. The ceiling, walls, serving area, tables and chairs are all covered in sticky notelets, the colours of the rainbow.

'Isn't it great?' Bea steers us inside.

Aunt Christine stops dead, folds her arms. 'It's a blinking mess. Where are we supposed to sit?'

'Don't be such a party pooper, Chrissie. It's a bit of fun.' Bea pulls out a chair at a table next to the stairs.

We sit, thumb through some notes stuck to the wall.

'Who puts these up?' I ask.

'The customers. They're good luck charms and messages. Some

will be from years ago.' Bea looks at the customers huddled in corners, framed by the multicoloured paper. 'Pretty, isn't it?'

I spot my fingertip on a red and white polka-dotted note – *Never forget how amazing you are. Cx* scrawled in black ink. My stomach twists, a thump in my heart. Clare was forever leaving me notes like this at university, on my door, on the fridge, on the windscreen of my car. She would pick the gaudiest of paper, scrawl her words of wisdom in thick black felt-tip pen. As the years went on, it became a text message or an email. A quote, a thought of the day, a 'I miss you'. Too many to recall, but one day stands out from all the others, the day our friendship ended.

***

I'm on my way, Clare texted.

Without breathing, I tapped back – *Please don't.*

Two hours later, sat in my kitchen, she had Patrick's latest love note crumpled in her fist.

'What's the fucker saying this time?' She flattened the paper on the table, read it out loud. 'Well, I be damned – *I hate it when we fight. Try to keep the place tidy. It will help. I love you. Patx.*' She tosses the note away. 'Where does he get off leaving you this bullshit? What the fuck, Soap? I notice the flowers aren't expensive florist ones any more, either. Just a cheap bunch from the petrol station down the road. He's got this sussed, hasn't he? He pitches a hissy fit about nothing and then gives you fucking flowers and a note. Which isn't an apology, is it? Please, Soap. This has gone on long enough. Get your things and come with me.'

I avoided her sticker stare, looked up at the ceiling. 'He's really stressed at the moment. My new job offer has come at the wrong time. I can't run out on my marriage every time we have a row.'

Clare slapped a palm onto the kitchen table. 'Don't. You're far from stupid, Soap. Nice try. But you don't believe that. Not really. These aren't arguments. You're constantly fighting. Actually, no, let me correct myself. He wears you down until you have no option but to argue back. Until you think you're the irrational one. What's all this crap about your job offer, too?' She swept the letter off the table. 'Argh. I'm madder than a wet hen. He should be pleased for you, not making you feel guilty. If he doesn't like his wife climbing the career ladder quicker than him, he needs to pull his finger out and do something. Not blame you.'

'You make it sound like he's a monster. It's not that bad.'

'But it is, isn't it? You mightn't have bruises or broken bones. Yet.' She winced, tempered her tone. 'This is not okay. If he's not shouting at you, he's not speaking to you; if he is speaking to you, he's trying to control everything you do. Sophie, please.' She gripped my arms. 'You're amazing and deserve so much better than this. Come on, you must believe that?'

'Stop!' I stood so abruptly, my chair clattered to the floor. 'Can you just go? Please.' I pulled open the front door, a thick sticky silence.

Clare swiped up her car keys. 'You don't mean that.'

'You need to go. He's right. You're always overthinking everything. He's not like that.'

'Oh, really.' Clare stooped, picked up the note, scribbled on the back. 'Well, I beg to differ.'

'It's impossible. The two of you like this.' I gripped my head, two hands. A pain. A beat pulsing. 'I can't do this any more. Go … Please.'

'So, that's it. He finally wins.'

***

She'd wrote *Never forget how amazing you are. Cx* in black ink on the back of his note before leaving that day. As she drove away, the emptiness howled inside me. I sunk to my knees, my head on the floor, and cried from the pit of my stomach.

A lightening touch of fear hits my nerves. 'People change, don't they?'

'What's that, Sophie-Anne?' Aunt Christine huffs.

'Sorry. What?'

'Look. See Beatrix. She's already comatose just from touching the wretched things. I bet this place is crawling with dust mites.' She wipes a fingertip on the table. 'I'll have a cup of chronic diarrhoea, please.'

'I think someone needs an early night.' Bea shakes her head. 'You okay, Sophie? You still with us?'

'What? No. I mean, yes. Fine. Sorry. Just daydreaming.'

Bea points to the menu on the blackboard behind the counter. 'So, what're we all having?'

I stretch to see the list. 'Are there any specialities?'

'Now, that's what I like to hear.' Bea frowns, flicks her chin at Aunt Christine. 'Good for you, Sophie. Your aunt should take note.' She holds up three fingers to the waitress. 'Cà Phê Trứng, please.'

'And what in God's name is that?' Aunt Christine throws her hands in the air.

Bea smiles, pats her arm. 'Cà Phê Trứng. Coffee. A local speciality. You'll love it.'

'Right. Well. Okay.' Aunt Christine adjusts the cardigan of her pastel lilac twinset. 'As you know, I like to try new things.' She scrapes her chair on the red-tiled floor, stands. 'I need the ladies. I'm guessing they have one of those. Although what state it will be in, who knows?'

'Stop moaning, Chrissie. What's got into you?'

Her lips purse. 'Can I not have an off day, Beatrix? I'm still cross about Sophie's bag being stolen, and I'm tired.' She looks away, clumps her handbag under her arm.

'I'll come with you. It's out the back if I remember rightly.' Bea stands, shepherds her forward.

As they walk away, they're like an old married couple in many respects. They laugh together, argue together, slip into a drunken haze together. I found them sitting on the floor of the top deck bar one night. Backs pressed against the railings, belting out the back catalogue of Frank Sinatra. Thankfully, there's been no repeat of the marijuana incident. Not to my knowledge, anyway.

The waitress places down three large cappuccino-sized cups, saucers, and small white jugs, each with a sticky notelet attached.

I peel off the coloured note. 'Excuse me. What's in this?'

'Cà Phê Trứng. Egg coffee.'

'Ah. You speak English. Egg coffee?'

The young waitress smiles, nods. 'It's a favourite in Vietnam. Strong dark Vietnamese coffee, egg yolk and condensed milk. We whisk the egg and milk into a fluffy foam, pour it over the coffee. It's popular with tourists.'

'Is this for me?' I hold up the notelet. She bows, strides back to the counter.

Written on a green two-toned heart, *Forgiveness is the greatest gift.* What the actual hell is happening today? Enough of these voodoo serendipities. And you, Kadek, for the love of God, get off my case. I heard you the first time, and I didn't understand you then. Give me a flipping clue or get out of my head. Seriously, it's full.

'Well, well. I wasn't expecting to see you here.' Two hands grip my shoulders. I twist around to find Oré and a younger, taller, leaner man, the same mop of brown curls shorn at the side, eyes cornflower blue.

'Hello. I could say the same about you. Another day off?' I pull my dress over my knees. Not that Oré and his friend can see my legs under the table, but covering my thighs has become a tick, something I do on impulse in company nowadays.

Smart in a navy linen suit, white t-shirt, Oré grips the chair opposite, two hands. 'Sort of. Twenty-four hours. Started at midday. How are you?' His brow creases concerned the same as when he had shown me into the back-office.

'Better. Thank you.' I take a sip. 'So, why are you here?' Coffee splutters from my lips. 'Sorry.' I wipe a paper serviette to my mouth, the table. 'That's none of my business. It's just not the sort of place I thought you'd like.'

'No?' He grins. 'Thought I'd be slumming it down on some street corner, did you?'

'Actually, I thought you'd prefer some swanky restaurant or bar. Slumming it doesn't seem your style.'

'Wow. I shout you lunch in the mountains, and you think I'm some Rockefeller. You're easily impressed, Miss O'Ryan. I'll remember that.' He slaps his hand on the shoulder of his companion. 'Sophie, meet Brad. Brad, this is Sophie.'

'Oh. You're his son. I thought you were in … Never mind.' I jump up, wiggle my fingers hello. 'You got together. That's great.'

'Ahh, Sophie.' Brad thrusts a hand into mine. Two firm pumps and a smile of straight white teeth just like his dad's. 'Good to meet you.'

What did that mean? Has Oré been talking about me? Why would he do that? We're hardly the best of friends. I nod, eye him from head to toe. He's the younger twin of his father. Except for those piercing blue oval eyes. His mother's evidently. Beautiful, intense, unforgettable. If I was in my twenties, I so would. 'I'm not sure what he's told you, but it's all lies.'

He nudges his shoulder into Oré. 'He never tells me anything. But Tap, she's a different story.'

I drop my eyes, sip my coffee with two hands, growl into the foam. Oré drops his head to the side, as if telling Brad to behave. 'He's teasing. Anyway, I can see you've got company. We'll leave you to it.'

'It's just my aunt and Bea. They're in the ladies. Sorry. The restroom. They're in the restroom.'

'Ah.' He looks over my head. 'Not any more, they're not.'

Aunt Christine looks up, stops mid-stride. 'Well, I can't leave you alone for one minute, can I, Sophie-Anne? Chatting up the crew again, I see. And who are you, young man?'

'Miss Collins. Lovely to see you again,' Oré shakes her hand. 'This is my little boy, Brad. He's working out here.'

'Christine, Oré. It's Christine.' She places a hand on her heart, swoons at Brad. 'Well, aren't you the mini-me?'

'Beatrix, looking as delightful as ever.'

'Oré, you're one big charmer. Join us.' Bea pats the chair next to her.

'You're fine. We're just leaving.'

Brad slaps his father's back. 'Pops, you stay. My scooter's outside. I've got another meeting in ten.'

'Oh. Okay.' Oré turns to us. 'Are you sure? I don't want to intrude.'

'Nae. You dafty. Pull up a chair.' Bea gestures for him to sit down.

Oré tugs Brad tight to his chest. Eyes closed, he nuzzles his face in his hair, draws in his scent. 'I love you, bud. Have fun. Stay smart. And call me.' He pulls away, kisses Brad's cheek. 'Say hi to that pain-in-the-butt girlfriend of yours.'

Brad waves goodbye, leaves. Oré snaps away, wipes a hand to his eyes. 'Right. Where were we?'

'Sit down.' Aunt Christine pats the chair next to her. 'Goodness. Isn't he the spit of you, Oré? Very dashing. And look at you, all smart in civvies. Got a date?'

'Ainti!'

Oré folds his arms. 'Nope. No plans. What do they say? All dressed up and nowhere to go. I'll probably wander around, grab something to eat and head back.'

Bea taps the table in front of him. 'You'll do no such thing.'

My jaw drops, eyes spearing Bea to the wall. Please don't. Please don't say it.

'You're coming with us.'

She said it. What the actual hell? I'm not in the mood for a cosy chat over food. Dinner – with him, with them, together. 'Jesus,' I mutter.

Aunt Christine jabs a finger into my knee, tuts. 'Play nice.'

Bea sips her coffee. 'We're just finishing. Then I'm taking these young ladies for something to eat. There's room for one more.'

I lean into Bea, whisper, 'I'm sure Oré has better things to do than hang out with us. Ow!' Aunt Christine kicks my shin under the table. 'How did you even hear me? That hurt.'

'That's kind of you, but I don't want to butt in.' Oré presses on his knees, as if he's about to stand.

'Oh, come on, Oré. As I tell my niece, live a little dangerously. We don't bite. Well, Sophie-Anne might fancy a nibble, but I promise to keep her in hand.'

'You can't help yourself, can you?' The grin stretching across my aunt's face mirrors mine. 'Enough, already.'

Oré stares at Aunt Christine, Bea, me, and places his palms on the table. 'Actually, you're right. Why not? Where are we going?'

'Ah. Master Oré, that's a surprise.'

18

Bea nods at the waiter. 'Who's for wine?'

Aunt Christine slaps her lips. 'I think I'm going to start with a beer tonight. Save the wine for dinner.'

'When have you ever drunk beer, Ainti?'

'I know. Get me. I'm feeling all frisky and modern.'

'Ha. I'll have a beer, too, please,' Oré says. '*Bia Hơi*, Christine?' She pats Oré's hand. 'Oh, go on then. You've twisted my arm.'

'Do you know what that is, Ainti?' I whisper.

'Not a clue.'

'And a bottle of Rượu nếp cẩm, please, for me and Sophie. I'd normally have it with dessert, but what the hell, we're on holiday.' Bea hands the menus back to the waiter. 'Have you been before, Oré?'

'Vietnam. Yes. Here. No.'

'Me neither. I think it opened last year. What about you, Chrissie?'

'I've only been to Hạ Long Bay.'

The lizard carved out of galvanised metal climbing the wall to my left becomes fascinating, seeing as I have nothing to contribute to this conversation, having travelled nowhere of interest in my life. Little miss even-more-inadequate is quite happy sitting hushed in the corner, thank you.

The waiter pours the wine, a deep purple hue. 'Whoa. I've never drunk anything like this before.'

Another waiter places down a wooden puzzle board carved with empty imprints and a black bag of coloured shapes matching those missing from the jigsaw. He motions for Aunt Christine to open her palm, hands her a blindfold.

'Oh.' Her face stony, she leans into Bea. 'I hope this isn't one of those kinky adult sort of places, Beatrix.'

'Chrissie, what are you like? You dafty. Nae. It's preparing you for the main restaurant. That's the surprise. We're eating in darkness.'

Aunt Christine crumples the eye mask in her hand. 'Why on earth would we want to do that? How will I know what I'm putting in my mouth?'

'That's the point, Chrissie. You won't. The owner set this up to help us appreciate how our senses work when we eat. You dinnae need to worry. I have it on good authority that the food is lovely. Look around. Most of the staff he employs are visually or hearing impaired or both. It's gonna be great.'

My mobile pings in my pocket.

'Sophie-Anne! Not again.' Aunt Christine shakes her head. 'Who in God's name keeps ringing? Give it to me. I'll tell them what to do with their endless bleeping.'

'Excuse me.' I leave the table, hover in the doorway. One eye on them, I flip open the phone.

TD: And?

Me: Sorry. I've been busy.

TD: And?

My finger hovers, ready to reply. When I don't, three grey dots appear, disappear, reappear. I look back at the table, Aunt Christine and Bea quizzing the waiter. Oré looks up, his eyes catching mine. He jerks his head for me to come back, pulls a goofy face like they're strangling him. 'Save me,' he mouths. I look down at the phone, back at him, his eyes on me. Another message pings. I snap the mobile shut, switch it off. Oré smiles, watches me walk back to the table, slip the mobile into my back pocket, sit down.

'Ready, everyone?' The waiter signals for us to put on the blindfolds.

I pull the blindfold over my head. 'Looks like it's go big or go home for us tonight, Ainti.'

Our host, Gia, guides us into the main restaurant. My breathing instantly magnifies, the blackness a visual silence revering awe to all other senses. The voices are loud, and, oh my goodness, the smell. What in the world has happened? Without using sight, the aromas circling us are the most fabulous recipe in the air, sweetness, sourness, fish-sauciness, a brackish taste tingling the tongue.

We're placed into our seats by Gia. Oré shuffles down next to me, the smell of his cologne thick in my nose, and so good.

The waiter clinks cutlery and china down around us, serving our appetisers, a tang of garlic, fresh bread.

'Is it soup?' I waft the aroma to me.

'How do you know that?' Oré says.

'I've just put my fingers in it.' I giggle, suck them clean one by one. 'It tastes very green.'

Oré hiccups laughter. 'How can it taste green? Hey, try this.' He pads the table, slides away the bowl, bumps what I assume is a plate in front of me, presses a fork into my hand.

'What is it? It smells cheesy.' I stab something, take a bite. 'Oh, my goodness.' I turn to question him, not knowing if he's looking at me. 'Is that fig? Balsamic? Maybe honey?'

'And chocolate?' The heat of his voice hangs on my cheek for an answer.

He catches me off guard, and I'm winded for a second. 'Chocolate? No.' I splutter, try some more. 'You're right. There's something, isn't there?'

'Aha, and I apologise. This soup is without a doubt green. I can taste mint. Damn.' Oré's spoon chimes against the china bowl.

'See. Told you.' I smile, sit a little taller.

'Are your eyes open or closed, Chrissie?' Bea says opposite me.

'Mine are most definitely open. I'm not missing a second of this. Isn't it extraordinary?' Plop, plink, glub. Aunt Christine catches my arm with her nails swiping at the noise. 'What the hell is happening?'

'I'm topping up your wine, madam,' Gia says.

'Oh. Yes. Of course. Is it that black stuff?'

'No. We moved onto the Sauvignon, Chrissie, remember?'

'Is it wise to mix beer with wine, Ainti? We'll be carrying you home.'

'Aah. Pocky cock, Sophie-Anne. Keep it coming, Gia. Keep it coming.'

'Oh, Chrissie, I'm so glad I met you.' Bea's words drip emotion. 'All of you. This is so much more fun with you guys.'

Julie A Russell

I hear her smile. 'We're glad too, Bea. This place is amazing. Thank you for bringing us.'

'A toast,' Oré says, a series of slaps as he pads his hand on the table. 'If I can find my wine, that is.'

'Good idea.' I feel around for my glass, lift it up over the table.

'To family and friends. They know us well but love us just the same. Ready? One, two, three.'

After a few near misses and a lot of laughter, our glasses clink. I blink my eyes, giddy, sip some more wine. My chuckling falters, his breath hot on my cheek again. I turn to him, heat tumbles my chest. 'Right.' I turn away, put down my glass, two hands. 'Yay. Is this the second course?'

'Have some broccoli.' Aunt Christine wealds it like a sword into my face.

'Ainti. What are you doing?' I flap her fork away. 'Put it down, and step away from the wine, for all our sakes. Please.'

'Now this you should try, Sophie?' Oré says. 'Open your mouth, and I'll–'

'Easy tiger.' Aunt Christine explodes into a fit of giggles with Bea.

'Give you a taste. A taste, ladies. Please. You're being very naughty.' His voice breaks with laughter.

'And drunk.' I fist-bump my aunt's arm. 'Behave.'

'Open wide for the choo-choo, Sophie-Anne. The Oré express is coming in.'

'Not funny, Ainti. Where are you, Oré? Give me a clue.'

'You keep still and I'll come to you,' he says.

Aunt Christine snorts out whatever is in her mouth. Pulls the napkin from my lap.

'Hey!' I lean into her. 'Not another word, Ainti,' I whisper, pivot back to Oré, eyes closed. 'Ow. That's my nose.' I reach out for his fork, guide it into my mouth. 'Is that coffee? Have I missed dessert already?'

'That's what I mean.' A couple of more bumps into my cheek, my chin, and he slips the fork into my mouth, again. 'Success,' he says. 'Coffee with duck? It's good, isn't it? Real good.'

His lips are a whisper from mine. I fumble for my glass, touch his hand, rest there for a moment longer than needed. His skin burns as I trail off the tips of his fingers, drag mine away. 'Oh my goodness.'

118

My gasp thumps hard in my chest, I sit up straight, dizzy. What the heck, Sophie? I hadn't come here for this ... I didn't want this ... not ever ... not now ... not yet.

19

Cruising the South China Sea.

I know I'm staring, but I can't look away. A hug, a kiss on the cheek, a snatched back hand. Candice scrapes apricot jam over a slice of toast, crunches it between straight white teeth, turns from Roy. A cup held to his lips, a hand pressing on a rutted brow. His eyes stay on her, always on her. She stares at the door, a stream of passengers; some pass by, others nod a polite good morning. Roy leans over the table, takes her hand.

'Stop it, Roy. People are looking. You're incorrigible,' she says.

Electricity sparks inside me, remembering Oré's fingers brushing mine, the lightness that skipped through me. Candice bats Roy's fluttering kisses away. He falls back laughing, bangs his fist on the table, and the room falls silent. The thud echoes against my mobile's buzz. I fumble to turn it off, knowing it's him, always him. The memory swells like a sickness from my stomach, choking, clawing at my attempts to swallow it down with gulps of lukewarm coffee.

In the same way, a bruise takes time to appear and discolour, people unravel. An unspoken fizziness of anger, an inflamed pressure sore below the skin blistering to the surface. A misery that touch, words, kindness can't reconcile.

***

I assumed my thumping on the front door would signal danger. I didn't want to scare her, but that's how I felt – scared. Rubber screeched upon tarmac, tremoring my body rigid. I snatched my head up and down the street, searched the car headlamps as they sped past, fearful he had followed me. I banged harder. 'Come on. Come on.' My sobbing surrendering to grief, the hurricane of pain whipping inside me. I pulled the holdall tight to my stomach, rain dripping from my nose. The lock crunched, the door edged open.

'Soap!' Clare pulled me in, slammed it shut. 'Jesus Christ.'

I buried myself into her, sucked in her smell like a cosy blanket. A pulse of muffled wails escaped my lungs.

'*Ça va?* What's happened?'

My eyes closed, welcoming the stroke of her hand on my hair – safe, for now. I pulled away, dabbed the bloodied patch on her shoulder. 'Sorry. I'm so sorry. Is it ruined?'

'Forget the fucking jumper.' She looked at my face. 'For Christ's sake, Soap, look at your neck? Did he do that?' She stroked the wound, fingers sticky with blood.

I inched open my hand, the Ailm charm, its signature branded hot red on my palm. 'I ... I ...'

'Hey. It's okay.' Her hug was full of everything, my body, my brain, my whole. 'I've got you.'

'I'm so sorry. I should've ...'

'Please tell me this is the end.' She rests her head on mine, kisses my hair.

Relief wept into my sobs. 'I don't ...'

'Oh, Soap. We'll sort it. I promise.'

***

'Can I get you anything else, ma'am? We're about to clear breakfast away.'

'Oh. Sorry.' A hand splayed against my chest I'm snapped back into the room. 'Do you need me to go?'

The waiter shakes his head, points at my mug. 'More coffee?'

'Please.'

The waiter tops up my cup, walks away with my half-eaten plate of scrambled eggs.

'May I?'

'Hey. Sure.' I motion for Oré to sit.

'I haven't got long. I'm on in an hour.' He sprawls back on the seat, hands clasped behind his head. 'Can't wait. It's always a blast on reception on a sea day.' A silent beat hangs between us. 'Recovered from the other night?'

I sip my coffee. 'Indeed.'

Our evening at Noir had ended in a raucous mess. Aunt Christine surpassed herself yet again. After misjudging her glass in the darkness, she downed hers and everyone else's drink. I suggested we leave after she toppled onto the floor, looking for her handbag. Wrathful drunken slurs of 'Do you mind' and 'That's not my arm,' greeted Oré's offers to help.

He smooths back his hair, drops his hands. 'What're your plans today?'

'Not sure. I might just find a sunbed and read.'

He nods, flattens a napkin. 'So, enjoying yourself yet?'

'Maybe.' My eyes don't leave his. The air thick with temptation.

'Maybe. That's a step up from no.' He grins, drops his gaze like a shy teenager.

'Maybe.' I place down my mug, smile, flick my eyes away.

'Right.' He loosens his tie, shirt collar. 'As much as I'd like to stay loitering around you all day.' He stands, tucks his chair under the table. 'I can't.'

I twitch in my seat, look down at my hands clasping my mug, nod.

'I didn't get a chance to ask the other night. How did you get on with the necklace?'

'Oh.' The room flattens. 'The insurance will pay, but I'm not sure I'll bother. It was my mother's. She died when I was pretty young.'

He steps forward, grips the back of the chair, two hands. 'I'm so sorry. That sucks.'

'Yep. A new one won't replace it.'

He sits back down, folds the napkin in half, then quarters. 'I learnt something a long time ago. We place far too much significance on things, even the most precious ones. It's the memories they hold that count.' He shakes his head, strokes his chin, his neck, his finger catching a gold cable chain I haven't noticed before. The heaviness in his eyes makes my chest squeeze. 'I hope it doesn't spoil the rest of your trip. I'm sure she wouldn't want that.' He stands, his expression distant, stiff. 'I'd better go.'

'Don't work too hard.' My breath catches as he turns away. 'Oré.' He looks back. I adjust my coffee mug on the table. 'Thank you.'

He nods, walks like he's pushing against an unseen wind out of the door.

'Where did that come from?' I mutter.

An ache coursing through my body stuns me silent. I swig the last of my coffee, collect up my book, tidy my chair under the table.

Outside, I yank a lounger into the shade, perch on the edge, open my journal. His half revelations leave so many questions unanswered. I like him. I do. An affable interest, the kind you might afford a friend. It's all I can offer. Friends encased with boundaries high enough not to topple on silly whims. It can't be any more. I daren't let it be any more, I write.

20

Da Nang. Vietnam.

Hands covering my mouth, I shield my laughter as a small child screeches and weaves across the crowded lobby, a mixture of horror and confusion on the other passengers' faces. Her scooting between the furniture reminds me of myself at her age, mischievous, tricksy, trouble. Several crew members give chase, dodging side to side like players in a rugby match obstructing her path. An unintended game of tag, which, to my delight, she is winning.

I jolt at the tap on my back.

'Couldn't keep away, hey?' Oré says.

'There's never a dull moment on here, is there?' I nod at the youngster rampaging past.

'Yeet!' Oré steps to my side. 'What the hell?'

The infant hollers, 'Out of my way.' Tears back across the room.

'Excuse me.' He strides to the counter, his expression stern. The child scoots past his legs and in one sweeping movement, he picks her up, grips her under his arm. He flinches, her fists and feet striking his torso to release his grip, aid her escape.

'Put me down. Put me down,' she screams, hands and feet thumping, kicking.

He drops her on a couch, barricades furniture to block all escape routes.

'Don't move. I mean it,' he says, a pointy finger. 'Stay there.'

Shocked by the firmness of his voice, I stroll over. Should he be doing this to a passenger's child or grandchild? Surely not. By the time I reach them, it's difficult to know who's sulking more, the child or Oré.

'Can I help?' I sit next to her on the couch.

'That's kind of you, Sophie, but we're okay. Her parents will be down soon. Aren't you on your way out?'

'Honestly, I don't mind. I'm only waiting for my aunt, and she's taking an age to get ready these days.' I offer my hand to the girl. 'Hi. I'm Sophie. What's your name?' She snatches her head from me, crosses her arms tight. I admire her doggedness, remember how I felt the same exasperation at being told to sit still and be quiet at her age. 'Who is she?'

Oré rubs his chin. 'The Captain's daughter. His wife's flown in for a few days. She asked Emelia from reception to watch her whilst she went on the Bridge.' He nods at a young woman, her uniform untucked, collapsed against the wall.

'She looks stressed.'

'Yeah. I don't think childcare is in her top ten transferable skills, do you?'

'Do you have some cards?'

'Sorry?'

'Playing cards. Do you have some?'

He drives a hand into his trouser pocket. 'Can I get them for you when you get back? I can't really leave her.'

His confused frown makes me giggle. 'Not for me. For her.'

'Oh. Sorry. Right. Ha. Yeah, of course.' Oré tugs a hand through his hair. 'Why?'

'I want to teach her to throw them around the room. Why do you think?'

'Oh. A game. Good idea.' He looks at the little girl kicking the cushions on the floor. 'I don't know. Shall I have a look?' His shoulders stoop like a child half listening.

'If you don't mind.'

'Will they help? I only know poker and blackjack. They don't seem appropriate.'

'We'll leave those until she's older, shall we? See what you can find. I'll watch her.'

Hands on hips, he watches the child scratch patterns into a cobalt blue velvet bolster, absorbed by how the fabric changes shape and colour with each scrape of her fingernail.

'Go. We'll be fine,' I say.

He returns with not one but six packets of unopened playing cards. 'I wasn't sure how many you needed.'

'So I see.'

There's a charm about him when he drops his business-like façade, lets his goofier, childlike side shine through. I tap out one deck of cards, build a tower. It tumbles to the ground, and her interest flickers. She pushes her chin onto the cushion, thumb in mouth, hands me the next card from the pack.

I rub my forehead. 'Do you know how to do this?'

She sits up, elbows on knees, chin cupped in her hands. 'You're rubbish.' She shuffles closer.

'You're not kidding. Want a go?'

'Aha.' Together, we stand card against card.

I offer my hand. 'I'm Sophie.'

She looks at my palm, pulls the ace of spades over her eyes.

'Do you have a name? Let me guess. Is it Jonathan?'

'No. I'm not a boy. That's a boy's name.' She picks up another card. 'Mummy says I'm not to talk to strangers.'

'Quite right.' That's put you right in your place, Sophie O'Ryan.

Oré sits down next to us. 'It's fine. You can tell Sophie. She's our friend.'

She pushes her hand into mine. 'Carrie. Carrie with a C.'

All right, now I'm even more confused. Why is he overriding her parents' wishes, and why is she listening to him? And why is he calling me his friend? 'It's nice to meet you, Carrie with a C. Are you sure you haven't done this before? You're pretty good.'

Carrie yawns. 'Where's Papa, Uncle O?'

My head turns slow-mo towards Oré. 'Uncle O?'

'He'll be down soon, Carrot.' He ruffles Carrie's hair, her eyes close as she rolls into his hand. 'Yeah. This little bundle of fun is my goddaughter.'

My expression pinches, confused. 'She is?'

Carrie squeals. Not an impish yelp but a cheerful cry at her father, smart in naval uniform, hurrying across the lobby. Her mother, elegant in a pink summer dress at his side.

'Papa.' Carrie jumps into his arms, pushes her cheek against his.

'He looks pleased to see them.' I stand, spin on my heels to Oré. 'So, what's going on, Uncle O?'

He pushes himself up, straightens his jacket, a two-finger salute to the Captain. 'What, me and Tom? I mean Captain Miller.'

'I'm guessing not everyone is charged with the moral upbringing of his daughter. Should I be impressed?'

'Absolutely.' He taps the playing cards into the deck. 'We went to Columbia together.'

'Columbia?'

'The uni, not the country.' Head cocked to the side, his brow puckers. 'Although perhaps I should suggest that. Sounds like fun. But no. Columbia University, New York.'

'You went to university with him?' I gesture at Captain Tom Miller. His daughter's legs slung on either side of his hips.

'Don't look so surprised. We have universities in the States. And even the lowly hired help can have an education.'

'I know that. I just wasn't expecting you …' My face creases, puzzled. 'Who are you?'

'Ah.' He clears the table of all traces of Carrie's game. 'There's lots you don't know about me, Miss O'Ryan. Good and bad.'

Carrie calls over to Oré. 'Uncle O, I gotta go.'

A glow of hot fuzziness flutters through me as they blow kisses to each other, mouth, 'I love you.'

He lifts an eyebrow. 'So, wanna find out some more?'

'About?'

'What are you up to this evening?'

'Me?'

'Yeah. You.'

'Oh.' I glance around the room. 'I'm not sure. Why?'

'Fancy a drink? A thank you for helping me this morning. I can tell you all about my sordid past with Captain Miller, and you can tell me about your secret talent for bewitching small children.'

A drink? With him? Alone? That's not part of the plan. I cross my arms around my waist, look at my shoes. 'I'm not sure what my aunt's got planned.'

'Oh. Okay. Another time, maybe.' His hands slap his sides. 'I'm gonna go, don't want to get on the wrong side of the boss. I've heard he's a bit of a tyrant.' He hesitates, rubs the back of his neck. 'That's a joke, by the way. He's not.'

A false smile hides the fact Clare is tapping away in my head – *it's just a drink*, she says. 'Oh, I know I'm going to regret this.' I wipe a sweaty palm on my trousers. 'Actually, Oré. Why not? A drink sounds good.'

He swings around. 'It does?'

Is it that obvious I don't want to go? 'Sure. But just a quick one.'

'Fantastic. I'll meet you in the Crow's Nest at nine?'

'Um, yes. Great. I'll see you later.'

A mixture of terror and exhilaration races through me as he leaves. Damn. This is why I don't do this kind of thing any more. You get all worked up, spend hours worrying about what to wear, and it always ends in disappointment, or they don't call, or they let you down, or worse. I fluff my hair between two hands, fake cry. I'll have to style my hair. Find something nice to wear. Put on make-up. What am I doing? I can see Clare leaning against my bedroom door, tutting *just be yourself*. My stomach knots, a growl of sadness. 'But I don't know who I am any more.'

'Talking to yourself again, Sophie-Anne?' Aunt Christine taps my shoulder. 'Sorry. Tammy popped in after you'd left, and we got talking. Did I miss anything?'

I link my arm into hers. 'Not much. Come on, let's go.' I pull up sharp. 'Tammy? Do I know her?'

21

Clare's words have elbowed me all day. So, here I am, being as much of myself as I can, ditching the heels and pinching my swollen feet into a pair of silver glittery ballet pumps, dug out of the post-Christmas bargain bucket in the boutique. Bombarded daily by fashion magazines, adverts, self-appointed stylists' top tips on the TV and social media, I had thought twice. A heel makes the leg look longer, Sophie, leaner, Sophie, and oh my goodness, couldn't you do with both of those, Sophie? But tonight, a little bit of my misplaced sureness has returned, and Sophie O'Ryan is stepping out in all her misfitted glory.

The Crow's Nest is a buzz of spirited serenity, the piano whispering a soft ballad, alongside the lazy swish of the ceiling fans. Men unwind in tailored suits, the women in dresses of silk and satin. Their laughter, their smiles, I soak them in, follow the path of dark green leather sofas creased comfortable to the bar. Dipped spots echo the stars outside, golden torchiere lamps sit on polished oak side tables, pitching a hushed yellowy glow against gold-flocked papered walls, timbered floors.

He sits waiting on a stool at the bar, one foot on the floor, tapping, spinning ice around a highball glass. He's early. I like that. Patrick was always late. Would enjoy letting me hover, spying my unease through the window before coming in, announcing – surprise. Which it rarely was. Oré jumps to his feet, smiling with his eyes, the darkest shade of chocolate brown. His hands fall easy to my waist, his kiss soft on my cheek and something cold slips down my spine.

'Wow. Look at you.' The edginess of his voice soothes the tightness in my jaw. Is he nervous too?

'Charming. Do I usually look terrible, then?' I sweep the hair from my shoulders.

'What? No. I didn't mean that. Jeez. Ignore me. I'm a bit out of practice. I meant you look lovely. Awesome. Is that better?'

'Hmm.' I hear the words, but it's a constant fight in my mind to believe them. The tempest of self-doubt itching inside. Has done since my teens. But I'm trying. I'm trying harder than ever. I shuffle onto the barstool. No tugging or smoothing tonight, my knee-length navy organza skirt floating like a best-dressed Oscar gown over my knees.

'Drink? Vodka? Wine?' He wiggles his eyebrows. 'A cocktail?'

'Yes. All of those, please, after spending another day with my aunt. Anything large, strong and wet.' What the actual hell, Sophie? Why did you say that out loud? He'll think you're a flipping alcoholic. I scan the length of the bar. The bartender clasps a tall-stemmed glass, lavishes cream foam onto a liquor of coffee brown over ice. 'What's that?'

Oré leans in close, a mouthful of minty fresh breath on my cheek. 'An espresso martini. Would you like one?'

Wine or vodka is the sensible option. Nah. What the heck? 'Yes, please.' Oh well. If he's already concluded I'm a social misfit with a drinking problem, I might as well go down with a bang.

I take the glass from the bartender's tray. The blend of chocolatey vanilla punches my nose, a rush of caramel coats my throat. 'Fuck me, this is good.' I slap a hand over my mouth. 'Shit. I mean, sorry.' I stare into the glass. Great start, Sophie.

'Ha. Glad you like it.' He clinks his glass to mine. 'Fucking good choice, Miss O'Ryan.'

A shaky laugh. I slump back into the chair. 'Thanks.'

He sets his cocktail down on the bar, strokes a finger along its stem. 'So, you were a pro earlier?'

I pull back, drink splutters from my lips. 'Sorry. Is that a compliment?'

'Don't be modest.' He takes a sip, eyes me over his glass. 'You were totally different … assertive. I've not seen anyone tame Carrie like that.'

'Well, she clearly listens to her godfather.'

'Touché. Seriously. How do you do it?'

'Years of practice, I guess.' Thirty years, to be exact. And he's right. I've always exhibited an instinctive air of confidence at work, one I've never been able to replicate outside. Frustrated actors – isn't that what they say about teachers? The best ones, anyway.

'So, I'm intrigued. Why leave?'

I push into the seat. Here we go again. He's been dying to hear this titbit of information since we went for lunch in Thailand. I take a long sip of my drink, leave his question hanging. 'It's just part of my life that's run its course. The job's changed, and I'm fed up with playing petty politics with children's lives, compromising everything I believe in because of government policies and shrinking budgets. Not that anyone's interested in my opinion.'

'Woah.' He gulps the last of his drink. 'That's pretty deep.'

'Are you mocking me, Oré?'

'No. That's not what I meant. Why do you say that?'

'Because ...' I take another sip, blink the fuzziness from my eyes. Rein it in, Sophie, before you say too much. 'Just because.'

'In my experience, most people will easily forgo their values when money and power are involved.' He fondles his glass, gives me a sideways glance. 'No. I'm a little in awe, if I'm honest.'

'Yep. Well, we'll see.'

He waves a hand at the bartender, points at my glass. 'Can I get another of those and a Dr Pepper, please?'

'Dr Pepper? You're kidding, right?'

'I know. I've got the tastebuds of a thirteen-year-old, but sadly, I'm on the early shift. Don't let me stop you, though.'

'The rule that must not be broken.'

'Ah, so you know.' He throws me a I-like-being-here-with-you kind of smile. 'What's the plan when this ends?'

'Sorry?' I slur, cheeks full of cocktail.

'After the cruise ends. You've chucked in your job. What next?'

'Oh.' I tap a finger on his chest. 'Still figuring that one out. Go home. Get another job. Face the music, again.' Shut up, Sophie. Shut up. 'Ignore me. It's just the drink talking.'

'Is that what you want?'

'Hey.' I nudge his arm. 'What's with all the questions?' I seize the fresh espresso martini from the bartender, mouth 'thank you,' take a slug. The bartender smiles at my blowing him a kiss. I attempt to swing one leg over the other, almost lunge off the side. 'Oops. Anyway, what about you? How does a college boy end up on his best friend's ship?'

'Who says we're best friends? Tom's such a show-off. I can barely tolerate him these days.'

'Not true. I saw you hugging. And stop avoiding my questions.' His eyes drop, watching me tap his chest again, emphasising each word. 'I've been superstitious, nope, suspicious from the start. So has Candice.'

'Has she, now? And, suspicious? What the heck does that mean?'

'You're cocky, aren't you?'

'Cocky?' He places down his glass, laughs.

'What?'

'Your accent. Cocky. It sounds funny.'

'See. That's what I mean. And then there's your aftershave.'

'My aftershave?'

'Cologne. Eau-de-the-tee-let.' I point to his shirt collar. 'The smelly stuff on your neck.'

He grins. 'Yeah, I hear you.'

Drink spills over my glass, splatters his jacket. 'Oops.' I pat a napkin on his chest. His eyes meet mine, drilling dark pools of temptation. I throw the napkin down, clean my hands on my thighs.

'So, you like my cologne?'

Jesus Christ. Look what I've started. 'I didn't say that.'

He rubs his chin, sips his soda. 'Oh, I think you did.'

'Hmm.' I wriggle straight. 'So, you're still avoiding my questions. Are you some kind of undercover spy?'

'Very good. I'm not a spy.' He leans in, whispers, 'But I am undercover.'

I pull back to see his face. 'Seriously? That's exciting.'

'I know, right?' He lifts his eyebrows, nods.

I lean an elbow onto the bar, cup my chin, refocus. 'Very. Whoa.' I slip off the counter, espresso martini splashing into the air.

'Hey, let me help you.' He grasps my glass, offers me his other hand.

'I think I've had a bit too much.' I press my forehead into his shoulder. His scent strikes me numb like a shot of ice water. Sit up. Sit up, Sophie. I smooth down my dress, flick hair unsuccessfully from my face. Something bubbles up from my stomach. I throw my head back, and I'm laughing tears, clutching my sides.

'It's gonna be a cheap date if you keep this up.'

I steady myself against his chest, my laughter tails off. A date? Did we agree to that? A thank you drink, he said. This is a thank you drink. Jesus. What did he mean by date?

Oré hands me back my half empty glass. 'Thank you,' I say. 'So, what do you do? For a proper job, I mean.'

'Aha. Now she's interested. Have a guess?'

'Oh. I don't know. A ruthless banker, something like that.'

'Wow. Remind me never to introduce you to my friends. Really?'

'I'm playing.' I'm not. 'Seriously, what do you do when you're not involved in clandestine games?'

'I'm a lawyer.'

I straighten, tip my glass against his. 'Now, I wasn't expecting that.'

'Thank you. I think.'

'What do you lawyerer, lawyer? Oh, you know what I mean.'

He tugs the cuff of his shirt down over his watch, laughs. 'Environmental litigation.'

'Nope. Not a clue.' I signal with my hand, something flying over my head. 'So, why do this? It makes no sense, Mr Oré lawyer.'

He takes a minute, before throwing his head back. 'I fucked up. Needed some time to clear my head.'

'Fucked up?'

He leans onto his elbow on the bar, looks at me as if deciding whether to tell me more. 'It's bad, and I'm not proud of it.'

'Okay. Spill. I'm confident I've done worse.'

He looks at me for a long, long moment. 'Okay. You need to understand. I've always been a lawyer. Damn good one, too. Does that sound arrogant? Maybe. Some guys had been hassling me for years to work for them on the other side.'

'The people who do the environmental thingies?'

'Yeah. They use the big prestigious law firms, pay big bucks. Well, bigger bucks. Tap and Brad had left, and in a moment of madness, I thought, why not?'

'Jesus, Oré. I thought you were going to tell me you'd done something awful.'

He slides his finger up and down the glass. 'It was a real big case. They knew we couldn't win. Stood to lose millions. So, they asked me to find evidence that would crush the claimant.'

'So?'

'It was obtained illegally, and not submissible.'

'And did you?'

He adjusts in his chair, scratches the back of his head, nods.

'Damn.'

'I know. I had a last-minute change of heart and tipped someone off. Got it thrown out. But it was done. I'd, what do they say, sold my soul to the highest bidder.'

'Wow, Oré. I hadn't put you down as the corrupt type. I bet they were pissed. That's, that's really serious, isn't it? Why do that? Why risk your career?'

'I've asked myself that question a thousand times. A moment of madness, anger, maybe. After Brad left, it was like I was drifting. Didn't know who I was any more. I sat back one day and realised I had invested all my adult life in him and,' he closes his eyes for a beat, 'I was lost. That's not an excuse. I know it was wrong.'

'Did you get in trouble?'

'Nope.' He sips his drink. 'It got brushed under the table. Wrapped up as an unintentional error. It wasn't, but I took that.' He leans back. 'But when you've danced with the devil, the devil sure wants to keep holding your hand. That's not me, not any more. So, I decided to take a break. Revaluate life. I'm not proud of it. See, power and money can seduce anyone.'

'Not me.' I shift in my seat. 'I don't know what to say. Does Brad know?'

'Hell, no.' He looks away, stares unseeing into the bars mirrored wall. 'Too much? Do you want to jump ship and run?'

I look down at my hands. 'We all have a story, Oré.'

'Um.' He looks at me like he knows there's more to that comment, but doesn't ask. 'Anyway, Tom's one of the good guys. He wanted to understand what it's like on the shop floor, so here I am. He gets what he needs, and I get to sweat the past year out of my system.'

'So, you're a snitch?'

Laughter roars from his stomach. 'A what?'

'A snitch. Grass. Telltale.'

'I get it. A snitch. I've never been called that before.'

'It's a terrible word. Never use it again. Bad. Really bad. The kids say it all the time in school. I hate it.'

He turns his head, wipes his hand to his mouth, conceals his amusement.

'So, what have you told Tom?' I attempt to strike a more serious expression.

'That it's damn hard work. He should pay them more. Give them more leave and ease this bloody drinking rule. It's killing me. Although to be fair, he just steers the ship.'

'Does he know you're telling people he just steers the ship?'

'Well. It can't be that hard, can it? Plus, he's got an entire room of people to do it for him. I've not seen him lift a finger the whole time I've been here.'

'He must love you being around with your eloquent wit and unwavering loyalty.'

'Good point.' He turns away, his shoulders shaking with laughter.

'Why didn't you just come on holiday?'

He taps his glass on the counter. 'I like to keep busy.' The sadness I saw at breakfast the other day clouds his eyes. He signals to the bartender for the bill. 'Anyway, it's kinda fun mucking in and doing something different. Or it would be if it weren't for passengers accusing me of assaulting their elderly aunts.'

'Stop it, James.'

His eyebrows pinch. 'James?'

'James Bond. 007. The spy who loved me.' I point at my glass. 'Shaken not stirred.'

'Right.' His shoulders relax, grin full-lipped. 'When you let your guard down, you're real funny.' He signs the check, folds the receipt into his breast pocket, slips off the stool. 'Well, that's where we're gonna leave it, then. Come on.' He offers his arm to steady against as I half jump, half stumble off the stool. 'Have you been to the casino yet?'

My palm on his chest, a heat rises within me, the desire to touch, to be touched. I snatch my hand away. 'Oré. I've never been to a casino.'

'What?' He loops his arm into mine.

'No. Not one.'

'Well, Miss O'Ryan, you're coming with me. It's time to teach you a few lessons of my own.'

22

Ha Long Bay. Vietnam.

Thump. Thump. Thump.

The cabin is loud with sunlight, its golden glow hugging me warm. My smile grows wide as I'm flooded with memories of last night, of expresso martinis, being awful at blackjack, high-fiving the croupier when red number nine came up twice on the roulette wheel, and eating dirty fries by moonlight on deck with Oré. I don't know what time I got back, but it feels like ten minutes ago.

Thump. Thump. Thump.

'Ainti? Can you get the door?' No reply. 'Really? I haven't slept in weeks, and the minute I do ...' I scramble out of bed, grab the white robe from the chair, pause at the dressing-table mirror to flick my hair from one side to the other, wipe away the smudge of mascara. 'Have you forgotten your key again?' I swing open the cabin door. 'I'm going to get you one of those lanyards and ...' Hands around my neck, I pretend to throttle my throat. 'Oh. It's you.' My hands slip down my sides.

'There you go again.' Oré shakes his head. 'Morning.'

'Um. Can you give me a minute?' I inch the door shut, fluff up my hair, wipe a saliva-wet finger at the last remaining make-up under each eye. What's he doing here? I sidle around, edge the door back open, tighten the robe's belt around my waist. 'Oré. Why are you here?'

'Charming! I thought I'd check in on you. She said you weren't great.'

'Who said that?'

'Your aunt.'

'Ah.' I suppress a groan. Of course she did. No doubt went looking for him this morning when she got nothing from me.

'She grabbed me in reception, said I should be ashamed for letting you come back in such a state. She was joking. I think.' He pulls his hands from his pockets. 'Is it a bad time?'

We're talking through a crack in the door, Oré. Of course, it's flipping lousy timing. 'I'm not dressed, and ...' I wave at the bathroom.

'Oh. Sure. I can see you're busy.' He raises his palm goodbye.

'Oré.' I creep the door open a little more, rest my head on its glossy wood. 'Thank you. I had a great time last night.'

He leans against the wall, his hand holding onto the doorframe. 'Me too. So much for a quick drink, hey? Will I see you later?'

A heat surges inside me. 'Sure. Laters.' I fall back on the door, snap it shut behind me. I contemplate whether to return to bed or sleep here. Another lighter rap on the door. I steal it open a slither. 'Can't leave me alone, hey? Did you forget something?'

'No. Well, yes. Your bank cards. We're in Hong Kong in a couple of days. I wondered whether you'd like some company to collect them.'

'Another day off? You must be in someone's good books.'

He taps his nose. 'I have connections.'

My grin grows in time with his. 'Are you sure?'

'Meet you in reception at ten?'

'Ten. Perfect.'

He nods down the corridor. 'I'd better go. Again.'

I wiggle my fingers goodbye. 'I think you better had, James.'

I wake up for the second time to a dark room. A slight breeze skips through the French doors, its coolness a Tangle Teezer brushing my hair. Against the stillness, Aunt Christine's alarm clock ticks in time with the thump in my head. 10.32 pm. Damn. I've lost a whole day.

'Ainti?' My gaze wanders the hazy edges of the furniture. Perhaps she's gone to dinner. No. There's no waft of perfume or hair lacquer choking my throat. 'Ainti?'

My shoulders tighten at the outline of the dress she'd hung on the closet before leaving. She hasn't been back. She wouldn't dare go to supper in the shorts and pastel twinset she was wearing earlier. I sit up sharp. What if something's happened to her? Oré said he saw her this morning in reception, but I've heard nothing since. It's not like her. Normally, she's clamped to my side like an oversized limpet. What if she's lying hurt somewhere? Or been arrested?

I tap the light switch. 'Jesus.' The ceiling light floods the room. I fist my hands into my eyes, flip it off. Padding my hand in the darkness, I flick on the bedside reading lamp, its yellow hue brushing every surface. Swinging my legs off the bed, I sit for a moment, choke back the wave of hangover sickness, haul myself up. 'Right. What are you up to, Ainti?'

On the sideboard is a note, handwritten, pinned down by a glass ashtray, a stubbed-out cigarette: *Chrissie, be at mine for 21.00. Bring the stuff. They're expecting us both. B x.* And that means what? Stuff? What kind of stuff? She wouldn't, would she? I sniff the roll-up. 'What the actual hell? You're flipping kidding me, Ainti? Not again.'

I slip into my Screw January T-shirt, leggings and glittery ballet pumps. My hair swept into a clip, I look like I've stepped out of an episode of *Fame*, except it's not the 80s, I'm not a dancer or a teenager, and if my aunt keeps this up, I definitely won't be living forever. My mind races with every worst-case scenario. What if Bea's a drug dealer? Some kind of cruising big wig narcotic peddler. If that's even a thing. Do old people deal drugs? She absolutely has the bling-bling lifestyle, and we don't really know her, do we? What if she's dragged my aunt into her underworld cartel? How will I bail her out with no bank cards? Oh my God. Ainti's going to die in prison. Her last days spent sleeping on a urine-stained mattress, eating roasted bugs and stale bread, and it's all my fault. I encouraged her, thought Bea was a good influence. You just never know, do you? I snatch up my key card. This is not good. Beatrix, you have a lot to answer for. Grooming my aunt like some kind of naive drug mule. How dare you!

I hurry down the corridor, an endless stretch of carpet this evening. Even the elevator slugs and crunches into action. I bow my head, fold my arms over my T-shirt, weave past passengers dressed in prim evening gowns and dinner suits. I mutter some ridiculous lie about finishing a personal training session late at the gym.

The lift door opens and I skulk around the corner, scouting Bea's room. Two women in evening dresses enter, and minutes later, some more exit. I creep up to the doorway, sidle into the cabin as another group leave. Bea pours wine whilst three other women huddle over the bar, their heads bowed. Aunt Christine's unmistakable cackle bellows from the other side of the counter like a bartender from a western movie, complete with a fist full of dollars. What the hell am I saying? A fist full of dollars? At least ten, if not twenty notes flap in her grasp. My throat chokes dry. I roll forward, a fit of coughing.

'Sophie-Anne. You're alive.' Aunt Christine stuffs the money under the bar.

Bea mouths 'hello,' shows her guests out of the door. I'm watching you, Beatrix. Every move you make, you narco trafficker, you.

'I was just saying to Beatrix we should check on you. How are you feeling?'

'What the actual hell are you doing, Ainti? And what's that?' I stab a finger at the counter, the hidden cash.

She slaps a hand on my shoulder. 'Always so dramatic.'

'Dramatic? A half-smoked roll-up in the cabin, people streaming in and out for no reason, and now you're hiding wads of cash under the bar. I've every right to be dramatic, don't you think?'

'What on earth are you going on about, Sophie-Anne? We got a bit carried away onshore and lost track of time. The cigarette's a menthol tonic. Well, that's what the man said.'

'Tonic? And you believed him?' I spy the piles of colourful fabrics covering the coffee table. 'What's that?'

A blush rises from Aunt Christine's neck to her cheeks. 'Oh … They're … That's …'

I dodge her outstretched arm, pick up a handful. Prize the materials of lace, satin, silk from each other, stare at Aunt Christine, Bea. 'These are knickers.'

They huddle together, wide, toothy grins.

I scan the cabin, two more holdalls stuffed to the brim with the same cacophony of vibrant-coloured fabrics. 'You must have hundreds here. What is this?'

'One hundred and sixty-two, to be exact. We've sold ten sets in the last hour,' Bea says.

'Sold?' I grasp the lingerie tight in my hand. 'You're selling these? Thank Christ for that. I thought you were … Never mind. Who's buying them?'

'Everyone. Five dollars a pair.' Aunt Christine rummages in a holdall, holds up a black satin bra and matching full-cut brief. 'We've got bras too.'

'What? Where did you get them?'

Aunt Christine stuffs the lingerie back into the bag. 'We started with a few spares from Marks & Spencer. But most have come from the markets.'

'Ben Thanh Market. The bags. I knew you were up to something.'

Bea takes the underwear from my hand, replaces it with a glass of wine. 'There was a gap in the market on here, Sophie. They weren't doing anything, so your aunt and I did.'

'It was your idea, Sophie-Anne. Start a pop-up, you said.'

'I didn't actually say that, did I?'

'Now, don't be modest. You've always been a big picture sort of person. Has she told you her school had the longest waiting list in Sussex, Beatrix? No, of course not. Far too humble. And why did they all want to go there? Because it's won loads of awards. One of the most innovative schools in the country. Made local house prices rocket, my friend Dolly told me.'

I gulp my wine, roll my eyes. 'Okay. Moving on from the biography. How much have you made?'

Bea stuffs the lingerie back into the bag. 'Minus the cost of buying them, about six hundred.'

'Dollars?' I splutter.

'Nae. Pounds.' She hands Aunt Christine a glass of wine. 'And they're still coming.'

'Fuck me.' I take another gulp of wine.

'Sophie-Anne! Language.' Aunt Christine places down her glass, folds her arms.

'Sorry. I'm sorry, Bea. But six hundred pounds. That's a lot of money.'

'Aye. Words got around. We've even had to set a timetable for when people can buy them.'

'Oh, Sophie-Anne. Yes.' Aunt Christine picks up her glass, takes a sip. 'It got ridiculous. They were turning up at the cabin day and night.'

'That's why Tammy was in our cabin. And the woman with the envelope.'

'Are you cross?' Aunt Christine puts down her glass, clasps her hands in prayer.

'Me? Why would I be cross? It isn't illegal, is it?'

Bea chuckles. 'Well, apart from a little tax evasion.'

I spit wine down my T-shirt. 'What?'

'I'm joking, Sophie. Look. If it helps, think of all the market traders' families we've helped over the past few weeks.' Bea grabs a handful of lingerie from a bag. 'See for yourself. They're excellent quality. We paid a good price too. So, everyone's happy.' She hands me a sample crafted in scarlet lace.

'Do people really want these? I mean, they're all—'

'Old?' Aunt Christine flicks her eyes at me. 'Sophie-Anne. I thought we'd got past all that ageism nonsense weeks ago. You, young lady, should know better. Do you think women stop wanting nice underwear and having sex because—'

'Whoa, Ainti. Stop.' I cut across her. 'Please don't give me that image in my head.' I pull a high stool from the bar, sit down. 'I get it. But red lace panties?'

'Have them! I think they should fit.' Bea rummages in one of the holdalls. 'We've got the matching bra somewhere. What size are you?'

Aunt Christine nudges her elbow into Bea. 'Better get a few sets out, Beatrix. After last night, I think she might need them.'

'I told you this morning, Ainti, it was a drink.'

'And I heard you.' She winks at Bea. 'No reason why you can't have a bit of holiday fun, though, Sophie-Anne. A little whoopee.'

'Whoopee? Are you being serious?'

Aunt Christine slaps my back. 'No need to be embarrassed. We're all doing it.'

'Are we?' Hands over my ears, I chant, 'Lah. Lah. Lah,' drown out her reply.

Bea and Aunt Christine link arms, strut up and down the room, singing, 'I'm In the Mood for Love'. Knickers waving in their hands, bras clasped over their clothing.

I look at the ceiling, shake my head. 'Dear Lord, give me strength.'

23

Hong Kong. Chinese Lunar New Year's Eve.

James: Morning! Reception at 10?

Me: On it.

Bea taps a napkin to her mouth, squashes it on the table. 'Okay. So, I've got a suite booked at the Peninsula. Two nights. Who fancies it?'

My eyebrows lift, a fork of pancakes and red berry coulis hangs at my lips. 'The Peninsula?'

'It's a hotel on the other side.' Bea waves her knife at the window. 'We'll be able to watch the fireworks without fighting through the crowds.'

I don't take my eyes off Bea. 'Fireworks?'

'Aye. The fireworks on the harbour.'

'Sorry.' I shake my head, place down my fork. 'You've lost me. I wondered what the lanterns were all about. Is it Chinese New Year or something?'

'Aye. It's gonna be a big night.'

'Oh, Ainti, you must go. You'll love it.'

'And you, Sophie-Anne. You're invited.'

I lay my hand over hers. 'Not this time. It's very kind of you, Bea. But I'm going to stay here and explore. On my own.'

'On your own? But–'

'On my own.' I squeeze my aunt's hand. 'You go have fun.'

'Oh, I don't know. I don't like leaving you. What if something happened?'

'Nothing's going to happen. You hate walking anyway.'

'I do not.' Aunt Christine swallows a fork of scrambled egg, her

144

face crumpled like a sulky teenager.

'Sorry. I thought that's why you insisted on sitting down every few steps.'

'Oh, stop apologising, Sophie-Anne.' She stabs at a piece of bacon. 'I'm not going either, then.'

Bea throws up her hands, tosses down her toast. 'Oh, Chrissie, stop being a heid-the-baw. Let the girl be. Sophie may not want to say it, but I will – she dinnae want you around all the time.'

'A what?' Aunt Christine drops her fork.

'A heid-the-baw. A dim wit.' Bea bites her toast, sticker-stares my aunt to her seat.

'I'm no such thing, Beatrix. And in England, it's rude to call people names.'

'Aye, you are. And I don't care.' Bea wags her finger at me. 'She's nae a child.'

'You know nothing about it. I can't go.' Aunt Christine stabs at some more bacon, thrusts it in her mouth.

'See. I keep telling her, Sophie. You're almost fifty years old and can look after yourself. You'd probably welcome the respite from us, yes?'

I smile. She already knows me so well. Aunt Christine pitches her fork clank on the china plate, scowls at Bea.

'Right, you two, enough. Bea, thank you for your kind offer, but no. Ainti, thank you for looking out for me, again, but I'll be fine. I want you to go.'

'But–'

'No, Ainti. This has to stop. I'm not going to do anything silly. I promise.'

Aunt Christine pushes her plate away. 'Oh, I don't know. Where will you stay?'

'On board. They're not throwing us off, are they?'

'Nae. Plus, the restaurants and shops will be open because of the holiday.'

'So, it's fine. Seriously, I'm all good. Go have fun.'

'But what if you get into trouble, or meet some wealthy business tycoon who whisks you away?'

'What?' I splutter my tea. 'Who's being dramatic now?'

Aunt Christine straightens the napkin from her lap. 'I worry about you.'

'I know.' I put my arm around her shoulders, press my head to hers. 'Anyway,' I straighten, sip some tea, two hands, 'I'm meeting up with Oré this morning. I can ask him to escort me back if that helps?'

Aunt Christine side-eyes Bea. 'Oh. Really. When did this happen?'

'Stop it, Ainti. I'm not having this conversation again. He's helping me pick up my bank cards.'

'Because they're so heavy.' She winks at Bea, turns to me. 'Okay. But make sure you've got your phone. We're only over there if you need us.'

Which would be fine, but where is over there?

'Oh.' Aunt Christine throws me a frisky pout. 'There's a bag of underwear in our wardrobe. Help yourself.'

'Just go.' I point a finger at the door. 'You heid-the-baw, you.'

Cool breeze flurries down the staircase into reception from an open door. I button up my jean jacket. Some passengers stray past, brows scrunching at signs warning them to disembark from the lower deck this morning.

'Let's go.' Oré scoops up my hand. 'I have strict instructions to escort you back on board later, to your cabin. I did offer to sleep in the corridor, but after some lengthy consideration, your aunt decided that wouldn't be necessary. Oh, and I'm to remind you to put the chain on the door.'

Damn you, Aunt Christine. Will she ever trust me again? 'I'm so sorry. She told me that at least ten times before she left, too. She forgets I'm not fifteen any more.' Or that I'm not about to swallow a dozen pills or step off the deck into the ocean. Not today, anyway.

'She also said I'm to tell you to stop apologising all the time. Apparently, you're working on that too.' His face bursts bright with laughter.

I nudge his arm. 'Stop it. You're becoming as bad as her.'

'Here we are.' He holds open the elevator door for me. 'Seriously, she seemed worried. I promised I'd keep an eye on you.'

I roll my eyes. 'Great.'

'Well, that's charming, isn't it? Thanks a lot.' Oré stabs the lower landing deck button.

'I didn't mean it like that. I'm more than capable of taking care of myself, thank you.'

'Oh, I don't think she means any harm. Hell, if it makes her feel better, let's do it.'

He stares at the elevator doors like a cat stalking its prey. Is he taking his promise to Aunt Christine seriously, or is something else veiling his thoughts?

'You okay? You look tired,' I say.

He lets out a long sigh, grips his palms to the back of his head before slapping them to his side. 'Brad and Tap were coming up for New Year. He called last night to say Tap's ill, doesn't want to leave her.'

'Nothing serious, I hope?'

He hesitates, bites his lower lip. 'She's pregnant. Morning sickness, they think.'

'Woah. Okay. I wasn't expecting that.'

'Yeah.' He looks down at me, back at the doors. 'Me neither. They seem happy enough, though.'

'I sense a but.'

'I worry about them. It's a big step, and they're so young. Things can happen, can't they?' The doors slide open, lines of eager passengers filing down the gangplank.

'Jesus. It's much cooler here, isn't it?' I pull the collar up on my jacket.

'Yeah. I think it's gonna be a case of acclimatising the further north we go. Do you want my coat?'

'I'm fine. But thank you.' I place a hand on his forearm. 'I'm sure they'll work it out. From what you've said, they seem to have their heads screwed on.'

'Hmm. I hope so. Come on, this way.'

I stride from the shopping mall, arms wide, hug the view of Hong Kong Island.

'Happy?' Oré steps to my side.

'Very.' I slip my new purse, complete with new bank cards, into my new bag. 'Thanks for coming with me.'

'No worries. Make sure that bag stays firmly fixed on your shoulder this time.'

'I will.' I grip the shoulder strap. 'Well, that's that then. I'll catch you later, maybe?'

Oré checks his watch. 'Sure.'

'You don't have to stay with me, Oré. Go, I'll be fine.'

'No. It's not that. I've got a forty-eight-hour pass, and,' he wiggles his eyebrows, 'permission to drink as long as I'm discrete back on board.' He pushes his hands into his jean pockets. 'What're your plans?'

'I don't know. I might wander around for a bit. See what's happening.'

'Hungry?'

The question catches me off guard. 'Yes. But you don't—'

'I know.' His smiling eyes surge hotness through me.

'Okay.' I bite down on the inside of my cheek. 'Do you know somewhere?'

'Nope. I haven't spent much time here, but I know a man who has.' He pulls his mobile out of his pocket, spins away on his heels.

I gaze across the harbour. A blast of steamy air, noodles, beef brisket, sweet potatoes roasting in a repurposed oil drum. A swell of blue-grey water, enraged at the ferries, boats churning its peaceful tide. Kowloon stands tall on the other side, a competition of skyscrapers vying for the best position, elevated views. The crowds surround me, like the seafront in Cambodia. My mobile pings.

'Hey. Ready? Noah's recommended some café a few blocks down.'

I jerk my bag closer, ignore the pinging inside.

'I've also sorted our plans for this evening.'

'You've done what?'

'Well, I was thinking. You've nothing planned, neither do I, so perhaps we could do something together? Make up for the other night when I watched you drink the bar dry.'

'I did not.'

'If you say so. Anyway, Noah's hosting drinks for a few friends, and we've got an invite. Cool, hey?'

'Who's Noah?'

'A friend from way back.'

'Won't people think I'm some kind of desperado rocking up with someone I've just met?'

'Six weeks,' Oré says.

'Six weeks?'

'Six weeks. Since we met. Give or take a rocky start because of your outrageous character assassination.'

How can it have been that long? How does he know it's been that long? Does he lie awake at night counting the days, bored, wanting this to end? I open my mouth to say something but don't. Thoughts of him in his cabin splash my mind. Do staff have double beds? The same soft cotton duvets? I twitch the strap of my bag across my chest, masking the heat rising. How is this helping, Sophie?

'Anyway, nobody's gonna be interested in us.' He wriggles his hips, shuffles his feet. 'The drink will be flowing, music playing. It's New Year's Eve, and we're in Hong Kong. You're not gonna get a better offer than that, are you? Come on, Soapy. Help me out. What's a guy gotta do?' He pouts his bottom lip, a playful sulky frown.

'Soapy?' The word curls up in the back of my throat.

'Sorry.' His expression twists serious. 'Did I say something wrong?'

My spine stiffens. 'No. It's just I haven't been called that for a while.'

'Is that a yes?'

I study him for a beat. 'I hope I don't regret this, James. On one condition.'

'Anything.'

'You don't leave my side. Not for a second.'

'Done.' Oré grabs my hips, attempts to conga me down the walkway. He slouches over, slaps his hands on his knees, panting. 'Ha. Not as fit as I used to be. Oh, I forgot to say. Noah says the women are all wearing red. Good luck, apparently.'

Nooo!

24

My reflection glows golden in the elevator's mirrored walls. I returned from lunch, tore everything from the wardrobe, trying to find something, anything clean that resembled evening wear and red, which equated to nothing. I don't wear red. Never have. It's bright, sassy and, well, red. I thought about pulling out, telling him I couldn't go, a cough, a sore head. But Clare was tapping into my thoughts, telling me it's *just a drink*. So, in a moment of spontaneity and desperation, I raced into the ship's boutique. Aunt Christine didn't need to find out about my further treachery, anyway this was an emergency.

Six hours later, here I am, heading down to meet him on the dock, running a hand over a figure-shaming wine-red full-length velvet gown. I've never been one for Spanx Higher-Power Panties, but oh my goodness, how I wish I had some now. I wanted something flowing, shapeless, tent-like, I told the sales assistant. I gave up protesting after she insisted I have a wonderful figure which needs to be shown off. 'Spectacular,' she said when I stepped out of the changing room. A stretch. She no doubt says that to every potential customer just to make the sale. I'm revealing every curve I've refused to show since forever, having to trust someone else's judgement that it looks okay. The matching wrap I'm gripping over my stomach like a comfort blanket, was her only concession, insisting I take it off and dispose of it later. I nodded, lied. This baby ain't going nowhere.

I study my mirrored image. Eyes, green, framed by smoky grey eyeshadow, a tumble of silky dark brown curls sweeping my shoulders. I have to admit, the beautician has done a fantastic job. Quite pretty, really. It's been a long time since I've looked like this. Who am I kidding? I've never looked like this. Even when I've attempted to dress up. So here I am, the stab of panic, self-loathing so strong it almost buckles my knees. The urge to eat it numb, strong. I turn away, face the muted blur of the steel doors. *You look fucking great*, I hear Clare remind me.

Oré watches me from the foot of the gangplank, a black dinner suit tailored to his form. His face shines dewy in the soft glow of the harbour lights. He takes a step back, smiles, and my heart bounces.

'Wow. Howdy. You look awesome.' He leans in, kisses my cheek.

'Why, thank you, kind sir.' I adjust the wrap over my stomach, suck up my unease. 'You don't look so bad yourself. Very dapper.' I sniff his neck, fan away its reek. 'Crikey, have you bathed in that tonight?'

'Here she goes again, entranced by my cologne. And yes, I have indeed put a little extra on for you.'

'Whatever. I'm so not interested.' I would never admit it, but I like the fact he thought of me whilst getting ready.

He circles his arm around mine. 'Let's go.'

Despite Oré's potent waft, I suck in the harbour air. Smoky, laced with garlic and ginger, the taste of burning from the restaurants and street vendors lining the water's edge. The occasional arc of fireworks crackle, splattering nightfall with a shower of rainbows. On one side of the harbour, vast vessels rest moored, protected by the shelter of the waterfront's defence. On the other, bursts of clapping mix with the crowd's spirited cries, the drone of music. Hundreds, perhaps more, jostle for privileged positions to watch the celebrations unfold, swaying to the energy of the pounding drums, dancing, zig-zagging dragons. The festivities reflect a canvas of colourful shadows on the mirrored floodlit skyscrapers, their insignia blazing against heaven's black.

Oré glances at me, slips a hand around my shoulder. I'm growing accustomed to how his eyes smile even when his lips don't. Something calms but equally excites me, as if we're best friends, about to embark on a new adventure.

'Here we are.' He tips his head towards the harbour's edge.

I stop, feet jamming to the ground like a dog refusing to walk on a wet day. 'We're going on that?' I attempt to sound casual, but the words come out slightly strangled.

'Yes. I think we are.' He shrugs, looks pleased.

The junk rises from the dock, a body of glossy brown teak, sails a blaze of red breath, full. Below a watery blackness slick to the bow, we step onto the walkway. Oré pulls my hand into his, clenches it tight.

'Oré,' mellow music circles us from the boat's sound system, 'In case I forget to tell you later, thank you,' I say.

'Yeah. I wasn't expecting it to be quite like this either.' He leans into me. 'By the way. You see these people. Every one of them is a banker or married to one. So be nice.'

'You wouldn't? I don't really think—'

'They're all egotistical bastards?'

'Crap.'

'Crap indeed. Relax, Miss O'Ryan. Your secret's safe with me.'

Garlands of red lamps strung from port to stern glitter like stars. A gentleman strides towards us, sweeps blond curly hair from his shoulders. 'Man, what an awesome surprise. What the hell are you doing here?'

'You invited us.' Oré pulls him into his arms, their eyes closed.

'Huh. I've missed that wit.' He presses his chin onto Oré's shoulder, hugs him closer, tighter. 'I mean it, man. It's been too long. Charlie's beside herself.' His eyes rest on mine. 'Hey, excuse my rudeness.' He pulls from their hold, offers me his hand. 'I'm Noah.'

'Noah, Sophie. Sophie, Noah. We've been friends for far too many years.' Oré slaps his back. 'It's good to see you, old man.'

'Sophie.' Noah tips his head. 'It's great to meet you. Thank you for coming.' He shakes Oré's hand two-handed. 'You're looking sharp. Something or someone's put the sparkle back into those eyes.'

A soft smile grows on Oré's lips. 'I'm good. Where's Charlie?'

'Did I hear my name?' A woman with an English accent strides towards us, a sharp-cut bob of flaxen hair, a scarlet organza ballgown. She seizes Oré's hands, plants a kiss on each cheek. 'Hello, trouble. I can't believe you're here.' Her nose crinkles, she slaps a palm flat on his chest. 'We'd thought you'd retired back in Chicago, old man.'

Oré kisses each cheek, swings his arm around Charlie's shoulder. 'Hey. I'm not ready for retirement just yet. Anyway, you're what?' He holds his chin, mulls it over. 'Four, maybe five years older than me?'

'How dare you?' Charlie fist-bumps his arm, mumbles into my ear, 'It's actually five and a half, but let's not swell his ego.' She clutches my hand in hers. 'Hi, I'm Charlotte. Everyone calls me Charlie.'

'Charlie, Sophie. Sophie, Charlie. Better known as a colossal pain in my ass,' he says in his best English accent.

She nuzzles under Oré's arm. 'You're wicked. Seriously, it's great to see you. Both of you. You're looking well. Is that due to you, Sophie?'

'Oh gosh, no. We're not … I'm–'

'Enough. Sophie's a friend.' Oré takes my hand, squeezes it hard. 'So, where do we get a drink?'

'Spoilsport.' Charlie shrugs, points to a group of people gathered at a bar.

'Right. Let me remove my wife before she says anything else.' Noah slaps Oré's shoulder. 'Help yourself. It's a free bar. We'll come and find you later.' He leaves, Charlie on his arm.

'You, okay?' Oré places his hand around my waist. 'Ignore them. Drink?'

'Soap, I'm gonna head to the restroom. Okay?'

Again, Soap rolls off his tongue. When he says it, my heart burns. I haven't decided whether that's a good thing. My head feels as clear as a summer day this evening, the first time since the accident. I haven't decided whether that's a good thing either.

'Of course, you go. I'll be fine.'

The skyscrapers are a floodlight shock of glass and steel against the night sky. A few weeks ago, I was skulking around Brighton, berating myself, clueless about what to do next, convinced I couldn't go on. Look at me now, sipping French champagne, about to witness one of the most incredible fireworks displays on Earth. All on a Chinese junk moored on Hong Kong Island. Crazy stuff! The strangest things can happen when you step out of your ordinary.

'Sophie.'

'Oh, sorry, Charlie. Just daydreaming about home.'

'Which is?'

'Brighton. You?'

'Southend.' She quaffs her champagne. 'Don't believe everything you hear about us Essex girls, though.'

'Jesus. No. I mean, I love Southend.'

'Me too.' She stares at the shoreline, the breeze snatches her hair. 'Gorgeous, isn't it?'

'Oh my, it certainly is. What an extraordinary place. Have you lived here long?'

'Fifteen years. My job's moved us around a fair bit. But we like it here.'

'Oh. Sorry. I assumed …'

'Ha. Don't worry. You're not the first.'

'No. That's no excuse. I should know better. Let's start again. What do you do?'

'It's okay. Most people think Noah's the driving force. I like to see the shock on their faces when I put them straight. Is that sadistic?'

'Not at all. I'd be the exact same.'

Charlie clinks her flute to mine. 'Yes, sister. Anyhow, I'm a lawyer. That's how Oré and I met. Recruited by the same firm in the US. When an internship in Thailand came up, we both jumped at it.'

'Oh. Were you and him … '

'Me and Oré? God, no. Nothing like that. His ego was far too inflated for me in those days. We clashed all the time.' She searches my expression. 'He does, however, seem quite taken with you.'

'Oh, no. I don't think so.' I choke on a mouthful of champagne. 'It's nothing like that.'

'Noah and I were worried he'd never leave Chicago again. He used to be such a free spirit.'

'Did you know his wife?'

'Who, Mia?'

I shrug, sweep hanks of hair from my shoulders, look out at the shoreside festivities. 'I don't know her name. Just that he met her in Thailand.'

'Yep. So sad.'

'He seems okay about it. I mean, he didn't say why they split, but it all sounds pretty amicable.'

Charlie follows my gaze, skimming the harbour. 'He hasn't told you, has he?'

My eyes snap to hers and I suddenly feel weak. 'Told me what?'

She swallows her drink, taps the flute on her chin. 'They didn't break up. Mia died.'

25

The fireworks snap, masking the stars with a spray of fresh graffiti. Oré lies slouched on a sunbed next to me on the *Tutum's* deck, an arm hooked behind his head.

'What time is it?' I lay back on the lounger next to him. He lifts his wristwatch to an inch of his nose. 'Twelvish. No. Hold on.' He scrunches his eyes into focus. 'Threeish.' He twists on his side, looks at me, his cheek pressed against the cushion.

'What?' I arrange the wrap loosely across my stomach.

'Nothing.' He rolls onto his back, shuts his eyes.

'Hey, big guy, don't fall asleep on me.'

A sideways glance, his gaze meets mine, soft, searching. 'Thanks for coming, Soap.'

'Oh, I think you would have been just fine without me. How many people do you know?'

'A few. They all loved you. See, not all bankers are arrogant assholes.'

My mouth screws into a pout. 'Funny.'

I curl my arms around my waist, stare at the cityscape, a shock of strobes and throbbing music.

'Are you cold?' Oré jumps up, pulls off his jacket, places it around my shoulders. He leans back on the guardrail, crosses his legs at the ankle. I watch him stare skywards and the world drifts away, leaving him, me, this night. He lowers his eyes back to mine.

'There you go again. What are you looking at?'

'You.'

I blink him away, push up against the bolster. 'Oré. Can I ask you something?'

'Sure.' He pauses for a moment, presses his thumbs into his

trouser pockets. 'Fire away.'

I've been rehearsing this conversation in my head since we left the party. 'Charlie and I got talking about how you met and Thailand.' I pause, taken aback by my emotion. 'I'm so sorry about Mia. I had no idea.'

He uncrosses his legs, turns away, leans two hands onto the guardrail, staring at the harbourside. He stays like that for a while. 'I guess that's the downside to seeing old friends. Your past has a habit of catching up with you.' He sits down, rubs at a scuff on his shoe.

'Charlie wasn't gossiping or anything. She just assumed I knew.'

'Oh, I know. Charlie's no gossip, and it's not a secret.' He looks over at me. 'Really, it's cool.'

The heaviness in his eyes slides into me. 'I'm so sorry.'

He closes his eyes, a crowing inhale. 'What did she tell you?'

'Just that she died.'

'Yeah.' He frowns, as if deciding whether to leave it there. 'It's not the easiest story to tell.' He scoots up his legs, lays onto his back. 'She wasn't meant to get pregnant. I mean, we wanted children. Knew from the day I met her, she was the love of my life.' He smiles like a memory is swelling in his heart. 'Funny, smart, strong-willed. Crazy when I look back on it. We'd only known each other six months before we got married. She was on a gap year working in Bangkok, teaching at one of the international schools.' He grips his hands behind his head, mischief in his voice. 'I proposed on our first date. Assumed she'd just say yes. Ha. Told me to get lost. But I wore her down. She gave into my charms, eventually. Who wouldn't, hey?'

'Modest as ever.'

'Yeah. I mean no. Jesus. I was much worse in those days, Soap. Much, much worse.' He jerks his head towards me before looking away, clears his throat. 'She was desperate to have a family. But she had a problem with her heart, pulmonary arterial hypertension. The hurt on her face when the doctor advised us not to have children broke me.' He stands, paces to the handrail, footsteps dragging. 'It's the worst feeling in the world, watching the person you love more than yourself in so much pain. There was nothing we could do. Not even money was gonna make it go away. Leaning onto his elbows, he takes a deep breath. 'Three months later, she's pregnant. Not planned. Well, not on my part, anyway. She's ecstatic. I'm terrified.'

'That must have been hard.'

He turns, reclines on the railing. 'We went back to the States. Got the best healthcare money could buy. Did everything right. Had it all planned out.' Oré clasps himself in a hug, stares into the night. 'She never saw him. Brad. Slipped away in my arms minutes after she gave birth. A heart attack, the coroner said. Twenty-four. Twenty-fucking-four.' The distant crack of fireworks fills the silence. He wipes away the fat tear running down his cheek. 'Do you know the worst thing?'

I shake my head. How could this be any worse?

'I begged her for months to have a termination. To get rid of him. Brad. Our son. I was so incensed with her. We spent the last months of her life arguing every single day, in constant fear of something happening, of losing her, of losing him. I couldn't go near Brad for weeks. I was so angry with her. With him.' He sucks back the tears. 'What kind of jerk would do that?'

I jump up, drop his jacket, the wrap draping my stomach, cross the deck. 'Oré, you loved her. I'm sure she knew that. You had every right to be angry.'

He turns to the shore. 'Yeah, well, it wasn't enough. And it certainly doesn't stop the guilt.'

Jesus. I know all about that. I bury myself in him, the emptiness wailing within me. 'Does Brad know?'

'Yeah. It's been hard, you know? I've been making up for it his entire life. Trying to be the best dad I can.'

I pull back, brush the creases from his shirt. 'Sounds like you've done a pretty good job.'

He sits back on the railing, lost in thought. 'Raising Brad sure made me a better person. I was such an asshole. Would have done it all for money and power. I was, what did you call bankers?'

'Ruthless.'

'Yeah. Definitely that. A total bastard. But he changed me. I'm not that person now. Second chances, hey?' Oré makes a strange sound, something between a laugh and a sigh. 'And now he's gonna be a dad. What the fuck?'

'I'd forgotten about that, grandpa.'

'Watch it.' His lips crease with the faintest of smiles.

A dull ache nudges me as he pulls a small gold wedding band on a chain from his top pocket.

'Worn it since the day she died. I took it off when I came here.' He looks at me. 'I should have done it a long time ago. When you lost yours, I panicked, put it back on. It's hard, isn't it?'

And there it is. Everything makes sense. His words that day at breakfast. The sadness clouding his eyes. He understands about my mother's necklace because he knows. He knows of devastating loss. Held onto Mia's memory, kept her close in the same way. He knows because of her, because of Mia.

'Will you wear it again?'

He fists it in his hand. 'No. It's been a long time. When Brad was little, he'd play with it. I liked that. I need to follow his lead, move on.' He pushes it into his pocket. 'I'm gonna give it to Brad. Perhaps he'll give it to Tap one day. Although, I'm not sure getting married is what young people do any more.'

For a moment, I thought my heart might crack. 'Charlie thinks a lot of you.'

'She's a good friend. She and Noah begged us to come back and live with them after it happened. But my family were in Chicago, so we stayed, and dear God, did I need their help. Children are hard work. How do you manage so many?'

I nudge my head into his arm. 'I'm truly sorry. It must've been hard when Brad and Tap left.'

'It's one of those times when you're forced to think about stuff, isn't it? Everything I built my life on was gone. Jeez. He reminds me so much of her. Headstrong, determined, but real gentle and kind. He's done great. Definitely takes after her.'

'Oh, I don't know.' I gather up my skirt, motion for him to sit down. 'I think there's some of his father in him, too.'

'Was that a compliment?'

'Don't get used to it. It's probably the drink talking again.'

'Ha. I won't.' Oré pulls me under his arm, my head resting on his chest.

'Brad's lucky to have you.' My eyes scrunch tight. Without warning, memories of my father squeeze my heart.

He presses his head into mine, his kiss like silk on my forehead.

'Thanks, Soap.'

The mix of his cologne and coconut lotion fondles my nose. A feeling, something transcending friendship, swirls between us, a yearning to be close to him, a knotted throb. He leans in, his touch burning like fire, lips lingering an inch from mine.

'No.' I shove him from me, stand up sharp. 'I can't.' A pressure in my temples, my vision foggy – alcohol, pain, grief. 'I just can't.'

Confusion slices his expression, he scrubs his hands down his face. He's done nothing to deserve the wrath rising within me, the panic clawing my throat. The magic of the evening breaks into a hundred tiny pieces, the thinnest of glass shattering in my hand.

He pushes up from the lounger. 'Okay. It's okay. I'll walk you back.'

'No. Please don't.'

His expression twists, grabbing my wrist. 'What's wrong?'

Anger bubbles from my stomach. Looking down at his hand a memory of rain-wet hair, the Ailm, bloodied flesh. 'What are you doing? Let me go.' I shake him from me, run across the deck and down the steps.

26

I fist my velvet skirt into my hand, tear down the corridor, back to the cabin. The door slams and I crawl into bed, bury my head into the pillows. Wind hisses around the balcony outside. A jolt, like a single domino toppling against another, and I'm back to that night, the passing cars whistling threats in the hammering rain, wet-slicked hair, Clare's blood-stained jumper. Doors slam in the corridor outside, and I can't fight it any more. Drunk on the tears slipping my eyes, the memory rips into my head.

***

The front door crashed shut downstairs.

'What the hell? Soph?' A thud of his shoes, his briefcase against the wall. 'What's going on?'

He was early. Patrick was never early. Not nowadays. Trying to hide was pointless. My bags scattered at the foot of the stairs, his feet. I fell back against the bathroom wall, my pulse roaring in my ears. 'You can do this.' I pulled my mum's fringed shawl from the radiator, pressed it to my face, damp, the faintest scent of peony perfume.

Footsteps pounding up the stairs. I felt the chill in my bones, as if buried alive in fresh snow. I pushed against the panic bubbling in my chest, squared my shoulders, opened the bathroom door.

'What's with the bags? Are we going somewhere?' He gestured me out of his path, stepped into the bedroom's ensuite.

'Not us.'

'Excuse me?' He spun on his heels, followed me back into the bedroom.

The pain burned, rising like a roar from my gut into my throat.

'I'm leaving.' I shuddered at the tremor in my voice.

'Oh. Since when?'

His stare scalded the back of my neck. I rammed the shawl into the holdall, pulled it off the bed.

'Are you going to tell me what the hell is going on?' He yanked my wrist, spun me into him, threw the bag back on the bed. His face reddened as he glanced at me, the door.

With both hands, I shoved him from me, snatched the holdall to my stomach. 'I'm leaving you.'

'Been on the double shot espressos again, have we? Stop talking fucking shit.' He unzipped his trousers, strode back into the bathroom. 'We both know you don't have the balls,' he yelled over his urinating. 'But don't let me stop you, though, babes. It's not like it's the first time, is it? You'll be back. When everyone's bored with you. Where are you going this time? That fucking whore?'

I flung open the bedroom door, ran down the stairs, his rage raining down on me. I knew leaving would make things worse, but I somehow hoped he would prove me wrong. But nothing was stopping me, not this time, not him, not my fear.

He jogged down the staircase; the veins pumping red in his neck, his finger thrusting into my face. 'You think you can ignore me?' He squeezed my throat, my cheeks, in one hand, crushing like a vice.

I fought to draw air, grabbed at his hand. His violence had never cast a physical blow, cut my skin, a blemish or bruise. His wasn't the type that could be seen. Until now, until he'd stepped over that line, too.

'What are you doing? Get off me.' I knocked his hand away, the snap of the chain sliced into my neck.

His fist daubed with blood itched inches from my face, the chain swinging through his fingers. Eyes closed, he inhaled long and hard, held out his palm, my mother's Ailm necklace. I felt his stare in my stomach, his roar hot and sour, drowning me.

He hurled the chain at me. 'Take it. You fat fucking bitch. Take it.'

My knees buckled. The Ailm striking my face, my chest, the floor.

'Get out. There are plenty more tarts where you came from, believe me.' He wiped a bloodied palm on his thigh. 'You should be grateful your mother died when she did. If I'd seen what a useless lump of lard you'd turn into, I'd have kicked you into touch long ago. Now fuck off.'

I fell against the wall, stooped down, stole up the Ailm. I didn't take my eyes off him, not for one second. The necklace clasped in my hand; I edged sideways to the front door, gripped the holdall, yanked at the lock. Come on, come on. Every creak twisted in my gut. The door swung wide, and I sprinted to the car. Patrick's hurls of abuse hunting me down.

'Hey. Everything okay, you two?' The voice, a man's, calm. Karl, our neighbour, climbed from his truck, nodded at Patrick. 'You okay, mate?'

Patrick's steps slowed. 'Women, hey?' He adjusted his jacket, shot me a hard stare, went back inside, slammed the front door.

Karl turned to me. 'You, okay? Can I do anything?'

I shook my head, placed one hand over the other to control the shake, jerked opened the driver's door.

'I'm going to stay right here until you've gone,' Karl said.

Tears of relief trickled my face. My gaze on his, I placed my hand on my heart, mouthed, 'Thank you.'

I threw the holdall into the footwell, stabbed the key in the ignition. A crunch of gears and I reversed out of the driveway. Treading the accelerator, my head struck the headrest, a wail of panic released from my lungs.

***

I sit up, my eyes darting the darkness for her, Clare, my safe place. Knees gripped to my chest, I rock, choking for air. 'I know. I've messed everything up. Jesus, I wish you were here.'

Crash! My head pitches up from the pillow. Aunt Christine huffs, throwing two large holdalls onto the bed.

'Please tell me that's not more knickers?' I punch my head back down.

'Ah, Sophie-Anne. I didn't see you there. No. No. Just a few souvenirs.' She throws a brilliant white gold braided bathrobe over her shoulders, 'the Peninsula' stitched onto the left breast pocket. 'Magnificent, isn't it?'

'Ainti, have you been robbing hotels again?'

'No. I have not. That's a terrible thing to say, Sophie-Anne. I've never taken anything from a hotel. Collected items to recompense for poor service, maybe, but steal, no.' She slips off the bathrobe, folds it on the bed. 'No. It was a gift. Look, I've got matching slippers too. Oh, and a shower cap.' She pulls item after item from the bags. 'A toothbrush, shower gel, hand cream.' She wags a finger at me. 'Not miniatures, mind. Chocolates, a basket of fruit, a bottle of champagne.' She heaves the last item from the holdall. 'And, an iron.'

'An iron?' I shake my head. 'When did five-star hotels start gifting electric irons? Unbelievable.'

'Well, I may have slipped that one in by mistake. Our one's a bit rubbish, isn't it?' She strokes it to her chest like it's a prized puppy. 'No. This isn't one of those useless travel types. It would have been a shame to leave it.' She places it on the bed, rips the cellophane cover from the fruit basket. 'Banana?'

I turn away, nestle my cheek into the pillow. 'No, thanks.'

'Why are you here, anyway? You're missing the parade.'

I scoop up my hair, scrunch it under my head. 'Didn't feel like it.'

'Aah. Heavy night, was it? What did you get up to?'

'Not much. I watched the fireworks on deck.'

'What? Is that all? I'll be having words with that concierge. If I'd known he'd throw you a damp squib of an evening, I'd never have left you.'

I flip over. 'Don't do that.' The last thing I need is her interrogating him. He's never going to speak to me again, anyway, for Christ's sake.

'Well, I expected better of him.'

I pull the duvet to my chin. The pain spreads and seeps like water damage through me, my mind skipping between Oré, Patrick, Clare.

'Sophie. Are you even listening to me?'

I draw up my knees, twist the duvet cover into clenched fists. A primal sound rises from the pit of my stomach to my throat.

Aunt Christine smacks down on the bed, pulls me into her arms. 'Oh my goodness, my sweet darling. Whatever is the matter, Sophie.

What happened?'

I dip my head into her shoulder, draw in short tar-like gasps. 'Everything's such a mess, Ainti.' The cost of last night surges me, of suffering, of pain, of grief, of my unbearable guilt. A reflection of everything that remains.

'Oh, my darling girl. I've got you. I've got you.' Aunt Christine's arms cloak me like a weighted blanket. She is and always has been my home, my refuge.

'I can't do it, Ainti.'

'I know it feels like—'

'No.' I shrug her from me. 'You're not listening. This will never end.'

She smooths the hair from my face, takes my hands in hers. Her voice, soft, calm, like the day she had sat on the floor and told me my mother had died. 'Sophie, what happened?'

I sink my face into her chest, the words silent, corkscrewing up into my throat.

'Deep breaths. Like she showed you. In one, two, three. Out, one, two, three, four, five, six.'

'One, two, three,' I repeat. 'One, two, three.' She kisses my hair, and my heart catches. 'He tried to kiss me.'

'Who?'

I lift my head, dagger stare her. 'Who? Really?'

'Oh.' She pulls me back, her voice slow and deliberate. 'And that upset you?'

I shuffle back, sit up against the headboard. 'No. Well, yes. Oh, I don't know.' I turn away, rub at a smudge of make-up on the duvet. 'We were having a moment. You know. When you're sharing things, and it gets intense. There's feelings and stuff. His wife died. Did you know that?' She shakes her head. 'In childbirth. Brought Brad up by himself. He gave up everything.' I swallow, look up at the ceiling, thump a fist on my chest. 'There's so much pain, Ainti. Mum, Dad, Clare, Patrick.' I wipe my eyes, catch the sobs in my chest. 'I'm so sorry. All I do is let you down. You've done all this, and it still isn't enough.' I bang my head back onto the bedhead, close my eyes. 'Why would I deserve someone like Oré?'

'Oh, really? You think that?' She puts her face close to mine, frowning, examining me like she can't quite believe her eyes. 'Oh my goodness, you do.' She draws up tall, takes hold of my shoulders. 'Right, young lady. Look at me. I've held my tongue for far too long. This has to stop. Now. Today.' Irritation cakes her words. 'Scolding yourself won't change what happened. All this, what doesn't kill you, makes you stronger nonsense, makes you think you should just get up, and be a tougher, wiser version of yourself. But terrible things damage us, Sophie-Anne. They change us. We can get through them, of course, we can, but let's not pretend it's easy.' She lifts my hands, kisses them before clasping them into her lap. 'Listen to me. You were not to blame. Clare was an adult. She knew what she was doing that night. She rolled the dice, and her number didn't come up. Do you think for one minute she'd blame you? Not a chance.'

I pull my hands from hers, open my mouth to speak.

'Uh, uh, uh. It's my turn.' Aunt Christine taps a finger on her lips, shakes her head. 'And as for that useless waste of space Patrick. He doesn't know how to love. Not you. Not anyone. You're not responsible for him, or how he feels, or how he behaves.' She inhales through her nose. 'It's not your fault, Sophie-Anne. Listen to me – none of it was your fault. Your understanding of love was so violated as a child. You were so young when your mother died, and as much as your father loved you, and he did love you, he was crushed. His whole world collapsed without her. He could barely look after himself, let alone a teenager. I don't condone what he did, but I've tried to understand.'

'Ainti, don't–'

'I know what you're going to say, but I promised your mother I would love you like my own. You've always done your best, Sophie-Anne. Have made me more than proud. But if you're waiting for when this is going to suddenly disappear or feel okay, you're wasting your time, my beautiful girl. You're blowing every bit of now. Redemption doesn't come from doing stuff, or others' forgiveness. It comes from here.' She places her palm on her heart. 'Inside of you.' She takes a moment as if collecting her thoughts, swallows the emotion in her voice. 'The past can't be any different. We can't change how these people behaved. But unless you let it go, accept it's over, you'll never move on. And I can't think of anyone more worthy of that, Sophie-Anne. I've seen you flourish a little more every day on this trip. Have seen glimmers of that little girl who used to trick me into letting her stay up late, who dreamt about exploring the world, who I laughed with until my stomach ached. I really like her. I think you do too.'

I wipe the back of my hand on my eyes, my nose. 'It's so hard.'

'I know.' She folds her legs up onto the bed, curls into me. 'Stop chasing the person you think you ought to be, or the life you think you should've lived. Sophie O'Ryan, I think you're pretty damn special, and it's time you believed it too.'

27

Cruising the East China Sea

Bea yanks me into her cabin, peers down the corridor like we're undertaking some covert operation.

'You okay, Bea? You seem a little on edge.'

'I don't want Chrissie to catch on. Did you manage to distract her?'

'Yep. She's currently wrapped head to toe in muddy seaweed, about to be launched into a floatation tank. The poor staff have probably already got their earplugs in, drowning out her snoring. I think we're good for a couple of hours. What's up?'

'It's Chrissie's eightieth soon, isn't it?'

'It is. On the twenty-first.'

'Aye. So, that's a sea day. Which is excellent news because I thought we'd throw her a surprise party.'

'Aw, Bea, that's a lovely idea. Count me in. What're you thinking?'

'And that's why you're here. Any thoughts?'

'Um, she loves big band music. Brat Pack stuff, modern stuff, too. She adores Pink.'

'Eclectic! I love it.' The doorbell chimes. 'I've arranged for one of the crew to join us to discuss our options. Can you put some coffee on?'

I throw my key card and mobile onto the bar, pick up a mug, start pressing some buttons. 'I've no clue how to work a barista machine, but I'll give it a shot.'

'Well, howdy, Oré. Come on in.'

I slap down the mug, duck under the counter. Jesus. It's been three days since that night, and I'm not ready to face him yet. I need to put some more thought into what I'm going to say, and I definitely can't do it in front of Bea.

'Coffee? Sophie's just making some,' Bea says, a rustle of paper, a shuffle of feet. 'Sophie?' More shuffling. 'Strange. She was here a minute ago.'

I pray the pad of footsteps is them heading back to the door, but my nose twitching at his cologne says otherwise. I look up to see two sets of eyes inspecting the dismay on my face. Without options, I flop to the floor, pat my hands on the ground.

'Lost something?' Bea says.

I jump up, tidy my hair. 'Um, teaspoons.'

Bea rattles a chrome caddy on the counter, a confused frown. 'On the top. Where they've always been.'

'Ahh, yes. Right. The top.'

Oré's grin pinches into a line when he spots me looking at him, clamps his notebook under his arm.

I wiggle my fingers hello. 'Hi. I didn't know you were coming?'

He nods, a smile that doesn't meet his eyes.

'You two sit down. I'll bring it over.' I yank at the portafilter. Stiff, it flies from my hand, my whole weight thrashing into the machine, toppling it from the bar. 'Crap!' Scooping up the pieces of the crumpled machine, I hand Bea the broken control knob. 'I think I've trashed it.'

Oré turns away, raises a hand to cover his laughter.

'Ha. Leave it, Sophie. Barista won't be on your resume anytime soon, will it?' She chuckles, tosses the broken part onto the counter. 'You two put your heads together. I'll go get Gino to sort this out. Back in a wee mo.' She ushers me towards the sofa, Oré.

I sit down, leave a good distance between us. A tart aroma wafts thick. Oré nods his head at the splash of coffee on my cheek, hands me his handkerchief, a square of folded white cotton.

'Thank you.' I wipe off the umber mess, hesitate before offering the handkerchief back.

'Keep it,' he says. Gone are the laughter lines. Instead, a sulky child, not getting their way, sits in front of me.

'Right. I'll get it cleaned for you.' I push it into my pocket, giggle as his nose crinkles, flicking open his notebook like the first day we met.

He jerks to face me. 'Sorry. Is something funny?'

I point to the jotter on his lap, his nose, decide not to mention how his quirky mannerisms amuse me. 'Are you having a nice day?' I bend forward, tidy some magazines into a neat pile on the coffee table.

'It's okay. You?'

I clear my throat. 'Good, thanks. But it's only ten o'clock, so plenty of time for something to go wrong, hey?' I reorganise the magazines into a fan display on the glass tabletop. 'Oré, I've been meaning to find you. About the other night.'

'It's fine. Really. I get it.'

'No. I don't think you do. I shouldn't have left like that. It was rude.' I pull up tall. There's so much I need to say, but can't, not yet. So, I start with the gentlest part of my story, the part he might recognise. 'I lost my mum when I was a child, too. When she died, my father couldn't cope. That's why my aunt stepped in. He'd always been absent, to be honest. He tried, but …' I stare over his shoulder at the wall. 'He couldn't do any better, and I couldn't make him.'

'I don't understand.'

'Nor do I really. When you started talking about Brad and what you'd done … It reminded me of him. Of how he just gave up on me.'

'Do you still see him?'

'Not much. He's in a care home. Has late-stage Alzheimer's.'

'Jeez. Soap, I'm sorry. I had no idea.'

'It's okay.' I adjust on my seat, smooth my trousers over my thighs. 'He had this innate ability to make me feel that if I could just do or be a bit more, he would …'

'But you've done so much.'

I shrug, look down at my hands. 'It never felt enough.' Our eyes meet. 'But you, you did everything you could for Brad. Gave up your job, friends, dreams. It hurt hearing you talk about him.' Thirteen-year-old Sophie flashes into my mind, gripping the steering wheel of Dad's latest sports car. My standing on the porch, waving goodbye, as he sped away. She didn't understand it wasn't about her, believed if she could just be a little better, more of everything, he would love her, and stay. 'I've spent a lifetime living up to his ridiculous expectations.'

He shuffles closer. There's no doubt within me. No debating whether his attempt to kiss me the other night was a step too far, that he had read the signals wrong. That night, something gave in me, a collision of our pain, our grief. A frequency between us, the touch of his skin, his smell, his smile melting into mine. It had charmed teenage Sophie, cowering within me, bruised and desperate to be loved, to break free.

'I'm not telling you for sympathy, Oré. I'm telling you because you did the right thing, and because of what you did, Brad isn't growing up with a thousand questions bumping around his head, like me. Wondering whether he's the reason you cry yourself to sleep, drink too much, eat crap, never smile, never laugh.' I take his hand. 'You're a great dad. Have been since day one, I have no doubt. Yep. Probably made a few mistakes you're not proud of.' I raise my eyebrows, tilt my head. 'Some bigger than others, hey? Haven't we all.' He tries to speak; I shake my head. 'Please don't.' I take back my hand, shift in my seat. 'Someone very wise helped me to see that sometimes we tell ourselves we want closure when what we're really after is a different outcome. I get it. Believe me, I get it. You did your best. It was more than enough.'

His eyes don't leave mine. 'Thank you.'

I nod. 'You're welcome.'

'I'm sorry too. I shouldn't have grabbed you like that.' He drops his head. 'What an ass.'

My mobile pings, bounces across the bar behind us. One, two, three messages. I raise my hands in prayer to my mouth, hold my breath for a beat until they stop. One, two, three more. I close my eyes. One, two, three more. I stand, snatch the mobile from the bar, switch it off.

Oré slides his notebook onto the coffee table, taps down his pen. 'Do you wanna tell me about that?'

Without looking at the screen, I slip it into my pocket.

He leans back, slips his arm along the back of the couch. 'The messages?'

'It's nothing,' I say in a way that indicates I don't want to talk about it.

'So why jump every time it goes off?'

Bea strides back into the room, followed by Gino, carrying three takeaway cups of coffee. 'What have I missed?'

'Apparently, nothing,' Oré says, his eyes not leaving mine.

28

Taipei (Keelung). Taiwan.

The silver envelope smells expensive as Aunt Christine rolls it between her hands, squealing. 'What is it?'

Bea circles her hand in the air. 'Nae idea. Open it, ye daftie.'

My aunt sinks onto the chair, its slender legs creaking as if they might snap at any moment. Its carved woodwork in distressed silver is a scandalous contrast to the cobalt velvet padded cushion. Wafts of sheer white voiles swath the ceiling, cascading like fountains around us, flowing onto stripped, dark-stained floorboards. Aunt Christine had scarcely taken a step before she slipped, saved only by my arm entwined in hers. Sculptured ebony side tables, dressers with curves worthy of the most voluptuous women, back onto whitewashed walls. The only gesture to its Taiwanese setting is burning incense, striking floral notes with hints of resin. It looks nothing like a clothing boutique. Where are the clothes?

Aunt Christine slips a fingernail under the gummed seal. The tenderness of her touch is a deliberate act to retain the paper. Later, she will preserve it in a book, add it to her box of travel treasures when she gets home. She squints at the rectangle of ivory card embossed with a silver script:

An 80th Birthday Celebration.
You are cordially invited to a party in honour of
Miss Christine Collins.
21.00 Wednesday 21st February 2018.
The Crow's Nest
Dress code: Formal.

'I'm speechless,' Aunt Christine says, hand on heart. 'Was this your doing, Beatrix?'

'And Sophie. Any excuse for a party, Chrissie, you know me.'

She takes my hand, gives it a gentle squeeze. 'Well, you're both very naughty, planning this behind my back. Thank you.'

To Bea's right, a woman appears, her petite frame offset by a bob of glossy black hair, a white satin smock dress.

'Ahh, this is Hoshi, ladies. You can't be having a party without something new to wear.' Bea stands, embraces Hoshi. 'She's one of my favourite designers and has kindly agreed to us having VIP access to her private collection. My birthday present to you, Chrissie. Have whatever you want. You too, Sophie. We're not leaving here until we're clad head to toe in bling and glamour. Right, who's first?'

Hoshi's assistants wheel into the room rails of garments. I shudder at the vibrant colour palette; the spotlights glinting against sequins, satin, silk. Every length, style, size. Each outfit a wonder on its own, but together a masterpiece like strokes of paint on canvas.

I rub the tightness from my eyes, flick through the gowns. Who am I kidding? I have no idea where to start. Dresses slip from the hangers into puddles on the floor. Hopping to my knees, I scramble to pick them up.

'Sophie, isn't it?' Hoshi holds out her hands. 'Let me help you with those.'

I climb to my feet, bundle the clothes into her arms. 'I'm so sorry. They kept falling off.'

'It happens all the time.' She eyes me from foot to shoulder. 'I think I have the perfect one.' She tosses the mound of fabric onto the chair, pulls out a dress, a swath of purple silk. 'Try this.'

'Um, it's gorgeous, it really is, but it's too short for me.'

'Sophie, will you trust me?' She places her hand on my arm. 'Come. I have a fitting room in the back. Try it on. If you don't like it, we'll find another. Deal?'

Concealed behind screens of cream satin, I turn away from the floor-to-ceiling mirrors, pull the dress down over my head, waist, thighs.

'Ready?' Hoshi inches open the curtain.

'No! I mean, not really. I can't wear this, Hoshi.' Elbows pressing into my sides, it takes everything I have to stand tall. 'It's lovely.

Stunning. But I can't.' My voice is a little firmer than intended. I jerk the hem of the dress down towards my knees. 'It's too short.'

Hoshi enters the screened-off space without invitation. Hands on hips, she looks thoughtful, leans against the wall. 'Sophie, you have an incredible shape to your legs. So, tell me, what's worrying you?'

'I like the colour. It's not the dress. It's my ... my legs.' My throat burns dry. 'Well ... my thighs. I don't like to ... I can't show them.'

'Why?'

Knees pushed together, flexed, I grimace, grip the hem tight to my skin. 'Um, I have marks. Scars.'

Hoshi waves her hand. 'May I?'

I don't want to say yes. I don't want her to look. For anyone to look. My jaw tightens, and the faintest gasp of 'Aha' escapes my lips as if someone else is speaking the words for me.

She lifts the hem, exposes my thighs. I look up, my hands fisting at my sides. I want to rip off the dress, leave, but my feet won't move as if held in concrete.

'You have many wounds?' Hoshi places a hand on my arm. 'An accident?'

I breathe hard through my teeth. 'That's why I need something longer. To cover them.'

'I see.' She tilts her head. 'Sophie, have you ever heard of the Japanese art of Kintsugi?'

'No. I've never been to Japan.'

'In Japan, it is believed that all imperfections are part of an object's history. To be admired, not hidden. That scars beautify an object. Kintsugi is the art of repairing fractures, scars. It is believed that to mark something painful with gold is to accept it as a precious jewel. To be admired, not hidden. In the same way, your scars are your jewels. Your story. To be admired.' She takes a tape measure from her pocket. 'I hope you will wear them with pride one day. But until then, will you let me brush them with my kind of gold dust?' Her hands, a carefree breeze, skim the dress over my hips. 'It will be my gift to you.'

'I can't accept that, Hoshi.'

She lifts her palm. 'It is my gift. It would be impolite to turn it down.'

She busies around me, lifting my arms, shifting my legs into position. Her kindness is impossible to bear. My hand on her shoulder, 'Thank you,' I say.

29

Cruising the East China Sea

Aunt Christine bounces around the party with her surprise escort, Anton, on her arm. A weaving river of excited revellers flows around her, swerving chairs and tables as if boulders unable to block their path. Plenty of people I don't recognise for me to question the validity of their invitations, but Aunt Christine and Bea embrace them all, so I assume they must be friends or at least acquaintances of their lingerie-selling sideline.

Thankful for my anonymity, I melt into the background. The crowd has an energy I haven't felt in the Crow's Nest before. The familiar shock of colour from the gowns complements starchy formal dinner suits of black and white. As the weeks pass, loyalty and solidarity have cemented these friendships. I can see why these people return time after time. A kinship between them, a community that dips in and out of each other, one of no judgement or expectation. A celebration of sameness, difference, life.

'Champagne, madam?' the waiter says.

'You're not kidding.' I grab a glass in each hand, suck in its hints of apples and pears.

'Thirsty? Ah, dinnae ken. Yer be oot yer face before we've begun.'

'Bea, I have no idea what you just said but it's lovely to see you. You're sounding very Scottish this evening.'

'Aye. I may have had a wee dram or two getting ready.' She nudges my arm. 'Hell. It's a party.'

I step back, inspect her outfit. 'Wow. You look gorgeous. You and Ainti are the belles of the ball.'

She spins around, curtsies. Her bronze-coloured flapper outfit, complete with an art deco feathered headpiece, sparkles in the spotlights. 'I could say the same about you, bonnie lassie.'

'Hoshi did a good job, didn't she?' I smooth the wide-legged purple pantsuit over my stomach, kick out the overskirt of purple silk and chiffon split to the thigh. 'I've not worn a pantsuit in my life.' I tighten the wide belt of emerald-green satin. 'It looks okay, doesn't it?'

'You look fabulous.'

'Hmm.'

Bea slides her hand into mine, promenades me along the edge of the dance floor. 'Sophie, what am I going to do with you? Head high, breasts out, and for one night only, rock the hell out of that outfit. And if all else fails, get as drunk as a skunk, and you won't even care. Right, I'm off to find more champagne. Enjoy.'

Arms lifted in hold, the other palm flat across his middle, Anton dances over, mimicking an American Smooth or perhaps a waltz, although it might be neither, knowing his lack of coordination.

'It's so good to see you.' I kiss his cheeks. 'When did you get back?'

'Ahh, Sophie-Anne. May I just say how striking you look this evening? That colour is outstanding on you. It really brings out the green in your eyes. You all look wonderful. Goodness, you're putting me to shame tonight. Fabulous. I'm quite wretched I left. But in answer to your question, I had plans to board again in Tokyo, but Bea called, and well, I do love a party. You've done a great job, by the way.'

'Not me. The crew sorted it out. Wonderful, isn't it?' I stroke a bouquet of glittering balloons, bouncing, twinkling rainbows on the wall, the floor.

A blast of trumpets and people wriggle to the beat on the dancefloor. The room swirls, a clutter of colour framed by the night sky backdrop from the floor-to-ceiling windows.

'Right. I think it's time we showed these amateurs how it's done, don't you? May I?' Anton grasps my hand, marches me into the middle of the dancefloor. Elbows jutted from his sides, he whips me from corner to corner, shouting *olé* as we turn.

My shoulders cave with laughter. 'Anton. Stop. Please stop. You're giving me a stitch.'

A deafening screech pours from the sound system. A clatter of unrehearsed notes, the instruments fall silent. On stage next to the band is Aunt Christine, microphone in hand, smoothing her long-sleeved bodice of marine-green sequins over the waistband of a longline, dusty pink satin skirt.

'Testing, one, two, three. Can they hear me? I've always wanted to do that,' she says. 'Firstly, thank you for coming. And thank you to my wonderful niece and dear friends for organising this soirée. Oh, and to the crew for making it happen. I feel very blessed. So, I'm told the band is ready for us to take over.' She converses with the conductor. 'Ah, yes. Quite right. We're not actually playing the instruments. So, hands off the bassoon, Anton. But we can sing with the band. How exciting is that?' She nods at the whoops of approval. 'Quieten down, you lot. They'll take any requests within reason. If you're short of ideas, they have a playlist up here. No Iron Maiden, though, Elizabeth. Sorry.' She cups her hand to shield the glare, searches the audience. 'So, to get things started, Sophie-Anne, I can't see you, but I know you're out there. As they say on *The Price is Right*, come on down.'

'What the actual hell is she doing?' I drop my head into my hands. What felt like a thousand eyes turn on me. I swivel on my heels, plant my face into Anton's chest. 'Tell her to go away, Anton. Please.'

'I've learnt it's best not to get on the wrong side of your aunt.' He brushes imaginary dust from the shoulders of my pantsuit. 'In moments like this, Sophie-Anne, it's best to take a deep breath and jump in feet first. Look, most people are pie-eyed, anyway. Come, fair maiden. I'll escort you to your impending doom.' He hands me a flute of champagne, loops my arm around his.

I gulp down the drink. My feet drag up onto the stage to where Aunt Christine and Bea are standing.

'Here she is.' Aunt Christine places a hand over the microphone. 'So, after your wonderful serenade on the first night, Beatrix and I were wondering if—'

'I wasn't serenading. You walked in on me singing. There's a difference. No. Ainti. I'm not doing it.' I look back at the crowd, a blaze of blinding spots. 'There are hundreds of people here. I'll make a total idiot of myself.'

'That's not true. You've a beautiful voice. We need someone to start the karaoke, and I want that to be you. Stop being so prissy.'

'Prissy?'

A queue of partygoers snakes down the side of the dancefloor, all eager to make a request.

'Look. You've loads of people wanting to sing. Choose one of them.' I turn to walk away.

Aunt Christine swings me back. 'Please, Sophie-Anne. Look, Beatrix and I will be singing with you. No one will even hear your voice over our cackles, will they? Please. It's my birthday. I want to sing a song with you.'

I grasp the microphone from her hand. 'You're really something else, do you know that?' Bea places an arm around my shoulders, waves her champagne flute at me. 'And you're just as bad, Beatrix. I thought you'd be on my side. Okay. One song.' I shuffle into position, my hand shielding my eyes from the stage lights. 'I'm never going to forgive you two for this.'

Aunt Christine shrieks, 'Yahoo,' claps her hands. 'Excellent. I thought we'd do this one.' She thrusts the song list at me, taps *Wide Open Spaces, The Chicks.*

'Are you sure? I mean, it's great, but it's not a disco song, is it?'

Aunt Christine pulls up tall. 'Perfectly sure, thank you.'

'Okay. And you're definitely singing it with me?'

Bea and Aunt Christine lift their microphones, grin.

I pull my feet together, pinch my eyes at the crowd, their shadowy outlines dazzled blurry by the lights. 'Right. Let's get this over with.'

'Okay. Testing. Testing. Ladies and gentlemen, for one night only, may I present my niece, Sophie-Anne O'Ryan, and, um, her, um, me and Beatrix. Yay!' Her words trail off into another squeal, lifting her arms into the air as if starting a Mexican wave. She leans into me, 'One last thing, Sophie-Anne.' She presses her tongue into her cheek. 'Try not to suck.'

'What?' I spin around, hand on hip. 'Are you kidding me?'

'Chill. I'm joking. You'll be fine.' She flaps her hand at me to turn around, sing.

I mutter the first line, tap the beat with my foot until the band thunders into the chorus, and I'm a little weightless, helped by alcohol, the reassuring hoots from the crowd. The tension flows from my limbs into every word. Anton was right, no one cares. They're either twirling across the floor or standing at the side, howling the lyrics back at me. I glance at Aunt Christine, Bea, who, despite their promise, are not singing. Instead, they're standing side by side, re-enacting some kind of strong woman physique competition. Flexing their biceps and pointing their toes to the lyrics. Tears of laughter streak my cheeks as I splutter the last words of the final chorus.

Applause booms across the room. Aunt Christine and Bea step to my side, holding my arms aloft. We bow to shouts of more, brava, my aunt punching the air. The lights dip, and the sight of the partygoers, full grins, cheering and clapping, squeezes my heart tender. Something towards the rear of the throng catches my attention. It could be Anton with two fingers in his mouth, whistling his appreciation, but it isn't. It's the man standing next to him, hands clasped in applause. 'Thank you,' I mouth to Oré, push the hair from my shoulders, climb down the stairs. One after the other, people surge forward, a chorus of congratulations, well done, a knowing nod. The next vocalist takes to the stage.

'Where did you learn to sing like that?' Oré says, striking in the same dinner suit he wore in Hong Kong.

'Thank you. I was terrified, to be honest.'

'Your backup singers were pretty special, too. Do you hire them out for weddings and bar mitzvahs?'

'Oh, my gosh. They're hilarious, aren't they? The Supremes we are not.'

His eyes journey up the length of me. 'Nice dress. New?'

'It's a pantsuit. Look.' I lift my leg, flap the pleats between my calves.

'And the footwear.'

I twist my UGG boots at him. 'Yeap. My favourites.'

'Cool. It, they, all of it – wow! It suits you.'

I open my mouth, ready to protest. He places his finger on my lips. 'No. We're going to take the compliment, Soap, aren't we? You look awesome. Best suck it up.'

The tap of a lone drum brush, the piano, trumpet, flute, Oré's smile grows of its own accord. He offers me his hand. 'May I have this dance?'

He twirls me onto the dancefloor, taps each foot to the side, leads me into ththe dance he learnt as a young man, the foxtrot to 'Fly Me to the Moon.' We circle the room, rise and fall, two beat steps, then one. He sways me in, out of hold, over his arm. His smile echoes mine. The drums crash into the instrumental. He lifts me into his arms, orbiting us around and around. My head falls back and I laugh so hard that the world stands still, falls silent.

Lowering me to the floor, I steady myself on his arm, catch my breath. He sweeps the hair from my face, and I'm a wind chime in a warm summer breeze, a fish gliding in cool, shallow, ice-clear water. I can't stop smiling, drinking him in like a strong, expensive wine, enjoy feeling tipsy.

He pulls my hand into his, curls his fingers around mine. 'I think you're awesome, Soap. I'm sorry I scared you the other night. Can we start again, again?'

30

Beppu. Japan.

Dove grey clouds hang dense, the smell of rotten eggs from swirls of white sulphuric mist dance like billowing smoke from the rooftops. It casts an eeriness on an already gloomy scene.

'I don't think much of your new cologne.' I smile at Oré's nose, crinkling into a frown.

'Very funny,' he says, guiding me onto the gondola.

The ropeway carriage swings with a musical creak. An onshore draft follows us, climbing the mountain slope. Below, the landscape soars, a woven tapestry of city, forest, sea. Roof tiles, weathered earthy red, ashen grey, tied by a spool of tarmac ribbons.

The car clunks to a stop. A puff of pearled white clouds swallows it whole. Hands swathed in woollen gloves, I press them into my pockets, follow the throng outside. A gust of bracing cloud fills my lungs, fresh air with brackish mineralised notes. Oré seeks a loose stone, kicks it down the path, like a child. I imagine he was not unlike Patrick in his twenties, suave, smug, partial to a large spoon of love bombing to get his way. Perhaps Oré is testament that people can, and do, change. He doesn't blame others for his choices, for how his life turned out, accepts his mistakes, owns them. If we allow them, our biggest mistakes can be the ones that help us most to grow.

Whiskers of white crystal splinter foliage and branch, as hoarfrost laces before us. Stepping onto a carpet of fog ringing the summit, rock crumbles beneath my feet. A snap of icy breeze fondles my cheeks tender. The air falls tranquil around us, broken by the purr of jocund voices, the crunch of footsteps.

'Jesus. It's so cold.' I tuck my chin under my coat collar. A line of iced coffee mountains churns the crisp, silvery clouds on either side of me. 'Looks like it might snow. I don't think we're going to see much this afternoon.'

'Oh, I don't know. I think the view's pretty good.' Oré casts his eyes from me to the horizon, rubs a finger to his lips, sits on a crag of rocks.

'Smooth, James. Very smooth.'

'Thank you.' A theatrical bow.

I like his playful nature, although I still find it hard to tell whether he's being serious or cutting a joke sometimes.

'This is amazing, isn't it?' I step forward, spin on a dance floor of frozen leaves, pirouetting to the ground into an almost split.

'Jeez.' Oré jumps to his feet, offers me his hand. 'Are you okay?'

Words fail me. I sit, legs spread wide. My laughter fused with random roars of 'Ow', like a wolf calling its kin to rally.

He heaves me to my feet. 'Are you sure you're not some kind of imposter? Surely school principals don't do this kind of thing.'

'There you go again, typecasting us poor academics. We can be fun.'

He sits, rests back on his palms. 'So, you are having fun? Admit it. You secretly love my company.'

I spill a handful of leaves over his head. 'Arrogant, overconfident and modest.'

He brushes himself down, stares over the edge of the mountain. 'I can't make you out, Soap. In a good way. You're a mystery not to be solved, aren't you? To think you started out as such an oddball.'

'Oddball? Charming.'

'Well, you were. Yeesh, Soap. You blasted me for maiming your aunt with a mop. A bloody mop. Thinking about it, I'm not sure you've ever apologised for that?'

'Let's not go there. You could've really hurt her, and you know it.'

'Woah. Admit it. You were pissed at something, and it wasn't me.'

'I was not.' My words trail off. His face wrinkles as if saying, are you sure about that? I look away. He doesn't need to hear about the madness that keeps me awake.

'Ha, I have a confession. On that first day, the mix-up with the beds. I didn't know what you were talking about. I'd never even seen a booking form.'

'I knew it. Rude.'

He rubs his Chelsea boots into the gravel. 'So, will you go back to teaching when this is over?'

'Hmm.' I brush a frozen leaf from my shin. 'If you'd asked me at the beginning of this, actually, no, if you'd asked me at the beginning, I would have told you to bug off and mind your own business.' I grin at how his face softens when he laughs. 'Seriously, I would have said yes. What else would I do?'

'But?'

A shot of fear hits my nerves. 'This trip's been great, but—'

'Sure, it has. You've met me.'

I bump his arm. 'Are you interested in what I've got to say?'

'Absolutely. Carry on.' Oré places a hand over his mouth.

'As I was saying, this trip's been great, but it's not real life, is it? We all have to go back and face reality at some point.' I slap my knees, lighten my tone. 'Unless you're Bea, of course, and just keep going around the world.'

Oré shuffles to face me. 'Maybe. But what if you could start again? Would you?'

Oh Oré, you have no idea. No idea how much I would give to do that. 'Are you asking for you or me?'

'Avoiding the question again?' Oré picks up a stone, skims it over the edge. 'Do you regret leaving?'

Elbows on knees, I rest my chin on fisted hands. 'I regret lots of things.'

He scrunches his brow, cocks his head at me. 'I'm a real good listener.'

I look down at my feet, slip my UGGs on the frozen ground.

'Soap, talk to me. Please. I know there's something going on.'

His words catch me off-guard. I look away. 'I can't.'

'Why?'

The silence is deafening. The sky knotted with clouds, frost cracking and sparkling like a carpet of tiny diamonds, the cry of a swooping bird.

'Do you ever dream about running away?'

He kicks another stone over the edge. 'All the fucking time.'

I jerk to look at him. His face is full of questions, as if he has seen my thoughts a thousand times but has never dared to ask. I look down at my hands.

'Why can't you tell me?'

I don't look up. My heart races in my chest, rehearsing how his face will crumple with disgust and judgement. I don't want to feel the pain of him looking differently at me because of it, of him leaving. 'It's not a topic you bring up in casual conversation.'

He takes my hands in his. 'Tell me.'

I look at him, drag my eyes down to my feet. 'I killed my best friend.' The words, quiet, rush from me like I have been holding my breath underwater for too long, stabbing through the surface, gasping for air.

He drops my hands, and my heart cracks. 'You did what?'

Our silence stretches across the mountaintop. A tightness coils my stomach. I can't look at the confusion staining his face, speak. The air rattles with the sharp cry of a gull. We both turn to the commotion and I'm glad for the distraction.

'What was that?' I say, stalling for time.

He turns to face me, compelling me to look at him. 'Sophie.' He rubs my arms warm, reaches for my hand again. 'It's okay.'

We're strangers, but there's something … something safe about him. Like his touch is pulling me behind a bolted door, shielded in trust and hope and love. 'No. It's not,' I whisper. We stay like this, whilst I try and compile the things I need to say in my head. Her loss too great for a simple sentence, buried, not forgotten, in a silent place. 'We … We were on her moped. My friend Clare. We'd just got off the train. Had been to London for the day. She insisted on dragging me to an art gallery every autumn. Ha. Said I lacked culture in my life. I liked it, really. Loved the cocktails afterwards more.' He strokes his hand down my back, my eyes close for a beat. 'The rain was awful. I'd begged her to get a taxi, but she wouldn't have it. We weren't dressed for it. Soaked to the skin.' My eyes drop to my feet, a tremble in my voice. 'She hadn't fastened her helmet. Wouldn't be told. I ignored it like always. Stop fussing, it's a ten-minute drive to yours, she'd say. We'd done it a thousand times. You know. It's one of those journeys when you get there and think, how the hell did that happen?' A sting behind my eyes, I draw the cold air through my teeth. 'It was so dark.' My heart cranks into high gear, punching against my ribs. 'I don't remember much. A flash of white light and we were on the floor. The smell of blood, splintered metal ...' My throat grips tight, like Patrick's hands are around my neck again. 'It felt like we were lying there forever.'

'Did nobody help you?'

'It was too late.' I shake my head, stare at the ground in front of me. 'They slammed us at the inquest. Painted her as some crazy biker. She had a caution for careless driving in her teens, apparently – who knew? It was a Vespa, Oré. A flipping put-put Vespa. The gaudiest, pinkest, most unforgettable bike you'd ever seen. Straight out of a Barbie collection. She loved it.' I ram my hands under my thighs. 'I couldn't get to her. She lay there reaching for me to help.' Without warning, my mind is a series of flashcards, rain dripping off my nose, torn skin, her whimpering *why*. I suck up the prickling in my throat. 'They said she died on impact, a massive head injury. But I heard her, saw her arm move.' My head falls back. I wipe away my tears. 'We'd been drinking.' I look at him. 'Only one, but it was enough.'

'Enough?'

'To blame her and attack me. The solicitor said if she'd survived, she'd have gone down for dangerous driving. She was a live wire, yes. But dangerous? No. It was impossible to hear them talk about her like that.'

Oré pulls me into him. 'Jeez, Soap. That sounds real hard.'

My heartstrings stretch so tight they might snap. 'No. I'm sorry. I– am– so– so– sorry.' Resting my chin on his shoulder, my eyes close, the burn rising within me, suffocating my words. 'You're right. I am pissed. With me, with her, with them. Every day. Every minute of every fucking day, I see it. I hear it. How could I be so stupid? I could've stopped her. I shouldn't have got on that flipping bike.' Pulling from him, I take off a glove, wipe my swollen eyes. 'I'm so exhausted with it all. I don't talk about it because I can't.' Shame throbs my cheeks, the anger inside me, white hot fiery rage. 'The thought of her dying alone like that crushes me.'

'Soap. I'm so sorry.' His arms envelop me, veil the chill in the air.

The sound of my mobile ringing in my back pocket is ear-splitting in the silence. 'You're fucking kidding me.' Without looking, I pull it out, push it into my thigh, shield its moan until it ends. The air turns thick with difficult. 'Sorry.'

He tips his head at the phone. 'Is that connected?'

I hesitate before turning the phone over. Flip it open. 'Kinda.' I nod for him to look as I scroll through today's missed calls and unread messages.

'Heck, Soap. Someone's keen. Who's TD?'

I flick it shut, push it back into my trouser pocket, a long draw of icy mountain air. 'Patrick.'

'Patrick?'

'My ex-husband.'

'Right.' Oré twists from me, sweeps some loose stones onto the floor. 'And?'

'He got back in touch after the accident. Helped me through it.'

He adjusts his jacket collar. 'Sounds like a nice guy.'

'I was a mess, Oré. He took care of everything – the police, the press, friends.'

'Are you and him?'

'What? No. I mean, he wants to, but …' I lay my fingers against my mouth. How much do I need to tell him? 'Our marriage was pretty bad.' I stand, walk over to the mountain's edge, 'There's this tug inside me that wants to believe he's changed.' I look down at my clasped hands, glance back at him. 'You forget, don't you?'

'How bad?'

I look out at the distant shoreline, a palette of melded greys unify sky into sea. A stark contrast to the blue skies and golden sands in the south. 'It started with the odd putdown.' I adjust my fingers back into my gloves. 'Sometimes it still catches me. It's like I'm floating outside my body, looking down on a movie scene.'

Oré looks away, breathes hard through his nose. 'Did he hurt you?'

I study his expression, a twist of curiosity, rage, sadness. 'Aha.' I straighten. 'He says he's changed.'

'Soap …' Oré rubs his chin, bites his bottom lip like he's fighting the urge not to say what he feels. 'Do you think he's changed?'

I look down at my feet, slide them up and down the frozen gravel.

'I don't know.'

Oré takes my hands, beckons for me to sit down. 'I'm gonna ask you again. Do you think he's changed?'

I turn to him, look away, shrug.

'Jesus, Sophie. Do you wanna know what I think?' I side-eye him, dip my chin. 'You're vulnerable, and he's taking advantage. End of.'

I throw him a there's-no-way-you-can-know-that look.

'Truth. Trust me. I know all about assholes like him.'

The granite-grey clouds crack like a turning page, catching the sun. Edged blossom pink, ruffling silvery swirls roll into line, spotted snatches of blue shining like sky puddles.

Oré picks up a stone, rolls it between his finger and thumb. 'Why TD?'

'The Dick. Clare renamed him in my contacts after we separated.'

'Ha. I would have liked her.' He tosses the stone, kicks it over the edge. 'I think that's your answer, Soap.' His arm slides my shoulders. 'You must miss her.'

My smile slips. 'Hmm. The crazy thing is, he couldn't stand her, and she loathed him.' Talking with him feels like the unseen scars inside me are being traced by the gentlest touch. 'She used to call me Soap.'

'Jeez. Why didn't you say something? I'll stop.'

'Don't.' He watches me straighten his jacket over his shoulders, brush out the creases, his face drowning in anticipation. I kiss his cheek. 'I like it.'

With eyes full of something, his body stiffens against mine. An air horn shatters our silence. Three blasts warn us that the last gondola of the day is about to leave.

He slides his fingers between mine, pulls me to my feet. 'Sadly, Miss O Ryan, that's our cue to leave.'

31

Hiroshima. Japan.

Aunt Christine sweeps cherry-red gloss across her lips. One long blast of hair lacquer and her face lights with a glow of golden joy streaming through the French windows.

'Ditched your usual cerise lipstick, Ainti?' I pluck a fleck of white cotton from between three polished brass buttons on her shoulder.

'I felt like a change.'

'I like it. New dress too?'

Navy, a flash of red pinching at her waist, her trademark pastel twinsets and cargo shorts, folded at the back of the closet. She looks down, skims it over her hips. 'Does it look okay? I haven't worn anything like it in years. Beatrix made me spend a small fortune in that blasted boutique.'

'Very sophisticated. You look perfect. Although, I thought you weren't going in there again?'

'Beatrix said I needed to get over myself. Hard to hear, but she may have a point.' Aunt Christine jolts at the rap on the door.

His smile beams as I swing it open. 'Sophie-Anne, how lovely to see you.' Plants a kiss on each cheek.

'Anton. I wasn't expecting you this morning. Are you the reason my aunt looks a million dollars? And get you all spruced up and dapper.'

He winds an olive-green scarf of thick cashmere around his neck, fastens the top button of his charcoal-flecked woollen overcoat.

I edge next to Aunt Christine, help her put on her best winter coat. 'You didn't tell me you were going out with him.'

A broad grin, her eyes avoid mine. 'I don't know what you're talking about.'

'I think it's wonderful.' Her eyes crease, a small smile as I kiss her forehead. 'You're wonderful. Where are you going?'

'I thought we'd stroll the gardens, get some local oysters, perhaps a quart of sake to warm us up. You're welcome to join us, Sophie.'

'I'm good, thanks, Anton. I wouldn't want to cramp your style.'

'Oh, I nearly forgot.' Anton steps forward, pins a pink rose buttonhole onto Aunt Christine's breast pocket. 'Gosh, you smell divine, Christine. Are those actual rose petals I can smell?'

'Oh, Anton. Get away with you.' She taps his arm, twists like a shy child on her heels. 'It's my new perfume. A birthday present from Sophie-Anne.' She pats the rose. 'Thank you. It's lovely.'

I give them an unspoken minute alone, feigning a sudden interest in a scuff on the sideboard. It's been decades since I've seen my aunt captured in this kind of moment, and it's charming, reminding me of watching her as a little girl on her boyfriend's knee.

'Ready? Shall we go?' Anton offers his arm. 'I'm not sure when we'll be back, but I'll take great care of her.'

'Before we sail, I hope, Anton?'

'Indeed. Very funny, Sophie-Anne. Very funny.'

I hold open the door. 'Have a lovely time, both of you.'

Aunt Christine swings around. 'Oh, and will you get down to that blinking salon and sort out your hair?'

'Hey?'

'It still wreaks of that eggy mountain. It's like sleeping next to a rubbish truck on bin day.'

'No. Does it?' I grasp some hair to my nose.

'It stinks, Sophie-Anne. Get it sorted. Today. Oh, and don't wait up.' Mischief laces my aunt's smile.

They stroll down the corridor, Aunt Christine giggles, Anton a throaty laugh.

'You're too cute,' I call after them. They don't turn around, lost in each other's company. I close the door, pick up the key card, fluff my hair in the dressing-table mirror. 'Okay. Time to get you sorted.'

The sun pitches a wintry summertime. I clasp my coat at the chill stepping onto the gangway. The distant call of workers, the thump of containers, the crunch of trucks signalling the harbour's days in full flow. A toss of my new hairstyle, its scent of fresh honeysuckle, overwhelms the waterfront's waft of raw shellfish, gasoline. I push my mobile into my pocket, humming Taylor Swift's 'Everything Has Changed'.

On the dock, Oré spins around. A stack of well-loved luggage bathes on the sun-struck tarmac.

An ache sears through me, drawing myself into a self-hug. 'Are you leaving?' My voice quivers.

'Who me?' He looks from side to side, checks that I'm addressing him. 'No. Why?'

Hands slapping my sides, the tension floods loose from my limbs. 'The bags.'

He smacks my back. 'Nope. You don't get rid of me that easily, Soap. Sweet though. Thanks for caring.'

'I wasn't.' I push his arm from mine. 'Caring, I mean.'

'If you say so. Nice hair, by the way. Very chic. What style is that?'

'This is a choppy bob with caramel highlights and a dab of hair oil for added shine.' I scrunch it in both hands. 'Thank you for noticing.'

'You're very welcome. Awesome with your favourite boots.'

'Ha. Yes. Thanks. So, who's leaving?'

'Oh, no one. New passengers arriving. I'm just waiting on the porters to come back and pick these last ones up. What're you up to? You haven't got long.'

'The museum, I think.' Behind us, a roar of laughter. 'What the actual hell?'

A cab driver bounces from one foot to the other, head bowing, offering a steady hand to his customers. Leaving the door to swing wide, two passengers weave towards us, arms curled around each other's waists.

'Yoo-hoo, Sophie-Anne. We're home.'

'Oh my goodness. Look at the state of them.'

Aunt Christine stumbles against Anton. It's a miracle they've made it back at all. Oré and I guide them up the walkway, lower them onto a sofa in the foyer.

'We can't leave them here like this.' I hand my aunt her bag.

A couple of happy drunks propped up against each other on the chair, Aunt Christine fumbles for something in her handbag, its contents spilling across the floor. She flips a whatever hand, gives up. Eyes squeezed shut, she rests her head upon Anton's shoulder. I fear they might plunge over the edge with each snort of laughter.

Oré gestures for the receptionist to help, scoops up my aunt's things littering the floor, hands them to me. 'They certainly know how to have a good time, these old guys, don't they? I think we could all learn a lesson or two from them.'

I drop my aunt's stuff onto the counter, slam a hand on my mobile, bleeping and vibrating in my back pocket.

Oré watches me pull it out. 'Is it him?'

I look at him, the phone, nod. 'Do you mind if I get this? There's something I need to do.'

He squeezes my shoulder. 'Go ahead. I'll sort out Romeo and Juliet.'

Fading into the corner, I answer the call. 'Hi. I'm glad you called. We need to talk, Pat.'

32

Osaka. Japan.

I can almost see the cogs whir in Aunt Christine's brain. She curls her manicured nails of lipstick-red polish into a fist, knocks the table. 'Gin.'

I throw my hands up. 'Already? We've barely started.'

She fans out three sixes, three nines and a run of nine, ten, jack and the queen of hearts. 'Sophie?'

I toss down my playing cards, a score of zero. 'Are you some kind of gin rummy card shark on the quiet, Ainti? No one stands a chance against you.'

'Nobody likes a sore loser, Sophie-Anne. Suck it up and move along. Game set and match to me, again.'

Anton taps the deck back into its packet. 'Another drink before dinner, anyone?'

'No need, Anton.' Bea strides up to the table, crystal flutes swinging in her hands. She pulls out a chair, motions for the bartender to place the ice bucket of champagne down next to her.

Aunt Christine smacks a palm to her chest. 'Don't sneak up like that, Beatrix. I almost peed my pants.'

'Sorry.' She sits down.

'How do you get away with it, Bea?' I nod at her outfit.

Her notorious flouting of the restaurant's smart-casual dress code continues. Tonight, she sports faded blue denim, red Dr Martens boots, a black Foo Fighters In Your Honour T-shirt, finished with a red military tailored blazer.

'What do you mean? It's vintage chic. Well, that's what I'll tell them.'

Anton passes around the crystal flutes. 'I'm not sure they'd have the audacity to tell Madam Beatrix what to do. She practically owns the ship.'

'Stop your nonsense, Anton.' Bea pulls the bottle from the ice bucket, pours each of us some champagne.

'Are we celebrating?' Aunt Christine asks.

'What, other than you two getting home in one piece yesterday? What were you thinking bringing my aunt back in such a state, Anton?'

'That sake can be a demon at times, Sophie-Anne. Although, I'm not sure I could make your aunt do anything she didn't want to.' He kisses her hand. 'She's quite the gritty woman when she wants to be.'

'Cheers to that and all the other strong women at this table.' Bea thrusts her glass into the air. 'A toast. I have a new great-goddaughter. If that's a thing. My goddaughter Zoey had a baby girl this afternoon.' Bea's smile beams, passing around a photo on her mobile phone.

I clink my glass to hers. 'She's adorable, Bea. Does she have a name?'

'Ava Beatrix.'

'Aah. That's lovely.'

Two hands grip my shoulders from behind. 'Howdy, folks.'

'Shit, Oré. What're you doing?' I say, lunge forward.

'Sophie!' My aunt tuts. 'Language.'

'Yeah. Yeah. I know. But he made me jump.'

'Pull up a chair.' Bea gestures for him to sit down. 'Champagne?'

'I wish I could, but I'm on duty. I've only got a few minutes. Christine, Anton, how's the heads?'

'Ah, yes.' Anton rubs his chin, pats a finger on his lips. 'Thank you for your assistance. It would, I fear, have taken a lot more to bring us down.'

'Ahh, the cards are out again, I see.' Oré slaps a hand on my shoulder. I can hear the smile in his voice. 'Building skyscrapers, are we?' He coughs, covering his laughter as Aunt Christine's nose wrinkles confused.

'Hilarious. Not.' I turn around to face him. 'My aunt's teaching me to play gin rummy. Although, the charlatan's not let me win a single point so far.'

'What would be the fun in that, Sophie-Anne? If I remember rightly, you said you'd rather stick hot pokers in your eyes than play cards with me. Not as easy as it looks, is it?'

'So,' Oré grips the back of Aunt Christine's chair, 'the reason I'm here is to talk about Tokyo. I've got some extended shore leave and wondered if you had any plans?'

'Oh. What a shame. We've got reservations at the Aman,' Bea says. 'Had to pull quite a few strings to get us all in.'

'Wow. Very nice. Not to worry. My friend's working on a new art exhibition, and I've twisted her arm into letting me look around before it opens.'

'I'm free.' My aunt, Anton and Bea's eyes pin me to the chair. 'I mean.' Tossing my hair from my shoulders, I try to claw back an ounce of coolness, giddy and hopeful. 'I'll just be mooching about, waiting on these guys. What is it?'

'I'm not sure. Some kind of digital art gallery. It's not open to the public until June. Should be cool. But I don't want to spoil your plans.'

'I love art.' Which isn't strictly true. Unless being dragged by Clare to the Tate every year counts. 'I'm in. I can go to the hotel another time. Is that okay, Bea?'

Bea pouts her lips, lifts her flute at me. 'Perfectly.'

'You're sure?' A buzzy energy in Oré's voice.

'Absolutely. Sounds fun.' I hold up my glass to him.

'Okay. Great. I'll be finished around lunchtime. Shall I call your cell when I'm done? Come find you?'

'Sounds good.'

'Enjoy your evening, everyone.' He raises a hand goodbye, leans into Bea. 'The Aman. I'm very jealous.' He wags a finger at the exit. 'Catch ya'all later.'

As I sip my champagne, it's difficult to grasp whether it's the fizz or fashioning plans with him that's making me feel dizzy.

'You were just gonna mooch about waiting on us guys, were you?' Bea tops up my glass. 'Can do the finest hotel in Tokyo any time?'

'Is there a problem?' I avert my eyes, tidy the drinks menu on the table.

'Not at all.' Bea coughs, swallows her laughter.

Anton smooths back his hair, chuckles. 'Better cancel Sophie's room, Beatrix. She's got a better offer.'

I put down my glass. 'It sounds like fun, okay? That's all.'

'Interesting.' Bea inspects my expression as if looking over half-rimmed spectacles, and I'm transported back to the night we met in the restaurant. 'I'm loving this new assertive Miss O'Ryan.' She holds up her glass. 'Cheers. What do you think, Chrissie?'

Aunt Christine looks down, takes a long slow gulp of her champagne. 'I think it's wonderful, Sophie-Anne. It sounds like a lot of fun.'

A wheeze of relief floats across the table. Anton's hand rubs her back. 'Well done,' he whispers, and my heart squeezes.

'Shall we drop into the spa, see if they can fit you in for a tidy up?' Aunt Christine flicks her eyes at my groin. 'You know. Down there. A Brazilian could be fun.'

'A Brazilian? Stop!' I shake my head at her before looking away. 'Can we change the subject, please? Our table must be ready by now, surely? I'm starving.'

The heater splutters smouldering air throughout the cabin. Aunt Christine sits hunched at the dressing table, pulls off my sunshine-yellow court shoes.

'They look good on you, Ainti. They go really well with those new navy pants.'

'Trousers, Sophie-Anne.' She rummages in her handbag. 'We're not American.'

'Ahh yes, that reminds me.' I reach into the bedside drawer, pull out a fold of paper, a photograph. 'This fell out of your bag in reception yesterday.' I smooth out the envelope, the same one from the bus in Thailand, *Chrystal* scrawled across it in blue ink. 'And this. It was inside.' I slide a black-and-white image of my mother onto the dressing table, her sitting under a tree, legs curled beneath her on a picnic rug. Behind, a lady, deep in thought, her head resting on a young man's shoulder, his arms circling her waist. 'That's you, isn't it?'

She looks up like an animal caught in headlights.

Mum was always teasing Aunt Christine about her men friends saying she had more boyfriends than items on the Gut Buster Breakfast at Brighton's Market Diner, which was a lot in those days.

But I can only remember meeting one, this one. Her sat on his lap at our house, arms draped around his neck. Their laughter bounced childlike despite their adult years. Aunt Christine stares into the dressing-table mirror, pulls a cotton wool pad across her face. With cleansing sweeps, the face she paints for the world melts away. It's easy to forget those we love were once young themselves, had a life beyond us.

I tap the photograph. 'Who's the hottie?'

The cotton wool pad stills on her lips. 'George.'

I slip the envelope alongside the photo. 'I knew I recognised it. Chrystal. It was him, wasn't it? He called you Chrystal.' I run a finger over his image, smart in a skinny suit and pencil tie. 'He just stopped coming around, didn't he?' It was hard to know at the time whether the sadness creasing her face was for him or her sister dying upstairs. 'Did he cheat on you?'

'Who George? Goodness, no.'

I hand her the photograph. 'This was taken just before Mum died, wasn't it?'

Aunt Christine folds the photograph in half, slides it back inside the envelope. She tugs her handbag from the floor, drops it inside, zips it shut.

'Is that why he left? Because of Mum.'

She flips the cotton wool pad into the bin.

'Ainti?' I circle my arms around her shoulders. In the mirror, her eyes close like a blackout curtain drawn across a window, the foot-dragging ache of her breath. 'Why did he leave?'

She shrugs me off her. 'He didn't want to be with me any more. It happens.' She stands, pulls a fresh nightdress out of the sideboard drawer. 'Time for bed.'

My aunt rarely lies to me, but her lack of eye contact always gives her away. She steadies herself against the bathroom door, falters for a beat.

Bea's words that night in Thailand flash my mind – more than you'll ever know, and something gives, like the bricks of my childhood home are falling around me. 'Was it me? Is that what Bea meant on the balcony that night? He left because of me, not Mum, didn't he?'

She straightens, a thick viscous silence between us.

I stare out the French windows. 'Jesus.' I close my eyes, press my palms onto the cool glass. 'Did you give him up to look after me?'

Aunt Christine spins me around, grips my upper arms. 'Now listen to me, young lady. The years I've spent bringing you up have been nothing but joyous. I wouldn't have changed it for the world.'

'But Ainti–'

'No.' She cuts across me. 'I will be eternally grateful that I saw his true colours when I did. Why on earth would I want to devote myself to a man like that? A man who expected me to abandon a young child. My sister's child.'

'Like my dad, you mean?'

'No.' She drops her hands. 'That wasn't the same at all. Your dad couldn't cope. His world had fallen apart.'

The violins playing in my head screech to a stop. 'Ainti. I'm so sorry. I wish you'd told me.'

'Why are you sorry? Yes, I thought he was the love of my life back then, but now, I realise he was just another in a very long line of prats. Perhaps I should've told you, but I didn't with the best of intentions.'

'Prats?' I repeat, smile at the frown creasing tight around her eyes.

'Prats.' Aunt Christine rubs my arm. We embrace, fall back into silence.

I lift my chin from her shoulder, drop my bag off the bed. 'There's something I need to tell you, too.' We all have secrets, some of which gnarl and fester until you realise that if you had only spoken them sooner, they might have been easier to hear. The words lay heavy, like a boulder in my throat. 'It's Mum's necklace. The Ailm.' My voice breaks, the chastised little girl rising within me. 'It's gone.'

'Gone. What do you mean, gone?'

'It was in my wallet when my bag got taken.' The words spill from my lips. 'I'm so sorry, Ainti. Patrick broke the clasp. I should've got it fixed.'

'Patrick? Patrick broke it. Why?'

I look down, my fingers fitted together. 'He snapped the chain.'

She studies my face. 'But how?'

'We were arguing. He grabbed my neck.' The pain in her eyes thumps deep into my chest.

'What? Why wouldn't you tell me something like that?'

It's one of those moments when you feel the memory swelling up in your throat. 'I didn't want to worry you.'

'So, you deal with it alone?' She steps forward, strokes my cheek. 'Oh, Sophie-Anne, how many times? It's okay to ask for help.'

I circle my arms around her waist, rest my chin on her shoulder again. 'Sorry. I thought I was—'

'I know.' She taps her head against mine. 'And the charm's definitely gone?'

I bounce my chin, nod. 'Why do you even bother with me?'

She pulls back, sweeps my hair from my face. 'Now listen to me. Your mum wouldn't want you to worry. It's not important. Believe me.'

'But—'

She places a finger on my lips. 'Our obsession with belongings can cloud what truly matters in life, Sophie-Anne. Trust me. Let it go.'

33

Tokyo. Japan.

The pavement glints in the late morning sun, damp with a trillion raindrops. Steely grey slabs pave the way to a concrete bunker held tall by elevated pillars, floor-to-ceiling windows. Huge lumps of stonework adorn the walls. At first glance, a melody of darker shades of grey until, on closer inspection, pebbles speckle its shell. In the garden, a bronze sculpture, The Thinker, reminds me of why I'm here.

Polished ramps spiral, rolling lines of daylight drawn from the ceiling, walls. Silken balustrades slip through my hand, climbing the gallery's uncluttered construction. Ambling the halls, my heart stings. It's been well over a year since I've stepped into somewhere like this. At the top of the slope, I stroll the final gallery. Works of art pitched to the walls, their reflections cast onto the floor, stained golden by the shine of uplighters, spots. A hush, bar the creep of footsteps. I close my eyes, count my breath in and out, force myself back to that day, our last day.

***

Tate Britain. London. England.

'Hey, she looks like you, Soap.' Clare says, perched on the bench.

'Charming!'

'Shush.' She nudged her shoulder into mine, giggled. 'You'll get us thrown out in a minute.' Clare scrolled her phone. 'It says here it depicts the plight of a beautiful and tragic woman.'

'I'm not tragic.'

'But you are beautiful.'

'And that's meant to make me feel better?'

'Seriously. You look like that.' Clare nods at the painting.

'Like what?'

'Sad. Lost. Depressed. Like your mind's full of stuff.'

I snapped to face her. 'I'm not depressed.'

Clare reclined, palms pressed on the wooden bench. 'Do you think she instantly regretted looking at him?'

'Who?'

'Lancelot.'

'Sorry?'

'Lady Shalott.' She tipped her head at the painting again, gave me a sideways glance. 'I'm worried about you.'

'Why? I'm having a lovely day.'

'I'm not talking about today, you numpty. I thought you'd have bounced back by now. What's wrong?'

I gazed at Lady Shalott. Her chin set high, lips parted full flushed red, skin ashen, wilted eyes. A reflection so familiar it hurt. 'Don't be silly. Nothing's wrong.' I swept some imaginary creases from my dress, adjusted my denim jacket. A longing hit me, but for what, I didn't know. I shook my hair, scrunched it between both hands. 'Anyhow, my hair's nothing like hers. I went to the hairdresser yesterday, so there.'

'Funny.' Clare clasped her arm around my waist, pulled me to her. 'You're amazing, sweet cheeks. I hate seeing you like this.'

'I'm fine.'

'You're right. You're a perfect example of okayness, who deserves so much more. What you need is a new direction. Look, you're smart, single, got no kids. How about doing something outrageous with me?'

'Like?' Here she goes again, imagining my life away.

'You always wanted to travel. Fuck it all, and do it?'

'It's a bit late in the day to pick up a rucksack and head off into the sunset, don't you think?'

'I think that's exactly what we need to do.'

'Jesus. You're on one today, aren't you? I'll think about it.'

'Promise?'

'I promise. Now stop hassling me. What's next?'

Clare pulled me up from the bench. 'Cocktails. Come. *Allons.*'

***

For Christ's sake. My phone vibrates, shattering the stillness. 'Okay. Okay.' I fumble it out of my bag, desperate to silence the other visitor's judgemental stares. 'Hello.'

'Soapy?'

'Oh. It's you.'

Oré laughs. 'There you go again.'

'Hold on. I'm going outside.' I huddle into a corner in the foyer. 'That's better. Sorry. Hi.'

'Are you okay? You sound tense.'

'No. No. All good. Done?'

'I'm leaving in five. Where are you?'

'The Museum of Western Art. Do you know it?'

'Crikey. No. But I'll jump in a cab and meet you out front. Soap?'

'Yes.'

'Can we pause being arty for a bit? I could murder a beer.'

Our next stop couldn't be more different, a tower of metal and glass inviting the eye heavenward. Slouching against the wall, we watch people queuing for a giant Ferris wheel. The scorn in my expression ensures Oré doesn't ask me if I want to ride.

'Zadzi. How are you?' she says, her voice overly familiar. My stomach hardens as the woman grasps Oré's shoulders, plants a kiss on each cheek. Likely the same age, her business suit, a crisp cut of sharp white lines.

'Hey, Brooky. Great to see you. It's been too long.' He clasps her to him, holds her a little longer than needed. 'Sophie, this is Brook. Brook, Sophie.'

'Hi.' She shakes my hand, sharp fingernails manicured in black polish. 'We're not open for a few months, but I can give you an idea of what it'll look like. Here you'll need these.'

Lanyards around our necks, Brook escorts us down a corridor of black walls.

'What the–?' I say. A projection of a flower-strewn lion follows us along the partition.

'Stroke it,' Brook says.

It roars from my touch before petals flutter to the ground, disappear. Oré spins around. 'What is this place?'

'Come. I'll show you.' Brook pushes back the unmarked black curtain.

A rainbow of virtual blooms dances at my feet. Music, light, picture united. Vibrant blossoms freckle across the floor, tumble the mirrored walls, my senses teased, imagining honeyed perfume, the soft caress of velvety petals. Brook, her white suit a canvas of colour, motions for me to stroke the flowered forest. A cascade of petals withers and fades at my fingertips. With each step, the images shift, reinventing themselves into a living piece of art.

'Look at this.' Brook slaps her hands on the wall. A spray of blossom appears, followed by a chorus of birds. Wisps of iced blue mark their flight as they glide to the darkest corners of the simulated garden. 'They've spent years creating the software and technologies. When it's finished, it will house around fifty pieces of art. The world's first digital art museum.'

'And you work here?' I run a hand down the mirrored wall.

'Yep. Pretty cool, hey? Let's just say it wasn't planned.'

Could she be any more impressive? Whilst I want to find reasons to dislike her, I have nothing but admiration the more we speak. Oré's face says the same. My annoyance at this surprises me.

'There'll even be a kid's area with trampolines upstairs.' Oré's eyes widen. 'Sorry, Zadzi. That part's not finished, so it's a no-go today. Okay. Let's walk and talk, and you can tell me why you're in Tokyo. It's a hell of a trip just to say hello.'

The music mimics the tumbling surf of the Hokusai-style waves projected onto the walls. Continuous jumps, swirls, circling us like stalking prey.

'Right, my friend. I'm gonna leave you to it.' Brook pulls Oré into a hug, and it pricks in my stomach, jealously. 'It's been great seeing you. Good to meet you, Sophie. Safe journey. When you're done, follow the corridor to the front. Security will show you out.' Brook holds up a hand goodbye, leaves.

The waves surround us, white-tipped. I picture home. The wind stroking my cheeks, the taste of salt on my lips, tousled hair.

'What do you think, Soap?'

'It's amazing. I can't imagine it full of people, though.' I stretch out my legs. 'How long have you known Brook?'

'We were at uni together.'

Does everyone he hangs out with come from that university, and are they all in such wonderfully interesting and exciting jobs? It's enough to make anyone feel inadequate.

'I haven't seen her in years. The power of Insta, hey? Handy, though. Otherwise, we would have missed all of this. Shame the trampolines aren't working.' His childlike frown makes me smile. He jumps up, the waves crash, displaced by his movement, crests of angry foam tossed into the air.

'Will she ever go back to the States, do you think?'

'No idea. By the way, I meant to ask. How did Christine take the news about the necklace?'

'She was okay. Cross I hadn't told her.'

Oré pokes a finger into the waves, steps back as they collide. 'Do you still think about your mom?'

'Not so much. Sometimes, they'll be a song playing or the smell of her perfume.'

'Ah, yes, your fragrance fetish.' He hops over my legs, playfully kicking them. 'And Clare?'

'Every day.' I close my eyes, run my hands down my thighs.

'How did the phone call go?' He doesn't take his eyes off me, scuffing his trainers across the floor.

'Oh. He didn't say much. Sounded a bit hurt, if I'm honest.'

'I bet.' His lips pucker like he's not buying a second of Patrick's transformation. 'He'll get over it.'

I curl my legs under me, my skirt slipping up my thighs. He presses his hands into his pockets, watches me wrench it down.

He nods at my legs. 'The accident?'

I look away, unsure whether I'm ready to reveal the broken parts of me, the wrathful ridges of red and purple scar tissue that contour across my thighs and stomach. The forever reminder of what I've done and lost. I inch up the hem of my skirt, over my knees, thighs.

'Damn, Soap.' He slips down next to me, kisses my hair, long and hard.

I tuck my skirt under my legs. 'It doesn't hurt any more.' I tap my forehead. 'Only in here.'

We sit in silence, the waves crashing, pulsing their steady rhythmic beat, calming the thump of my heart. Will he stay or go, now he knows? Will it kill his want, shift his perception of me? I couldn't bear to only see pity in those dark eyes.

He springs up, holds out his hand, heaves me to my feet. 'Hungry?'

I curl my fingers around his. 'Aha.'

'For?'

Slapping my lips, I grin. 'Pizza.'

'Pizza. Well, she does it again. We're in Japan, with some of the best restaurants in the world, and she wants pizza. Yeesh. You're full of surprises, Soap.' He pulls me to the door. 'Come on. Pizza it is.'

34

'You don't have to do this. We can go somewhere else,' I say.

Oré removes his jacket. 'Hell no. You want pizza and pizza you're gonna get. Plus, this place came highly recommended by the guy on the subway. You shouldn't question the locals.'

'He was a Canadian tourist.'

'And your point is?'

'Anyhow, I'm not talking about the pizza. I'm talking about everything else. I know you're only doing this for me.'

'You're so wrong, Soapy. Come on. It'll be fun.'

The host sweeps open the door to the booth, instructs us on how to order refreshments and select the songs.

Oré tips the host, clicks the door shut. 'Right.' He sits down on the row of padded seating along the back wall, flips open the iPad, presses a remote at the TV screen the size of a small car. 'You sort the food. Anything hot and spicy and a house beer for me. Let's get this party started.'

I pick up the phone, order our food and drinks, giggle at Oré, pleased with himself for flooding the room with multicoloured spots and music. I slip onto the seat, whilst he positions himself on a small square of stage. Microphone in hand, he spins around, gyrating his hips to the beat, a sultry pout satirising Billy Mack in *Love Actually*. He faces the TV, wiggles his behind, ignores the words scrolling the screen, makes up his own, before belting out the chorus of 'Don't Stop Believin.'

I'm laughing, tears leaking from my eyes, clutching my sides. 'You're terrible.'

'Most rock stars are, Soapy-Anne.' He strums an air guitar, lunges up and down. 'It's all in the butt action. If I hadn't gone to law school,

I could have been another Hendrix.' He strums the final notes away, takes a bow. 'Okay, Aretha. Get up here and show me how it's done.'

The waiter enters, sets down our food and drinks, leaves with a smile. The aroma of freshly baked dough and onions fills the space between us.

I take a bite, thumb through the iPad, pick up the mic. 'Okay. Let's face it. I couldn't be much worse, could I? Can you press play, please?'

I turn to the wall, look over my shoulder, straight-legged, swinging my hips from side to side, delivering my best Britney Spears. A slice of pizza droops from Oré's mouth. Eyebrows lifted, he shakes his head. I have no idea what's come over me. I will almost certainly regret this in the morning, but now, I recreate the vocals and choreography to 'Baby One More Time' in front of an almost stranger. Complete with hair flick, slap to the hip. Oré is gracious, doesn't laugh. He doesn't smile, either. He is indeed speechless, eyes drenched wide.

The music fades, and he's on his feet, applauding. 'Hell yeah.' His eyes journey the length of me, and I'm warm all over. He hands me a slice of pizza. 'You're wasted, Soapy. Why are you not doing this for real? You're so good. And look at you, dancing all …' He pulls at the neck of his sweater. 'Phew.'

I drop my face into my hands, heat tumbling my chest. 'Hmm. Maybe not.' I scroll the iPad again, select another track. Another slice of pizza crammed into my mouth, I toss hats, boas and comedy thick-rimmed oversized glasses out of the prop box. I hang a plastic guitar around my neck, throw another to Oré, pull on a short mod-style wig. The thud of the bass, and a 'Town Called Malice' blasts into the room, and I summon Oré to the dance floor with my finger. He shrugs I-don't-know-this-one-but-what-the-heck shoulders.

'You don't know The Jam? Sacrilege.'

Strumming our guitars, he copies me lunging forwards and backwards, the occasional uncoordinated air kick.

'Ooh yeah.' We collapse on the floor, a heap of arms, legs and laughter.

'Oh my goodness, Oré. Thank you.' We toss off the props. 'I can't remember the last time I laughed like this.'

Head pitched against the wall, he pulls off his wig, smooths back his hair, tight sweaty curls. 'Me too. Where is Malice, anyway?'

I can't take my eyes off him, my heart catching in my throat, a trail of pounding beats. 'So, what's next?' I stutter.

He rubs the back of his neck, stumbles up, taps the iPad. 'Another?'

'I don't think I can take any more of your howling.'

'Rude.' He scrolls through the songs. 'A duet. Something super cheesy.'

'Or something where you don't sing, maybe?'

'Not kind, Soapy.' He pulls me up. 'Here. Take this.' He thrusts the microphone back into my hand. 'I'll be Ewan McGregor. Come on, Nicole Kidman.'

'Not something I've ever been called before.' I reach over, drain my drink, take his hand.

The song Come What May seeps around us. My words falter as he pulls me against him, his hand slipping my waist, my fingers stroking his back, his stare in my stomach. I cup his face, press my lips to his, the freshness of passion, our pure, vulnerable selves.

35

Oré grabs my hand and my heart jams. There's a freshness in the air, slate grey rain sprays the skyscrapers, a blur of lights and neon signs pulse into the night sky. A protective arm, he guides me against the swarms of people jamming the Shibuya Crossing.

'Are you warm enough?' he says.

I nod, squeeze his hand, our smiles endless.

'Come on. Let's go before this gets any worse.' He pulls me onto the road.

The road grows into a maze of intersections. Hordes of people troop from four directions, the middle, a scrum of arms, legs, bumping torsos. Engine's growl on either side, their headlights probing the driving rain. The crispness in the air is gone, gasoline biting the back of the throat. The rain no longer falls easy, striking my skin like needles. We edge forward, the junction traverses, opening wide.

My mobile buzzes in my bag. I shift the strap on my shoulder, grip it tight. A rumble. A thunderous snarl. Slick with rain, my hand slips from Oré's. A van, jet black, screeches inches from my feet. Shrieks, howls, twisting my nerves. Hands clasped to my head, my lungs scream, ears roar. 'James.' I suck the damp air thick with fumes deep into my lungs. 'Oré! One, two. One, two. One.' Panic chokes my words silent. The squeal of rubber on tarmac. The skid before the thud. Cries stung with fear. He's gone. Swallowed by the crowd. I spin side to side, push through the growing mob of spectators. 'Oré.' The van sits still, a crumpled hood, headlights scorching the blur of people scattering the road. I close my eyes, throw my head back. 'No. No. No. Not again. Please no. Not him.'

I blink to focus, and for the briefest moment, everything is as it should be. A mind trick, a split second of calm when nothing's wrong.

Then the swell pierces my senses, a tsunami, no backwash, no retreat. Bedlam. Acrid smells. Mangled metal. Headlights echoing off wetness. Cries. The roar of engines. Sirens. I spin around, push against the masses. The crunch of splintered glass on the soles of my boots. 'Oré. Please. Where are you?'

I clutch my bag to my stomach, the rain pounding like razor blades. How is this happening to me again? Terror pours through me, choking me numb, tearing like the roughest wave, swamping, pulling me under, again and again. Its snarl demands I cower, to remember my limitations. 'No!' I scream.

I snatch the phone from my bag, punch at Oré's name – 'Hi, you've reached Oré. I'm currently sailing the seven seas. No, seriously, I am. Leave me a message, and I'll get back to you.'

Gripping my chin, I loosen the tightness in my jaw, jab redial. The voicemail torments my patience. 'For Christ's sake, Oré. Where are you? Call me.' I slip the phone into my pocket. Arms splayed, I separate the crowd, fight my way through. 'Think, Sophie. Think.'

'Sophie!'

I spin giddy towards him. 'Oré?' I take a second look, blinded by the misty air. Hands balled into fists at his side, sandy blond hair weeping with rain. 'Where ...' I blink away the wetness. My mind zigzags like a wasp. 'How?'

'Thank fuck.' Oré grabs me from behind, clasps me tight, sinks his face into my hair, my body shaking against his. 'Soap. Are you okay? Where the heck did you go?'

The fist of volcanic panic balled in the pit of my stomach erupts. 'Where did I go? Seriously? Are you kidding me?' I push him away hard, search the crowd.

'Woah. Easy, Soap.'

'Easy?' A guttural roar blasts from my lungs. 'It's him, Oré.' I point at the river of people pushing against each other. 'He's here.' Tears slip unchecked down my cheeks. My emotions jagged, insides tight.

'Who?' He grips my shoulders.

'Patrick.'

Two-thirty in the morning, a handful of people sit scattered around the Crow's Nest Bar. The bartender clinks glass against glass, restocking for tomorrow's pre-dinner rush. I lift the vodka and tonic to my lips, breathe in the squeeze of lemon, its chill rushes my oesophagus numb.

'Are you okay?' Oré tugs a hand through his hair, a thousand other questions on his face. 'What happened?'

I fight the panic scratching my words, fist the itch in my eyes. 'He was there, Oré.' I lean onto the table, hands shielding my head like debris is tumbling onto me.

'Patrick?' His voice trails like a tap dripping dry.

I side-eye him. 'You think I'm lying?'

He rubs my back. 'No. Of course not. It was real busy. Are you sure it was him?'

I stare into my glass, stroke the trickles of condensation. The face fits my memory, sheeting rain, dripping wet hair, clothes sodden to skin. 'No.' My head falls back. 'Jesus. I don't know. I'm turning into a paranoid mess.'

Oré cocoons me into him 'What? No. He's been fucking with your head for months. It's gonna take time.'

I unwind in his arms, smooth his shirt, crumpled, wet, to his chest. 'You need to change.'

'So do you.' He nods at my feet. 'They're trashed.'

I peel the sodden UGG boots off my feet, toss them onto the floor. Two hands, I slick back my wet hair. The heaviness in his eyes makes my heart ache. 'Hey, I'm okay.'

He cups my chin. 'I know. I wish there was something I could do.'

'But you can't. The only one who can sort this is me, Oré. Only me.'

36

Petropavlovsk – Kamchatsky, Kamchatka. Russia.

Anton salutes. 'Right. Get comfortable, ladies. I'm off to see the pilot.'

'Hold up, Anthony, I'll come with you. I'm bursting for the ladies.' Aunt Christine stumbles out of the helicopter into his arms, and they can't stop grinning.

Anthony? I don't even think Anton is short for Anthony. Can they get any more adorable? After her revelations about George, watching them walk away arm in arm, I'm grateful they've found each other.

Bea unstraps the seatbelt from her chest. 'How are things with you, Sophie?'

'Good, thanks. Better.' My Tokyo mind games whipped everything into painful focus. When we started in Sydney, I was angry, exhausted, hated myself, my life and pretty much everyone in it. Losing Clare had plunged me into a vulnerability shitstorm. I came on the *Tutum* to please my aunt, but she was right, it's been everything I needed and more. The fog of my childhood, Patrick, the accident, beginning to fade in my head.

'And Oré?'

I look out at the snow-tipped mountains that scar the milky blue sky, place my palm on the window, welcome its bite of iciness. 'I've stuff to work through.'

'He seems a good guy.'

'I don't need to be fixed, Bea.'

'Sophie, what's wrong?'

I breathe slow and hard through my nose. 'Trusting me is one thing, but believing in a man again, well …' I adjust in my seat, turn to face her. 'Anyway, what's your plans after the cruise? Are you staying on?'

'Nae. I'm gonna head to Banff for a bit. Spend some time with my goddaughter and the wee bairn.'

'Is that home?'

'Aye. Moved there thirty years ago to be with Alice.'

'Alice?'

She rubs her neck, stares out of the window. 'My partner. Ex-partner.'

Kadek sitting cross-legged on the porch in Bali smokes my thoughts. It's the only other time Bea mentioned that name. 'The photos in your cabin. Is that her?'

'Aye.' She twists a silver band around her ring finger, drops her hand, looks back outside. 'We separated before I got here. I wanted to travel. She didn't. Not her thing, apparently. She gave me an ultimatum,' ache scuffs her voice, 'and here I am.'

'No. Will you see her? She might've changed her mind.'

'Nae. I doubt that. She's as stubborn as me.'

I place a hand on her arm. She turns back, smiles. 'I'm sorry, Bea.'

'Aye. It's been a real tonic meeting you both. I love my life, but having people to share and laugh with, that's a blessing. I'd forgotten how much I miss that.'

'My aunt's a total gift, isn't she?' I roll the past two and a half months through my head. The beautiful places we've been, the friends we've made, the truths we've learnt, are still learning. 'Do you have other family?'

'My parents are dead, and my sister, let's just say she didn't get over the shock.'

'Of your parents dying?'

'Me and Alice.'

'Howdy, ladies.' Aunt Christine climbs in, secures her harness. 'Thank goodness for that. I thought I was going to pee myself.'

I jerk my head at Bea, refastening her safety belt, roll my eyes. 'Thanks for that, Ainti.'

Anton adjusts the mic to his mouth, looks over his shoulder. 'Ready, ladies? Alexei, let's go.' The engine roars to life at his hand signal.

Excited squeals fill the cockpit as the rotor whirs. The blades swish, gathering speed, the landing skids hover off the ground, pitching us to the left, right.

I grip my ear defenders, glance at Bea.

'Life can be short, Sophie. Give him a chance,' she shouts.

I stare out of the window. The mountain peaks a celebration of blue, grey slate, crowned with silken white powder, like a gloss of molten ice cream. My lips part, a smile growing from inside. 'Bea.'

'Aha.'

'There's something I need to do. Will you help me?'

She pats my knee, grins. 'Sounds intriguing.'

37

Crossing the International Date Line

Aunt Christine and Bea perch on the bed, willing me to step forward, to look in the mirror. I drop the sarong to the floor, skim my hips, the reddish-purple ridges slashed in hot lines across my thighs, crisscrossing unseen onto my stomach. My new swimsuit drops from one shoulder, wide diagonal ruched sidestrokes dyed three shades of dark blue, exposing everything I've hidden since the accident, my pain, fear, disgust. I'm starting from where I am and moving with it, facing the burn of what's happened, the wounds that will forever lacerate my skin and mind.

Aunt Christine steps to my side. 'You look beautiful, Sophie-Anne. Ready?' Her hand strokes my back, she kisses my cheek. 'I couldn't be prouder of the wonderful woman you've become.'

The words catch in my throat. 'Thanks, Ainti, and thanks, Bea, for helping me with the costume.' I pull up tall, suck in my middle, tie the sarong back around my waist. 'Okay. I'm ready.'

Rainbow lights play upon the swimming pool, skipping to the beat of the music pumping from floor-to-ceiling speakers. Strings of pearl white lanterns thread like necklaces across the pool. Woody piquant smoke billows from the barbecue, the syrupy aroma from the whirl of a candyfloss machine pushes against the bleachy chlorine. We slip into the crowd, feed off their smiles, the sound of happy chatter fusing with the thump of the band. In the pool, partygoers flow like shoals of fish in vibrant swimwear in and out of the water.

I push to the bar. 'Vodka and tonic, please. Ainti, Bea, what are you having?' No answer. I spin around, slam a hand on my mouth, shield my laughter. Anton, Aunt Christine, Bea and Oré stand arm in arm in a line. Chins high, hips dropped one leg in front of the other, my aunt and Bea swathed in high-leg neon pink swimsuits with plunging necklines. The boys in matching fluorescent yellow budgie-smugglers, so tight I avert my eyes.

'We knew this evening would be hard for you, so we've made it a little easier.' Bea throws open her arms. 'Ta-dah.'

'You guys.' We clasp each other in a group hug, my nose twitches at the cacophony of perfume, hair lacquer, fruity shampoos. 'Jesus. I love you.'

Oré takes my hand. 'Come. There's something you need to do.'

My eyes scan him from head to toe.

'I get it. I'm hard to resist, but please try to control yourself,' he says.

'I'm trying.' I burst into hiccups of giggles. 'How can I refuse a man in neon yellow pants?'

'Pants? How dare you? No. No. No. These are the best Speedos money can buy. I don't think I've ever worn anything like them in my life, but looking at the admiring glances we're getting, Anton and I may start a new trend. Either that or we could be about to get lucky.' He twirls me through the crowd, wriggles between the revellers. 'Ready?'

'For what?'

He points at the water. 'I know you want to.'

I turn to him, his smile buffing his eyes. I nod like an excited child, tug off the sarong, fling it onto the floor.

'Now that's what I'm talking about.' He whoops, shouts, 'Yahoo,' yanks me over the side.

We plunge into the water. A rush of happiness soaks my skin, an emotional return to my childlike self. I rise to the surface, splutter into his arms.

His hand smooths back my hair, strokes the water from my face. 'You look awesome.'

'It feels so uncomfortable, but thank you.'

'Wow. Are you accepting another compliment? What have you done with the old Soapy?'

'Stop it.' I push him away.

'Sophie-Anne.' Aunt Christine crouches over the pool's edge. 'Stop canoodling. They're doing the sky lanterns soon. Get dry and we'll meet you outside.'

'Canoodling. I haven't heard that in a while.' Oré heaves himself out of the pool, offers me his hand. 'Well, come on. Christine is not the kind of lady to be kept waiting.'

Wrapped in warm clothes, I tuck my chin under my coat, clasp the guardrail. Hot breath billows into the icy air, stars sizzle a perfect midnight sky.

Oré nudges into my side, hands me a lantern. 'For you.'

I stroke the thin layer of white parchment stretched over a domed bamboo frame. 'What do I do with it?'

'You light it here and send it up into the sky. It represents releasing your worries and new beginnings. I thought you could light one for Clare.'

I stare into the distance, lean back into his arms. 'This might sound mad, but I hear her sometimes, you know. As clear as anything in my head.'

'I used to talk to Mia all the time. She was forever interfering with Brad. I told her to get lost more than once.'

'Do you still hear her?'

'Not any more. I like to think we've made our peace.'

I suck the dryness from my mouth, look up at the stars. 'I love and miss you more than you'll ever know, my beautiful friend.'

Oré strikes the base. The lantern ignites into flames, drifts from my grasp, twirls free against the wintry backdrop. He clasps his hands around my waist, my back resting on his stomach, chest.

'Okay?' He kisses my hair.

'I am.'

'Good, because I've got something to tell you.' His tone's edgy.

I turn to face him. 'Sounds serious.'

'Yeah. It is a bit.' He scrubs the back of his neck. 'I quit this morning. I'm finished on here.'

My heart and every ounce of faith I have mustered in him shatters. 'You're leaving? When?'

38

He doesn't answer, tugging me down the stairs and along an unfamiliar corridor. I can't look at him, hot galling blood gushing through my veins.

'Here we are.' He opens the door to a cabin, flips on the lamps, stops mid-stride, a tentative smile on his lips. 'Good, hey?'

I blink away my uncertainty. This was always going to end, but the thought of him leaving strikes hard. Bigger than ours, the cabin isn't huge like Bea's, but still furnished with the same customised features, two low-slung sofas, a wall of bi-fold doors.

'What is this?'

'It's mine. Until I leave.'

'Oré, you're not making any sense. Are you leaving or not?'

'I didn't say I was leaving tonight.'

What does that mean? I point at the emperor-sized bed swathed in a quilt edged with gold thread. 'Could you ask for a bigger bed next time?'

'Cheeky.' He taps a controller. 'Smoke on Water' blasts the room 'Yikes.' He thumps the stop button. 'Not the vibe I'm looking for.'

My smile reflects his. Even when I'm screaming with frustration, he charms me. Silky music fills the space between us. I tap my foot to the beat, a rush of nervous anticipation in my stomach fiery.

'Drink?' He shakes a tumbler at me. 'Vodka?'

'Please.' I slip through the bi-fold doors onto the terrace, the wind warm and cool at the same time, the alcohol, or maybe it's the burn of fear, that everything I've been learning to love will be ending soon. A field of stars stretches so large, luminous, that you can almost touch them. Echoes of lanterns quiver on the sea's surface, twirling to the distant throb of the pool festivities. I rub myself cosy, the wind whispering through my hair.

'Here.' Oré hands me my drink, closes the doors behind him.

The calming wash of the waves on the ship's sides, so quiet, so peaceful, like time has paused. A line of lanterns bobs out to sea, dancing to different heights on the same stream of sea air, some faint, flying high, some bright, lower on the horizon. We stand in silence for a few minutes.

'Beautiful, isn't it?' Oré leans onto the guardrail, nods at the night sky. 'Our galaxy is one of billions in the universe. You're standing on Earth in the Milky Way galaxy in the Laniakea.'

'Excuse me?'

'Been a stargazer since I was a little boy. Got my own telescope and everything.'

Oh my goodness, that sounds sexy rolling off his lips. 'Anything else?' I sip my drink, the ice taps cold against my lips. Enough of this teasing me with erotic secrets and whatnots. I'm going to burst, Oré. Burst. 'When do you leave?'

He sips his bottle of beer. 'I wasn't planning on going anywhere. Do you want me to go?'

He's both infuriating and delectable with his boyish frown. 'You said you'd quit.'

'I didn't quit to leave. I'm just pissed watching you have all the fun. Tom's happy. So, I'm coming over to the dark side to do some touristy stuff with you.' He searches my eyes. 'You don't want me to?'

'I didn't say that. I mean, I'd like that. You staying. I'd like that very much.'

'Me too.' He slides open the door, steers me inside. 'I've got something to show you.'

I throw my jacket over the chair. It's no good. I might explode if we keep flirting like this. One of us needs to make a move.

He places the bottle down, picks up his cell from the bar. 'Meet baby Zadzisai.' His face beams, holding up a sonogram image.

I take a closer look. 'What the actual hell? Look at that.'

'Cool, right?'

'Very, and they're the spit of you. All alien-looking and wrinkly.'

'Hey.' He squints at the image as if checking for these similarities. 'Seriously, they're all doing well. Tap's back at work. Brad's more chilled. Baby's due late September, apparently. He's asked me to go over and stay with them when this ends.'

'That's great news. I'm so pleased for you all. Can you relax now?'

'I just want it to be okay for them, you know?' Oré clasps the bottle, shuffles it between his hands. I see the roll in his throat. 'Soap.' His tone falls soft. 'You can tell me to mind my own business, but why don't you have children? You're so good with them.'

I didn't anticipate this swerve, place the tumbler down, sit on the sofa. 'After losing my mum, and, well, my dad being my dad, I didn't see it as something I wanted to do. I don't regret it. Don't get me wrong, I love being around kids. I just never had the same maternal kick my friends felt. I suppose you think that's weird?'

'Nope. I respect a woman who knows her own mind.'

'Well, you're in the minority. I've spent most of my adult life justifying it.'

From the gasps of horror about my making a conscious decision not to get pregnant, to the shamers who told me I would forever regret my choice when it was too late, to those convinced I was hiding Patrick not being able to conceive. When one of Aunt Christine's elderly lunch club friends dared to utter the word barren to me, she frogmarched her out, telling her not to come back until she'd learnt some manners.

'I prefer to sit with the nonconformists.' Oré's arm glides around my shoulders, lips honey smooth, kissing my neck. I snatch up the tumbler, sloshing its contents around the glass. He pulls back, runs a thumb over my collarbone. 'Say if you wanna call it a night? I'll walk you back.'

'No. I want to be here. Jesus. This sounds ridiculous. All of this has been great, and you and me, well,' I look down at my hands, grip the glass tight, 'it's been a long time.'

He leans in, places my drink on the table. 'I like you, Soap. I like you a whole lot, but I'm cool whatever.'

'No.' I definitely didn't want whatever. 'I do want this.' I drop my head into my hands. Could this be any more embarrassing? Come on, Sophie, you're a flipping adult, start acting like one. 'I'm not saying this very well, am I? It's not that I don't want to. I do. But ...' I clear my throat. 'It's been a really long time.'

His head falls to the side. 'Do you think you've forgotten what to do?'

'Really?' I shove his arm. 'That's all you can say?'

'What? I'm trying to lighten the mood.'

'Well, it's not sensitivity personified, is it, when I'm baring my soul?'

Oré shuffles taller against the sofa. 'You're right. Sorry. This isn't the time for jokes.'

I swallow a few times, relax my dry mouth. 'To be honest. I'm scared I want to, and I'm scared you might not want to. And then I'm scared you'll do it anyway because you're a man.' I sound like an idiot, stop.

He pulls a goofy grin. 'We're both pretty scared then.'

I toss a cushion at him. 'It's not funny, Oré.' I love this satirical twang to his humour.

'It is a bit.' He pulls my shoulders until I face him. 'Look. We'll work it out. It's been a while for me too, and I'm just as scared. Especially with you.'

My eyes meet his. Heat surges through me. 'I don't know what especially with you means, but I think I like it.'

He raises an eyebrow. 'Although I am a man. And even if I didn't want to, apparently, I still would. Not that you're typecasting.'

I bump a fist into his arm. 'Stop it.'

'Soapy, you're funny and definitely the most extraordinary woman I've met in a very long time. A bit annoying, but hey, I can live with that.' He strokes a hand on my cheek. 'You don't get how awesome you are, do you?' He reaches across me, presses a few buttons on the remote. The soft tone of James Arthur floats from the sound system.

'I love this song. Oh—'

He lifts my chin, slips the tip of his tongue softly along my lips.

His arms circle my waist. The warmth grows deeper, and I'm spent, totally and utterly done in. I place a hand on the small of his back, my kiss fiery, urgent. 'Take me … Please.'

His growl a new sense of energy, tugging my dress up over my head, tossing it on the floor. 'Is this lingerie a Christine and Bea limited edition?' He runs a finger down my bra strap to my navel.

The laughter bubbles up from my stomach. 'Sorry. I can't help—'

'What are you doing?' He lifts his head.

'It tickles.'

'Um. I'm trying to be erotic down here.'

'So I see.' I hitch up his shirt, run a finger along the waistband of his trousers, smile at his throaty moan.

Rolling his hips, he shifts onto his side, half on, half off the couch, pushes his jeans from his legs. 'For fuck's sake.' He flips onto his back, kicks turning into full-on rocking, tugging at the denim, boxer shorts bundle around his ankles.

Throwing my head back, I'm laughing. Tears prickle my eyes. 'Oh, stop it,' I wheeze. 'You're killing me.'

'I've still got it, hey, Soap?' He slumps his forehead into my shoulder. 'What the heck, Zadzi?'

I stroke his hair, kiss his head. 'Are you finished with all the sexy unveiling?'

'Nearly.' He wiggles his eyebrows, runs his hand around my back, unclips my bra. 'See?'

'Aha. You've definitely still got it, James.'

He pulls me to my feet, nudges my thighs apart, lifts me until my legs wrap his hips. 'I could put my swim costume back on if you like.'

'If you do. I'll leave.' I yelp as he feigns my slipping from his arms. 'Don't drop me.'

He carries me over to the bed, lowers me down, pushes his nose to mine, our mouths soft, open. The crisp cotton sheets, fresh, slip easy against my skin.

Flipping me onto my back, he drags a hand across my thigh, tracing the scars onto my stomach. My body jolts.

He pulls away, his eyes full of concern. 'Shall I stop?'

I slip off his shirt, run my hand over his chest. 'No.' The musky bite of his cologne, strong in my nose and throat. 'You smell so good.' Gripping a fist of silken curls, I pull him to me, my heart forever stained.

He peels off my panties, his kisses like feathers on my body. His tongue sweeping my breasts, stomach, thighs, the slices of blemished skin. He pauses, looks up, 'Okay?'

We become an interval of hands and moans and sweat. I have no idea when the music stopped, but the room is quiet except for the countdown of a ticking clock, and us.

He sits tall, straddles my hips, pulls a foil square from the bedside table. Despite our years, it feels like the first time, awkward, exciting, unrehearsed.

'It's been a while since someone's whipped a condom out on me.'

'Have you never heard of safe sex, Miss O'Ryan?' He curls a hand around my waist, tugs me to him, growls. 'Now, where was I?'

Our bodies come together, backs arching, my knees drawing up to my heart. I gasp into his mouth, every part of me tense. I have, I realise, wasted too much time. The thought of this ending, of us ending, steals my breath.

I grow dizzy, a rush of helplessness, my face buried into his neck, my fingers digging his skin. His hips roll against me, once, twice … My whole body feels it, head to toe and back again.

He groans, his body trembles silent on top of me. My head falls back onto the pillow. I lean into his hand, stroking my cheek, draw him to me with my eyes.

'Well?' He pushes a strand of hair behind my ear.

'Well, what?'

'How did we do?'

'Are you kidding me? We were flipping great.'

'We were, weren't we?' He flips onto his back. I lay my head on him, curl my leg over his stomach. 'Your hair's so soft.'

'You're stroking my leg.'

'I know.' He laughs like a child laughing at their friend being caught out in class.

I bounce my head on his chest. 'You cheeky whatnot. I shaved them this morning, I'll have you know.'

'Ah, so you've been planning to seduce me all day, then? I've heard about women like you.'

'Says the man with a spare condom in his bedside table.'

'Busted.' He turns to face me, watches me for a beat, runs a finger down my cheek. 'Have you decided what you're gonna do? When this ends.'

The one thing I'd rather not talk or think about. 'Not really. I could do with some more time.'

He lifts onto his elbow. 'So, let's do it?'

'Do what?'

'Take some more time. Travel. You and me. We could stop and see Brad and Tap. I can show you Chicago. You can show me Biton.'

'Brighton.'

'Yeah, there too.' His eyes search mine. 'We get on okay, don't we?'

I'm the first to look away.

He pulls from me, falls back onto the pillow. 'Or maybe not.'

My heart rips. 'We're not eighteen, Oré.'

'What's age got to do with it? Don't go all conventional on me.'

'Conventional? What do you mean by that?'

'Doing what everyone expects you to do, rather than what you want. Whose life are you living, Soap?'

I lay down, stare at the night shapes shifting on the ceiling. 'It's such a big decision.' I roll over, press my head on his chest. 'Can I think about it?'

'I'll take that. It's not a no.' He kisses my hair. 'Ignore me. I'm getting over-excited. It's cool either way.'

But it isn't. My indecision has cut him. I reach up, kiss his cheek, snuggle under his arm. My head dances to the rise and fall of his chest. The old me would have said yes to make him happy, crushed by his dejection. But I'm not that woman any more. At least, I'm trying not to be. The next six months flash my mind. What about a job, money? My mortgage, bills? Savings don't last forever, do they? What about Aunt Christine? It's not easy to say yes, is it? He knows that. I have a hundred reasons why I can't go. *And a hundred reasons why you can*, Clare whispers.

39

Sitka, Alaska. US.

We giggle like small children on the way back to my cabin. Oré's arm around my shoulders, parading the corridors wearing fluffy white robes and cabin-issue slippers. Never has a walk of shame been more shameful.

'I've got another one for you, Soap. If you could perform with any musician, alive or dead, whom would it be?'

'Oh, that's easy.' I shimmy my hips. 'Tina Turner. I l-o-v-e love her.'

'You're quite a diva underneath all this seriousness, aren't you?'

'Imagine doing something that makes thousands of people happy.' He squeezes my shoulder. 'You do.'

'Hmm. Did. What about you? If you could sing, of course.'

'Rude!' He smooths back his hair, 'Without a doubt, TBG.'

'Who?'

'The Big Guy. Sinatra. Big band, cool clothes, smooth moves.' He spins from my hand, mimics Rat Pack dance moves.

'Jesus. My aunt idolises Sinatra. Perhaps you should date her.'

'Dating? Is that what we're doing?' He grins like a teenager. 'I'd like that.' Oré tips his head down the corridor. 'Now, wait a goddamn minute. What have we got here?'

Pressed against the cabin door wearing last night's clothes, Aunt Christine and Anton stand locked in a passionate embrace.

Oré leans into me, whispers, 'Have they been up all night?'

'Like you can talk.'

'True. But I have to say, Soapy, if you're still getting your kicks like Christine at her age, you'll be okay.'

'She's incredible, isn't she? They both are.'

He slips his fingers between mine, and we sidle up to the door. A sideways glance from Aunt Christine, she steps from Anton, smooths down her clothes.

'Sophie-Anne, don't be creeping up like that.' She pats her palm to her cheeks, rosy, hot. 'Why are you skulking around the corridors in bathrobes, anyway? I thought you'd be at breakfast.'

Anton gives a one-finger salute. 'Sophie, Oré.'

'I think we're doing the same as you, Ainti.' I drag my eyes over them, head to toe. 'What have you been up to?'

Aunt Christine presses her key card on the lock. 'Anthony, I'll see you later.' He lifts her hand, kisses it gently, holds open the door. 'Well, Sophie-Anne, can you bear to put Oré down for a few minutes?'

'Laters, James.' I blow Oré a kiss, step inside, press my backside to the door, click it shut.

'James, is it now? A strange choice of nickname.' Aunt Christine pulls off her earrings, shoes.

'Homage to his 007 alter ego. A story for another time.' I hip-kick off the door. 'Looks like you had a good night?' I steady myself on the sideboard, take off my slippers.

'I did, thank you. Things got going for you two, then?'

'Got going? What sort of phrase is that?'

'You know what I mean. God knows he's waited long enough.'

I flop next to her onto the bed. 'Who would have thought we'd be having holiday flings at our age, hey?'

'We don't stop living because we're getting older, Sophie-Anne. We just do it better. Anyhow, you two are hardly past it.'

I nudge my elbow into her arm. 'Not judging by last night.'

She taps my knee. 'Please spare me the details.'

'Seriously though, Ainti, I like Anton.'

'Indeed. He's very charming.'

'I should hope so if you're spending the night together.'

'Don't be so crude, Sophie-Anne.' She shuffles into bed, tucks the covers under her arms.

I twirl the bathrobe belt between my fingers, lean back onto the sideboard. 'Oré's asked me to go travelling with him.'

One eye peels open. 'Did he now? Interesting. When?'

'Whenever, I think. Maybe after this.'

'How do you feel about that?'

'We've not known each other long, have we?'

She adjusts her head on the pillow so she can see me. 'And?'

I shrug. 'I can't, anyway. What would you do?'

She shuffles up tall against the headboard. 'Stop right there. I may have started this cruise not letting you out of my sight, but things have changed.' Ache stings her voice. 'We've changed.' Her eyes hold steady on her handbag slumped on the dressing table for a minute, George's letter inside. 'If you don't want to go, fine, but don't blame me.'

'I'm not,' I say, vexed. 'I worry about you.' My concern for her scores my heart, and as much as she snubs it, I feel the same duty to her she has afforded me for the past four decades.

'Anyhow, Anton and Beatrix have asked me to join them on their next cruise, so there's no need,' she says.

'And you're going?'

'Why not? I need to pop home, but–'

'Nice of you to tell me, Ainti.'

'I just have.'

'That's not what I meant.'

'Oh, stop sulking like a grumpy teenager, Sophie-Anne. This isn't about me and what I'm doing. What are you going to do?'

'Is that why you're doing it? Not to burden me.'

She folds her arms, turns away, mutters something before looking back. 'Don't be so ridiculous. I have no intention of being a burden to you or anyone else. I'm going because I want to.' She pauses with a drawn-out groan, flattens the bedclothes. 'Sophie, whilst you can't see it, you're still so young. You need to live your life. If not for you, do it for me and your mother. Please. What is it you say? You're cramping my style.'

'Charming. I thought you liked having me around.'

Aunt Christine slips down under the duvet, presses her cheek into the pillow, closes her eyes. 'Stop being theatrical.'

Lying next to her, I curl my arm around her middle, rest my chin on her arm. 'What if we don't get on? Or he ends up hating me or something.'

'Goodness. Are you penning a tragedy in your spare time? And what if it goes right? What if you're destined to make each other blissfully happy? What's the worst that can happen?'

'He murders me and steals all my money?'

She shakes with laughter. 'Yes, you're right. There is that.' She pats my hand. 'You're quite unhinged. Do you know that?'

'That's not very nice.'

'Well, I think we've established he's no serial killer conman, haven't we?'

'Have we?'

'Well, you're sleeping with him. What does that say about you?'

'That's mean.'

Eyes closed, she nuzzles into the pillow. 'I think you're just looking for excuses. What do they call it, self-sabre whatsit?'

'Self-sabotage?'

'I've got a case of déjà vu. Didn't we have a similar conversation when we booked this trip?' She peeps at me from one eye. 'You'd rather go back to a job that sucks the life out of you and people who live for those gossip rags, would you? Oh, come on, Sophie. Find some Collins grit.'

'I don't know what I want.'

'Yes, you do, Sophie-Anne. You've been reimagining your life for weeks, months even.' Aunt Christine thumps the bed. 'Life can be short. You know that better than anyone. If it doesn't work out, you end up back where you started. So what? Wide open spaces, Sophie-Anne, isn't that what you sang? Jump ship, go make some more mistakes.'

I lower my head, tighten my grip around her. 'I'll miss you.'

'And I you. But we're only ever a plane ride away.'

I shuffle up the bed, place a kiss on her cheek. 'I love you, Ainti.'

'Yes, well. I have something much more pressing on my mind. It's your fiftieth in two days and we need to get things sorted.'

Crap. I'd forgotten about that. 'I don't want a fuss. Maybe we can just have a nice dinner or afternoon tea?'

'Oh, we can do better than that.'

I lift from the bed. 'Did you hear what I said? I don't want a fuss. Please don't.'

Aunt Christine plumps the pillow under her head, hums Stevie Wonder's 'Happy Birthday'. I love her, but she also infuriates the hell out of me.

'Ainti. I mean it.'

'I heard you. I'm not listening, but I definitely heard you.'

40

Cruising The Inside Passage. Alaska. US.

Oré grips his hands behind his head, lays back on the pillow. 'Hey, as of today, you're sleeping with a toy boy.'

I stroke his cheek, the scratch of stubble makes his nose twitch. 'I like the idea of having a younger man in my bed. When's your birthday?'

'24th December.'

'Aw, that's cute.'

'I am cute.' He flips me onto my back, his body pressing down on mine. 'Happy Birthday, Soap.'

'Thank you.' My heart flutters, stretching for a kiss as he rests his chin between my breasts, his eyes the warmth of auburn flames, looking up at me. My kind of heaven right here.

'So, what's it like to hit half a century?'

'Much the same as yesterday. My mind says I'm in my twenties, and that's where I'm staying. I just wish my body–'

He places his finger to my mouth. 'Uh. Uh. Uh. I'm taking a stand. No more putdowns.' He sits up, kisses my nose. 'Anyway, I like your body.' He pushes off the bed. 'Wait here.'

He makes no effort to cover himself, returning with a bag tied with purple ribbons.

'For me? It's so big. What is it?'

'Open it, you dafty.'

'You're spending far too much time with Bea, you know that right?' I lift out the large box, open the lid, unfold the tissue paper. I forget to breathe. 'Oh my goodness. I love you.' I lift out the UGG boots, stroke their softness across my cheek, draw in the smell of new leather. 'Where on earth did you get them?'

'Yeah, well. Your old ones are trashed, and I know how much you love them. Are they okay?'

'Oh, Oré. They're absolutely perfect. Thank you.'

'Really?' His voice falters, eyes searching mine. 'Not the most conventional fiftieth birthday gift. I can get you something else.'

Something gives inside, hot and bright. 'I love them.'

'Phew.' His shoulders relax. 'We clubbed together our tips on reception to buy them.'

I roll my eyes, kiss his lips. 'Of course you did.'

Sitting on the side of the bed, I slip them on. I cross the room, unfold my arms, naked except for the boots in the mirrored wardrobe. This body has seen fifty years of life, mostly healthy years, and even before the accident, I had ignored her, chastised her, hated her. I hold my arms lax to my sides, drag my eyes from head to toe, eyeing how she swells plump across my breasts, hips, thighs that kiss, my skin sagging a little looser now. At the scars, a token of unforgettable pain, sorrow, survival. The hand on my heart, masking the ones no one sees. This body has been breathing for fifty years and this is me. More exposed, alive and loved than ever.

Loving yourself isn't about looking in the mirror and worshipping what you see. It's adoring who we are, so we don't want to keep hurting ourselves. Of letting go of whom we think we need to be. To stop numbing the haemorrhaging shame with alcohol, and work, and food, and money, and drugs, and sex. To reach inside the wounds, snatch out the pain and find peace. Kadek, I hear you. I finally hear you. Forgiveness isn't about ignoring what's happened to me or giving others penance for their actions. Forgiveness is accepting it can't be any different. To step out of my past and find freedom on the other side. We think our hands are tied, but they're not.

Oré slips his arms around my waist, kisses my neck. 'I think this is my favourite look on you.' He nudges his head at my reflection.

I turn, run a hand through his crop of soft brown curls, the faint taste of last night's cologne, his coconut oil lotion. 'Me too. Thank you.'

The doorbell punctures the silence. His forehead presses into mine. 'Damn.' He leans down, scoops a robe from the floor, hands it to me.

'Who's here at this time?' I throw it over my shoulders.

'I'm hoping it's breakfast unless we're about to be ambushed by the three amigos again.' He pulls a towel out of the bathroom, fastens it around his waist.

'Don't let my aunt hear you call them that. You'll be knocked right off your pedestal.' I knot the bathrobe belt, loop it around my finger. 'James, before you open the door. I've been thinking about what you said the other night. If the offer still stands … I'd like to come with you.'

Oré steps toward me, feet dragging like he's processing what I've said. His smile, wide, echoes mine. The doorbell chimes again. 'Yeah. Yeah. I'm coming, dude.' He tugs me to him, spins me in the air. 'And today's meant to be your birthday. It's gonna be great, Soap. I promise.'

I pull back, tap my palms on his chest. 'I know. Let's start with a month. Okay?'

'Absolutely. We'll make it up as we go.' The doorbell rings again. Its tune lingers a little longer. He thumbs over his shoulder. 'I think I'd better get that.'

As he springs to the door, I imagine a future with him in it. Doubt still rains through me. Changing our lives and hoping for something better has no certainty. Perhaps indecision is part of the adventure. Can you do something new without it? He glances at me, smiling with his eyes, as he guides the porter in with our breakfast tray. I turn back to the mirror, bouncing on my toes. I'm happy, we're happy, and for now, that's good enough.

'Happy birthday, ma'am.'

A knife slice of icy air carves into me. I clasp the robe tight across my chest, turn as if time has slowed.

41

'Thanks, dude. I've got this.' Oré clatters plates around the table, catches my stare stabbing him. 'You okay?'

Neither one of us move as I turn and face him. 'You ...'

'We're fine, bud. You go. I'll sort this.' Oré waves the porter towards the door.

He shakes his head, smiles. 'Hi, I don't think we've met.' The uniformed porter holds out his hand to Oré.

Arms limp at his sides, Oré studies him. 'I'm sorry, you are?'

'Patrick.' He towers over Oré, three, four inches taller. 'No? Okay, dude.' He draws back his hand, tugs it through his thick, sandy blond hair.

Oré looks at me, back at Patrick. 'Excuse me?'

'Patrick. Sophie's husband. Oops, a slip of the tongue. Ex. Ex-husband.' He offers his hand again, slaps it to his side when Oré doesn't respond, spins on his heels to me. 'So, babes, fifty, hey?'

Behind him, ice laces the glass pane circling the outside terrace. The sea, a black-and-white photograph. The occasional stripe of white sunshine through knotted clouds glitters the surface like a skating rink. Yet, Patrick being here is a gale raging. The root of so much of my fear, standing barely three feet away.

'Why are you here?' I wince at the tremor in my voice. The shackle of memories whipping my brain – torn flesh, the sweet, metallic taste of my blood. I turn to Oré. A surge of something travels from my head to my toes and back again.

'How did you get on board?' Oré's question fires like a dart.

Patrick sits, pours himself a cup of coffee, a splash of cream. 'Been checking up on me, have we? Did you know that, Soph? Sweet, hey? Nah. Don't beat yourself up, old man. There might have been the tiniest mix-up of passports. Would you believe I picked up my brother's by mistake? He's a fucking prick, of course. Hasn't noticed. God knows why you'd even get one if you've no intention of going anywhere.' He takes a sip, grimaces, spoons in one, two teaspoons of sugar. 'Anyway, you and him?' He waves a finger between Oré, me. 'Who would have guessed?'

'Why are you here, Patrick?' I signal for Oré to back off.

'Well, I'm a little pissed, actually. Isn't that what you say, darling? Pissed. Such a classy turn of phrase. After everything I've done. Poof.' He clicks his fingers like he's conjured a cloud of smoke in the air. 'Spinning some bullshit about needing space. So, I thought I'd drop in and see what's happening.'

Oré strides to the armchair, his eyes on Patrick, slips on his uniform jacket, slides a hand into the pocket.

'Why'd you do that, Soph?' Patrick rips off a piece of croissant. 'I thought after everything that happened, we were getting somewhere?' He sweeps pastry flakes from his suit trousers, leans back, crosses his legs. 'What can I say? I'm disappointed.' He turns to Oré. 'Has she told you? About her fifteen minutes of fame. Being splattered all over the news at home.' He draws an imaginary line in the air as if reading the newspaper headline. 'Headteacher Slammed for Friend's Death. Or my personal favourite – Drink Drive Disaster. Catchy, no? I thought so.' He searches Oré's expression, the blood pumping fiery through the raised veins on his temples, itching Oré to bite back. 'Oh …' Patrick stands, reaches into his back pocket, pulls out a red velvet gift box. 'I almost forgot. Happy birthday, babes.' He hands me the box, leans in for a kiss.

I thrash my head to the side. That uneasy moment when someone misses your cheek, a fumble of footsteps as he swerves to regain his balance. I toss the box onto the bed. 'Why are you here?' I say.

Patrick walks over to the bi-fold doors. 'I have to say. I never thought you'd end up somewhere like this. But it did all,' he rotates a finger at the side of his head, 'send you a bit ditzy woo-woo, didn't it?' He turns to Oré. 'She can't remember a thing about it, which is unfortunate, or perhaps fortunate.' He leans back onto the doors, the sole of his shoe pressed flat on the glass. 'Shame. You were always the highflyer in our family, weren't you, darling? Landing on your feet time after time like some scrawny, weathered pussy. Although scrawny isn't perhaps the word we would use nowadays, hey? Maybe, more of a tubby tabby?'

Oré steps towards him. 'Are you kidding me, you—'

'Oré. No.' My eyes on Patrick, I adjust my robe, fingers tapping into its softness. One, two, three. One, two, three.

'What's been your favourite?' He sits back down, sips his coffee, taps a napkin to his lips. 'Vietnam, Taiwan, Tokyo.' He points a knife at the gift box, scrapes butter on some toast. 'Open it.'

A tightness grips my chest, eyeing the box on the bed. My mind commands my feet in opposite directions, as if warning me not to take another step.

'Go on.' He waves the toast at me. Side-eyes Oré. 'You'll never guess.'

Picking up the velvet box, it sits soft in my hand. The hinged clasp stiff, I lever it open, lift the chain from the cushion. The necklace falls cool into my palm. 'What have you done?'

A splayed hand on his chest. 'What? You don't like it?'

I look at him, my hand, him again. 'It was you?' I grip the Ailm charm, my mother's necklace, into my fist. 'You stole my bag?'

'Now, that's debatable, isn't it? Someone's stolen is another man's found.'

'Why, you—' Oré lurches at him, hands lifted to throttle his throat.

'No, Oré! Please.'

He freezes, adjusts the towel around his waist, mutters something under his breath.

Patrick stands, pretend stumbles backwards, smooths down his suit trousers, jacket. 'Easy, dude.'

'Why, you—'

'Oré, no.' I tug his sleeve to stop. Nod at him to step away. 'So, you've been watching me like some sick pervert? And Tokyo? Was that you too?'

Patrick stabs his finger at me, his eyes ice-blue pools. 'Shut your mouth.' He drops his hand, moves a step closer. 'That was rude. I apologise. I wanted to do something nice, surprise you for your birthday. Thought I'd take a little break too. The necklace was my little joke.' He throws his hands in the air, steps forward. 'SURPRISE!

Shall I put it on for you?'

'I've had enough of this bullshit.' Oré slaps a chair to the ground.

'Oré, stop. Please.' The pain coils my heart, Oré's eyes not leaving Patrick.

He turns towards Oré, flattens out his suit lapels like he's helping him to get ready for a date. 'Chill, old man.' He rubs his chin a few inches from Oré's face. 'That's quite a look you're rocking.' Patrick picks up his half-eaten toast, waves it at the towel tucked around Oré's waist. 'I must say, darling, I am surprised. Fucking the staff. Things must be desperate. But now, you're just another damaged plaything, you've got to get your kicks somehow, hey?'

Oré's knuckles itch white, fisting his hands at his sides, lips pursed, a thin white line.

'I told you I needed time to clear my head, so why do this?' I place down the charm on the table.

Patrick swallows, tosses the toast on the plate, walks to the windows. 'Is it hot in here? It is, isn't it?' He tugs open the door. Steps outside.

'Soap.' Oré reaches for me.

I squeeze his hand, shake my head, follow Patrick onto the terrace.

He's leaning over the handrail, fanning his palm against the breeze. Resting back on the banister, he crosses his feet at the ankle. 'Come here, you. It's a bit nippy.'

My mind is cotton as I slip into his arms, lie my head on his chest. A twitch inside me, deep, old, making me giddy for a second.

He draws me in, deep panting gulps, strokes the tips of his fingers down my spine, and I'm transported back to our first date, a breeze tousling our hair, him cradling me in his arms. 'I should have told you I was coming. I get it. It's a shock.' He buries his face into me, a silent moment between us. 'I missed you. I thought ...' His chin rests on my head, his heart thumping in my ear. 'After the hearing, I thought we were ...' His grip tightens, vice like. 'I don't understand. We were getting on so well. And then you ...'

'It's been hard, Pat. Clare—'

He pushes from me, his posture rigid. 'Is that bitch always going to get in the way? After everything she's done.' He grips the guardrail, two hands, a long, growling exhale.

'What?' I stumble over my words, clasp the robe tighter across my chest.

He jerks his head towards me before looking away. 'That do-gooder whore. Anyone would think you were fucking her.' He turns to face me. 'Were you fucking her, Soph?'

'Excuse me?'

'She was always there, wasn't she? A leech, sucking the life out of us.' He grips his hands behind his head. 'She just couldn't resist twisting the knife one last time, could she?'

'What are you talking about?'

He drops his arms, agitated steps up and down the terrace. 'Oh, really? A fucking liar, too. Well, now, isn't that interesting? She didn't tell you?' He studies my reaction. 'That I came around to yours.' A roll in his throat. 'She didn't tell you?'

I shake my head. 'I don't know what you're talking about.'

'I'd found some of your stuff in the loft. Blah, blah, blah in my face as soon as she opened the door. The fucking interfering bitch never knew when to stop, did she?'

'Why didn't you just leave them?'

He jabs a finger into the space between us. 'Listen.' The words spit from his mouth. 'You never fucking listen. She didn't listen. Lecture after fucking lecture.' He snaps his hand at his ear like a child's crocodile puppet. 'Nah. Nah. Nah. Nah. Nah.' He collapses onto the lounger, scrubs a hand over his face. 'She was always plotting, you know. Trying to get one over on me. Ha.' He looks up at the sky. 'How did that work out, bitch?' A ragged breath, he waves for me to step closer. 'You don't understand. I wanted to see you. Not her. You. I love you, Soph.' There's an ache in his voice. 'Always have.'

Beside him, I crouch down, slip my hand into his, stroke my thumb on his skin. 'I know.' Dizzy, my heart thumps wild in my chest. 'What happened with Clare?'

'You see.' He yanks back his hand. 'This is what I mean. I thought you …' He stands, clutches the railing, looks at the horizon. 'She kept going on and on. Non-stop nag, nag, nag in my ear. Nah. Nah. Nah. Get your life in order. Sophie's moved on. Fuck off out of her life. I thought …' His words taper off into a mumble.

'What? You thought what?'

He spins, his eyes burning, full of hate. 'Years I invested in us, and you think you can just walk away?' His fist thumps his chest. Forearms chiselled like stone, he throws his arms in the air. 'I worked just as hard as you, but it was never enough.' He tugs both hands through his hair. 'You and her spouting lies to everyone. Have you any idea how hard it is to watch your wife overtake you, year after fucking year? To be told, by some jumped-up, overentitled whore, that you're a fucking defect. You were supposed to put me first.' He slaps his palm on his chest. 'ME.'

Something fizzes up from my stomach and I'm laughing. 'You're kidding me, right? We're not living in the flipping dark ages, Pat. Do you want me to apologise for being good at my job? I worked hard to get to where I am. What do you want me to say? You're a shit teacher. Okay. You're shit. Always have been, always will. Your dysfunctional arse should be as far away from kids as possible.'

He lunges towards me, raises his hands as if to clasp my neck, my face. I step sideways. He slips, stumbles onto the deck. Hauling himself up on the guardrail, he darts out his tongue, moistens his lips. A hand slips my back, Oré.

He points a shaky finger at me. 'She did this. Clare fucking Fox. She infected you. We were doing fine. But oh no, you had to listen to her lies. I know all about it, you know ...'

'Oh really? What do you know?'

'About you and her. The photographs, the diaries. It was all there, in those fucking boxes. Did you want me to find them? Is that why you left them there? To throw acid onto my wounds.' He slams his fists on the guardrail. 'That dirty whore trashed my marriage.' He steps towards me. 'Did you think I was stupid? I saw how she looked at you.' He flicks his tongue in and out of his mouth like a snake tasting the air. 'Taste good, did she?'

I stiffen, my breath hard in my chest. 'What the fuck are you talking about?'

'YOU AND HER.' Dropping his head in his hands, he claws at his face, a guttural roar. 'It was me.'

'You're not making any sense, Pat.'

'That night, you fucking idiot. He stabs a finger into his chest. 'IT

WAS ME. I drove the fucking dyke off the road.'

I take a step closer. 'You ran us off the road because you thought I was fucking her?'

He cuts me a sharp stare, nods.

I'm shaking so violently, my lungs gasp for air, white fiery rage bubbling from the depths of me. 'You piece of fucking shit! I loved her, you bastard. You fucked up bastard.'

'You love me.' He slams his chest, one, two, three times.

Something, hot and bright, rushes me, my mother, my aunt, Clare, rising together like a roar from the pit of my stomach. 'No, I don't, Pat. I know now, I never have.' Electricity sparks under my skin. I charge him, two palms crashing into his chest, tossing him backwards over the lounger onto the deck, smack into the barrier.

'Damn, Soap. Good move.' A splinter of sunlight winks in Oré's hand. He grabs the sleeve of Patrick's jacket, cuffs him to the barrier. 'The lady has spoken, asshole. It's over.'

Patrick pitches straight against the glass, crazy laughs. 'Ha. But it isn't, is it? Because I won. Hearing them crush the whore in court, shredding her reputation into teeny tiny pieces. Oh, it was so worth it, babes. A tap on the accelerator, and boom, she's gone. Bye, bye, Clare.'

'Why?' I kick out, strike my boot into his thigh, again and again, and again. 'Why?' The memory rises from my gut, a stabbing pain, thick slices of it into my heart. Clare's body broken, twisted like roadkill dumped in the gutter. I stumble backwards, clasp the burn in my stomach. *Why?* she says, sobbing, her hand reaching for mine. My breath catches for a beat, falling forwards like I'm about to throw up. 'She knew.' I turn to him. 'She knew it was you.' I straighten, look out at the ocean, draw in the sea air through pursed lips, the taste of gasoline, rotting scum. My finger stabs an inch from his face. 'This isn't over. Do not.' I spear the tip of my finger a centimetre from his nose. 'Do not underestimate the grit of a Collins' woman.'

'Good luck with that one, darling. What makes you think they'll believe you this time?' He shakes his head, rolls his eyes. 'Woo-woo. Woo-woo. The crazy lady's back.'

'Because this time, asshole, she's not on her own.' Oré picks up his mobile phone from the table, waves it at him. 'It's all on here, fucker. Every word.'

'Says the creepy dickhead porter. As if anyone's gonna be interested in what you've got to say.' He flips him off with his hand. 'Fuck off.'

Oré places an arm around my waist, guides me through the bi-fold doors. He pulls a walkie-talkie from his pocket. 'He's all yours.' The door bursts open, and a stream of security guards spills past onto the terrace.

I slump onto the bed, fall into him, close my eyes as his face sinks into my hair. 'Is it enough?'

His chin bounces on my head. 'To get the case reopened, probably. A conviction,' he shrugs, 'I doubt it.' He tightens his arms around me. 'But hey, we're gonna have plenty of time to build a case against the weasel. He won't be going anywhere for a while, theft, passport fraud, stalking.' He whispers in my ear, 'impersonating a porter.' My thin laugh makes him pull back. 'Aha. I know, right?' He puts a finger under my chin, lifts my eyes to his, 'We'll get him, Soap. I promise.'

42

Aunt Christine prods me to shift over, rests her head against mine. 'I'm sorry I wasn't there, Sophie-Anne.'

'I know. But I think one Collins woman knocking the shit out of him was probably enough, and before you say it, I'm not apologising for my language. Not today.'

'Well, I hope you gave him a good wallop on the shines from me.'

She looks pale, cosying up against me, curling her fingers between mine. It no longer frightens me to see this side of her. This woman knows how to face vulnerability, she sees uncertainty and welcomes it with open arms. She isn't afraid to speak it, she isn't afraid to feel it, and she isn't afraid to live it.

'I'm going to miss you, Sophie-Anne.' She wipes her eyes, shuffles up straight. 'Oh, my goodness, pull yourself together, Christine.' I lean into her hand as she strokes my face. 'You've been so brave.'

I roll over, pull out the red velvet box, snap it open. 'Here, I want you to have this.' Peeling open her fingers, I give her the Ailm charm.

'Never has a charm signifying inner strength been more deserved, hey? I appreciate the gesture, my dear, but I don't want it.' She lays it back in my hand, folds it shut. 'I've never told you this, but your mum giving you that Ailm was never about you. It was her constant reminder to me to keep kicking your bottom if you ever slipped into her lane and out of mine. Ha. Oh yes, she knew what she was doing, even at the end. It looked pretty around your neck, but I knew why she'd put it there. I thought my work was done when you stopped wearing it. How wrong I was.' She pauses as if running something through her mind. 'You had so much spontaneity as a child, Sophie-Anne. But as you grew, I watched you become more and more fearful. More and more like her.'

'Are you saying mum regretted her life?'

'What? No. She just wanted better for you. We wanted better for you. I brought you here to give you time and space, to find that audacious little girl we adore.'

'And you didn't think a chat might suffice?'

'You're kidding, aren't you? You've experienced first-hand what happens when you wrong a Collins woman. We never take kindly to being told. I could've tried a million times. You wouldn't have listened. Look how long it took you to leave that blasted job.' She turns to face me. 'Sophie-Anne, you don't need me, your mum, Oré or Clare telling you what to do or how to be. You need to believe in yourself again.'

I roll over to face her. 'Ainti, I'm sorry.'

'Sophie-Anne—'

'No. Hear me out. I'm sorry you had to make all those sacrifices for me.' I breathe through the scratch in my voice. 'But I'm grateful you did. What would I have done without you, hey? You've taught me so much. Not always appropriate things, to be fair, but interesting.'

'Never a dull moment, ha? So, what bit of wisdom will you be taking from this trip?'

'What other than don't marry a complete bastard?'

She stickers me silent, smiles. 'Other than not marrying a complete bastard. Ooh! Wash your mouth out, Christine.' She looks at the ceiling. 'Sorry, mother. I just want you to be happy, Sophie-Anne. I'm thrilled you've got Oré to do it with, too. Not that you need him, of course.' She slaps my arm, giggles. 'Although, if I were your age, I definitely would.'

'Ainti! You're terrible. What about Anton?'

'Ah, sure. He's special too. I'd take both of them with me and let them fight for my affection. Ha. I do make myself laugh.'

'I love you, Ainti.' An ache squeezes my heart sore, burying my face into her shoulder.

'I know.' She pats my hand, shuffles her legs off the bed. 'Look at the time. We need to get ready. Nobody, not even your bastard ex, is going to spoil tonight.'

'Ainti!'

'I know. Get me being all assertive and modern, again.'

I squeeze Oré's hand. 'Why are they clapping?'

'I tried to stop her, Soap.'

Bouquets of gold and silver balloons arch over the Crow Nest's entrance. Transformed into a private bar with a dance floor and band, hundreds of guests stand, applaud us to our table.

'Who are these people?' We take our places at a table for five. 'Ainti, this is lovely, but we agreed to a quiet drink after dinner.'

She flicks her chin, waves a hand. 'Puh. So, I got a bit carried away.'

Oré places a hand on my knee. 'I love the dress, Soap. Very Tina Turner. And look at those boots.'

'Bea and Ainti got it for me.' Initially horrified by its length, the hem sitting just above the knee. A silver sequin chain dress, a Hoshi original. Cut loose on the shoulder, its long sleeves tapered at the wrists, accompanied by my new UGG boots. 'You look great too.' I had growled inwardly when he arrived at our door, white shirt unbuttoned at the neck, hanging loose over beige linen trousers.

Bea has not let me down, either. Her trademark leather biker jacket tops a black wide-leg pantsuit over white pumps. Anton is in formal attire, complete with a silver bowtie to complement my dress, he said. But Aunt Christine has stolen the show, swathed in an evening gown of tiny gold sequins. A mermaid cut split to the knee, finished with gold glitter court shoes, a black pashmina draped across her arms. A lifetime away from the knitted twinset and olive-green shorts she arrived in. This is the Aunt Christine I remember from my childhood, bright, sassy and a whole lot of trouble.

'Well, Sophie-Anne. What do you think?'

'It's great.' I kiss her cheek. 'Thank you.' I skim over the fact that I only know the people at our table. It doesn't seem important. She's happy, which makes me happy.

'Goodness me. What have you got on your feet?' Aunt Christine waves a hand at my boots.

'Aren't they fabulous? Oré got them for me.' I twist my right foot on its heel.

My aunt glares at him. 'Boots? Interesting choice. Strange. But interesting.' She taps her hand onto mine. 'If nothing else, we've established he's not a money-grabbing conman, hey? Just the serial killer traits to eliminate.'

Oré frowns, looks at Aunt Christine, me. 'What?'

'Ignore her.' I shake my head, place a hand on my stomach, curbing its growl.

'Well, will you look at that? Something you want to tell us, Sophie-Anne? Aunt Christine holds her hands in prayer, looks up at the ceiling. 'Thank you, Lord.'

My raised eyebrow is a question.

'Being all touchy-feely with your stomach. It's not too late, you know. You can get a—

I hold up a palm between us. 'Stop. Just stop. I'm not pregnant.'

'Shame.' She leans into Oré, lowers her tone. 'You can use an egg donor nowadays, Oré. I've looked into it.'

'Why? Why would you do that?' I turn to him. 'I'm so sorry. Just when you think she can't get any worse.' I place the wine on the other side of the table, out of her reach.

'Anyway, any idea where you're going because I'm loving all this friends-with-benefits malarky, Sophie-Anne?'

Drink splutters from my mouth. 'Excuse me?'

'Christine, you're the best.' Oré slips an arm around her shoulders, kisses her cheek. 'Brilliant. Just brilliant.'

'Wherever you go, I hope it's fabulous,' Bea says.

Anton lifts his glass into the air. 'To Sophie and Oré. What was it T. S. Eliot said? Those that risk going far will find out how far they can go. Something like that. Bravo. Well done, you two.'

Oré sips his drink. 'We've no firm plans, yet. I wanna show Sophie Chicago, catch up with my dad. Then we're heading over to Tap and Brad for when the baby comes.'

'My, he's introducing you to the family, Sophie-Anne. Oré, something you want to tell us?'

'Ainti. Stop.'

'I'm only joking.' She taps his arm. 'Look after her. And for goodness' sake, please don't bring her back.'

We all look at each other, laughter erupting around the table.

'You're unbelievable, Ainti.'

'Well, it's true. Exchange or refunds are no longer available, I'm afraid.' She nudges her shoulder into mine. 'I'm only playing. I wish you both much happiness. Oh, yes, one more thing. I know we're not talking about earlier, but Oré.' She straightens her glass. 'Handcuffs? Just hanging around in your pocket, were they?' She dips her head to the side, a quizzical frown.

He clutches my hand under the table. 'One of the security guys, perhaps?'

My aunt runs a polished metallic gold fingernail through the condensation on her glass. 'Perhaps, indeed.'

Like the sea below, our laughter floats between us. These people have taught me the value of time, the need to embrace life, and not take any of it for granted. To ignore others' unwritten rules, timelines, what they tell us we should believe, should do, how we should or shouldn't feel.

'Come on. Time to get your Tina Turner shimmy on.' Oré tugs me out of my seat. 'Anyone else coming?'

Aunt Christine flips him away. 'You youngsters go. We'll join you in a minute.'

The vocalist growls the intro to 'Proud Mary'. Oré spins me onto the dance floor, thrusting into me from behind, his arms sliding mine like wheels on a train. He clasps my hand, twirls me into his arms, parading us across the dance floor, not unlike our first tango lesson. You'd be loving the passion smouldering between us now, Candice.

The last crack of a cymbal and the music stalls. Shaking my hips against Oré, we work our way off the floor. His hand slips mine, Aunt Christine beckoning him back with a wag of her finger, grasping him in a waltz accompanied by The Big Guy's 'Moon River'.

I climb onto a bar stool. The bartender shakes a cocktail shaker at me.

'Oh, go on then. Espresso Martini, please. Just one more before …' Something gives inside me, and I'm alone in my head. The peace, a trap door crashing open in my heart. There's a space, her ghost-like shadow gone. The bartender pours the cocktail into a tall-stemmed glass, my grief surging like a river, swirls of sludge and silt, running a mountain pass. Oré's face turns on me. 'I'm sorry,' I mouth, slip off my seat and out of the room.

43

Vancouver. British Columbia. Canada.

'Careful, Oré, you'll tip us in the drink.' Aunt Christine clutches his arm in hers, cuts to me. 'Although it might solve a few problems around here.'

'You've no one but yourself to blame, Ainti. A wise woman once told me we should be able to choose what we want to do and how we do it.'

She shrugs. 'Yes, well. You shouldn't listen to old fools like me.'

Oré pats her hand. 'Look, Christine.' He points at the car. 'I've got you blacked-out windows. They'll think you're a film star when you arrive at the airport.'

'You're such a darling, Oré. If Sophie dumps you, call me. I can slot you in with Anton.'

I turn to face him. My footsteps heavy, drawing him into my arms. 'Say hello to Brad and Tap for me.' A shallow gasp calms my breaking voice. He lowers his lips onto mine, and my heart aches, swollen, sore. 'I'm sorry.'

Last night, my throat thick with his rich scent, I told him I had to go back. He cocked his head, took a moment. 'I'll come with you,' he said. I stroked his face, reminded him that Brad needed him more, that he would never forgive himself or me if something happened and he wasn't there. I know if I stay, I'm doing it for my aunt, for him, for Clare. It's hard to believe that I'm letting him down, causing him this much pain, but for the first time, I realise I can't compromise my own, not even for him.

He rubs a hand on my back, and electricity shocks inside me. 'Shyla will call you in a couple of days. Get things rolling. If there's something to be found, she'll find it.'

'Thank you.'

'I love you,' he breathes warm on my cheek. He hasn't told me to stay, he doesn't have to. The grip of his fingers on my shoulders says it for him. 'Call me.'

'I will.' I brush a hand on his arm, turn to Bea. 'Hey, you look after yourself.'

'Aye. I'll be seeing you, Sophie.'

Anton puts his arm around my shoulders. 'Ready?'

The wail stuck in my throat tells me no as I turn to him. 'Aha.'

I take Anton's arm, knowing I might change my mind at any moment. My heart pinches conflicted, with leaving Oré behind, with the need to get justice for my friend.

'Come on, you two. We're going to miss the flight. Anthony, can you grab my shawl, please? It's chilly.'

'Coming, sweetness.' He slips his arm from mine, strides to the car, circles his hand in the air.

One foot in the car's footwell, I hesitate, turn back to the *Tutum of the Sea*. There is nothing more important than discovering what we believe about ourselves and the world. It's a fallacy to imagine we master this at any age. We can but keep trying, keep loving, keep growing, keep living, trust life. Learn to be comfortable with the uncomfortable. Because this is where adventure lives. The sweet spot, some might say. I blow a kiss to Bea, Oré, slip into the car.

We turn onto the highway, and the past three months snap my mind like a slide show. This is not over. It will never be over. I have seen what my life can be, discovered an enthusiasm buried for four decades by self-doubt, addiction and the expectations of others. Only I can rediscover that childlike wonder still pulsing through my veins, and finally, live life on my terms.

Epilogue

Six months later. Phnom Penh. Cambodia.

'Sophie-Anne, is that you? Oh, my goodness, look, Beatrix. Sophie-Anne's on TV.'

'Ainti. I can't see you. Switch the camera on.'

'Why do I need to take a photograph?'

'Not a photograph. The camera on the laptop, so I can see you. Where's Bea? She'll help.'

'Aye. I'm on it, Sophie. Look, Chrissie, here.' Aunt Christine and Bea's sun-toasted faces erupt onto the screen.

Waving into the camera, I mirror their excitement. 'Look at you two, looking all golden and summery. Where are you?'

'La Gomera in the Canary Isles. We're off to Dakhla in the morning,' Aunt Christine says.

Amazing, my aunt can't turn on a computer but ask for next week's cruise itinerary and she'll relay it by the day.

'Wow. It only seems like yesterday I dropped you both off in Southampton. How's it going?'

'It's lovely to be back. We're in Bea's amazing cabin and Anton's right next door.'

'Where is Anton?'

'He sends his love. He's on a kayaking tour of the island. Can't sit still for toffee, that man.'

'Didn't fancy it, Ainti?'

'Goodness no. I've no interest in splashing around on a plastic ironing board.' She playfully hits Bea's arm. 'I do make myself laugh. Anyway, did you see your dad before you left?'

'I did. The care home seems lovely. I'm not sure he recognised

247

me, but it was good to say goodbye.'

'Karma, Sophie-Anne. Blinking karma.'

'Ainti! Let's not go there. It was sad.'

'You feeling sad for him? What about you?'

'Ignore her, Sophie. I'm very proud of you.' Bea looks at Aunt Christine's scowl, nudges her arm. 'We both are. I'm sure Kadek will be smiling, too.'

'Beatrix's much more forgiving than me.' Aunt Christine folds her arms. 'And what about Prat-Dick?'

'Christine! Language,' I say.

'Yeesh. Yes, Mother!' I love how her nose wrinkles when she laughs. I miss it. 'Naughty, Christine.' She slaps the back of her hand. 'Beatrix's such a bad influence.'

'What? Yer bum's oot the windae.'

'My bottom's perfectly fine where it is, thank you, Beatrix. Now, where were we? Oh, yes, Prat-Dick.'

'They've reopened the case. Some new evidence from CCTV, apparently. Shyla, our solicitor, is hopeful. We'll see.'

'Karma,' Aunt Christine coughs.

'Will you give it up?' Bea chuckles.

'What?' My aunt shrugs. 'It's true. Anyway, moving on.' She slaps the counter, bumps the laptop. 'Oops. Are you still there?' She peers into the screen like it's a tiny peephole. 'Ah, there you are. So, how are you?'

'Good. Still in Phnom Penh. The first women's centre opens next month. Oh, and hot off the press, I've started training as a counsellor. Which is very exciting.'

'Aye. That is. Good for you, Sophie. You look well. Glowing.'

'Thanks, Bea. The flat finally sold too, so I should get the money through soon.'

'Marvellous.' Aunt Christine claps her hands. 'Will you buy somewhere else?'

'No. I'll be moving on in a few months. New projects spring up all the time out here. I'm loving the uncertainty of it all.'

'And Oré?'

My smile grows of its own accord. 'All good. He's been in Thailand working on some legal stuff. I'm waiting for his call to tell me he's landed.'

'Oh, I don't like the thought of you being on your own, Sophie-Anne.'

'Ainti, I'm fine. The people are lovely, and it's a beautiful place.'

'Yes, well. Be careful.' She tucks loose waves of hair behind her ear. 'How is it going with Oré? Any news?'

'Ainti, no. As I tell you, every time we speak, we're doing our thing, our way, which doesn't involve getting married or egg donors. Anyhow, what about you and Anton? Bea, are they impossible to be around?'

'Nae.' Bea presses her head against Aunt Christine's. 'They're an adorable pair. I'm very grateful to have them both.'

Aunt Christine runs a finger on the screen, no doubt caressing my cheek. 'We miss you, Sophie-Anne, and Oré.'

'Me too, Ainti.' I blow her a kiss. 'We're hoping to come see you at Christmas. Let us know where you'll be.'

'We will.' Sadness cracks Aunt Christine's voice.

'Oh, I nearly forgot.' I pick up my phone. 'Bea, I'm sending you something.'

The phone pings on her screen. Opening the message, their smiles beam.

Aunt Christine looks up at me, back down at the image. 'Oh, Sophie-Anne. It's the baby.'

'A beautiful little girl. Kitti Mia Zadzisai. Eight pounds two.'

'Goodness. A right little whopper. Just like you were.'

'She's perfect. Oré's completely in love.'

'Ah. He's such a sweetie, that man. And a handsome one at that. How's Tara and Brad doing?' Aunt Christine says.

'Great. Tap's really well. They're living just down the road from us now, so we see them loads.'

Aunt Christine frowns. 'I don't understand why you call her Tap. With Oré calling you Soap, all you need is Brad to be a bathtub, and you'll have a complete bathroom set.'

'It's a long story, Ainti.' My mobile buzzes across the table. 'I've got to go. That's Oré calling. Bea, message me when you're next in port with good Wi-Fi.' I blow kisses at the screen. 'I love you. Take care. Love to Anton.' The icon hovers over the leave-call button. I savour their smiles and waving hands for the last few seconds. 'Bye. See you soon.'

Acknowledgements

Thank you ...

To Sam: for being brilliant. I hope finishing this book inspires you that anything is possible with hard work and tenacity.

To my dearest Aunty Gloria, for being a constant source of joy. Your unwavering love and support for me and my dreams are immeasurable.

Debbie G, for believing in me more than I ever have. Jumping Ship and I are where we are today because of you.

Debbie M, for your friendship and love during what has been years cloaked in happy and less happy times. Thank you for your patience and enthusiasm in reading so many early drafts and for falling in love with Sophie.

To Ellie Hawks, my fabulous editor, for her invaluable feedback and advice. You have inspired me to achieve more than I thought possible. Check Ellie out at elspells.com.

To James, Stefan, Joe, and Chris at spiffingpublishing.com, for making publishing this book easier and more enjoyable than I imagined.

My Parents, Keith and Margaret, for the countless hours I have spent working at various tables across their home and their endless supply of tea. To the staff at East Sussex National Hotel, especially Nicoleta Shetty, for their kindness and for letting me sit at the back of the bar on numerous weekends, surrounded by coloured pens, notebooks and journals.

I'm also grateful to those who surrendered themselves to aid my research and early drafts: Loo for motivating me to dream bigger and Penny for being an all-around beautiful person. I'm so sad Rich never got to see Jumping Ship published, but I know he would have been its greatest fan. To Karl, for his wisdom about cruise ships, so much of the finer details would have been lost without you. To Jane for the loan of her spare room and keeping me fed. And Chris, thank you for your selfless charity and listening ear over countless years.

I have worked with many fantastic people over the past five years. Thank you to everyone at the Cheshire Novel Prize, most notably Sara Cox, for encouraging me to believe that Jumping Ship could be more than just a bottom-draw draft. To everyone at Curtis Brown Creative, especially Lizzie Enfield, my fabulous mentor who helped me knock this novel into a first draft, and the Talking Cats, my fellow students, a special shout-out to Lauren Spencer.

And finally, to those family and friends who may not have contributed to this book directly but still believed I would get it published one day.

If you have enjoyed reading Jumping Ship, sign up for the newsletter at www.jarussellwrites.com for exclusive news and bonus materials.

Printed in Great Britain
by Amazon

40221084R00142